Lineups & Lyrics

Coach's Playbook Series
Book 1

Tina Gallagher

Lineups & Lyrics: Coach's Playbook Series Book 1

By: Tina Gallagher

Published by Galsalla Press

Copyright © 2026

Cover Design: Qamber Designs & Emporium

Editor: Jeannine Luby

All rights reserved. No part of this book may be reproduced in any form or by any electronic or mechanical means, including information storage and retrieval systems, without written permission from the author, except for the use of brief quotations in a book review. All characters in this book are fiction and figments of the author's imagination.

For my indie author friends who keep proving that some of the best series ideas come from floating in a pool or hanging out at the tiki bar.

LINEUPS & LYRICS

TINA GALLAGHER

Chapter One

Benny

I eased into Lot B, the one closest to the player and staff entrance. Bergmann Stadium towered ahead of me, all red brick and clean lines, the kind of place that wears its history proudly.

The parking lot stretched out in front of me, empty save for a few cars. The midday sun cast long shadows across the pavement, and the quiet sat heavy, as though the space was waiting for something to stir it back to life.

I killed the engine and sat there for a second longer than I needed to. If anyone asked, I'd call managing the Lagerheads a great opportunity, a shot to run a team and put my stamp on it. But deep down, I wasn't sure I was ready to be back here.

Coming home carried its own weight. This town was full of people who knew me before the big leagues, before my name meant anything outside of Waypoint. They'd be watching, and it felt like more than just wins and losses on the line.

Taking a steadying breath, I opened the door and got out of the car. Each step toward the entrance felt like a walk into uncharted territory, the weight of the unknown settling on my shoulders.

The security guard handed me a visitor's pass and made a quick phone call. After a brief exchange, he gave me a nod and motioned for me to follow him.

"I'll take you to Tessa," he said.

We took the elevator up to the third floor, and then down the corridor passing framed jerseys and action shots of players that lined the walls. I'd walked halls like these in stadiums all over the country, but this one carried the gravity of home...whether I wanted it to or not.

As we turned the corner, I spotted Tessa Bergmann, leaning casually against the doorframe of the conference room.

I gave the guard a quick nod and muttered, "Thanks."

He offered a tight-lipped smile before turning back toward the elevator, leaving me to make my way down the hallway toward Tessa.

As I approached, she smiled like we'd only seen each other last week instead of what...twenty years ago? She exuded the same energy she'd had in high school—poised and a little untouchable. We'd hung out in the same circles back then, and I'd gone out with her sister Margot a few times. It was weird seeing her now and thinking about back then—realizing how much had changed, how much hadn't.

"Benny Reed," she said warmly, extending her hand. "Thanks for coming in."

"Happy to be here," I said, shaking her hand.

"That's good." She stepped aside so I could walk in. "We're thrilled to have you. And I know the community is going to be ecstatic when we announce you're the new manager." She smirked. "Although with the way the gossip mill works in Waypoint, they probably already know you're here."

"Wouldn't surprise me," I said with a grin.

"Let's have a seat." She gestured toward the table. "Would you like something to drink?"

"No thanks, I'm good."

We sat across from each other, the soft hum of the room filling the space between us. Tessa folded her hands on the table, a casual smile still playing on her lips.

"So," she said, glancing at me with a tilt of her head, "are you all settled in yet, or still drowning in boxes?"

"A little of both," I replied with a laugh. "Moving always feels like putting together a puzzle that never ends, but it's slowly coming together."

We shared the usual small talk—the weather in Waypoint, what's changed since my last visit, and how the town's main street managed to feel both familiar and different. The conversation flowed easily, light and comfortable, like old times.

She was telling me about the food truck festival happening next weekend when the door swung open. A woman walked in, and her face looked familiar, though I couldn't place it right away. She gave a quick, apologetic smile.

"Sorry I'm late."

"No worries." Tessa said with a smile, then turned to me. "Benny, you might remember Quinn Logan from Waypoint High. She's the investor I told you about."

I stood and shook her hand. Her name wasn't just Waypoint big, it was recognized worldwide. I vaguely remembered her from high school, but we'd never really crossed paths. She'd been quiet, kept to herself, while I was busy being the guy on the field.

"Nice to see you again," I said.

"You too," she replied, her tone courteous and measured.

We took our seats, and Tessa launched into an explanation of Quinn's investment—what it meant for the team's future and growth. I nodded along, but my attention was only half on her words.

Thanks to my nine-year-old niece Grace's obsession with her music, I'd learned more about Quinn in the past few years than I ever did in school. I could hum more of her songs than I cared to admit, and the truth was, they're actually pretty good.

I didn't recognize her right away because she looked so different from the flawless images plastered on billboards, magazine covers, and Grace's bedroom walls. This Quinn was softer, more natural, and less polished.

She caught me studying her, and when our eyes met briefly, she looked away. I turned my attention back to Tessa.

"We'll be installing a new scoreboard, plus updating the video boards throughout the concourses and improving the sound systems. It's been a while since my dad modernized the place when the team moved up to the majors, so these upgrades are a big step forward." Her gaze settled on me. "Any questions?"

"None for now," I said.

"Great." She smiled and glanced down at her tablet. "My first order of business is finding a new general manager. I'm working with a consultant who's handling the initial outreach and gauging interest from potential candidates. He's putting together a list of names for us to consider. I'm counting on you to help refine the shortlist and participate in the interviews."

"Of course," I said. "Any changes to the open coaching spots since we talked?"

"The list I sent you last week is current. So, we'll be looking to fill several key positions."

At least no one else has bailed. Still, I've got to hire half the staff in the next couple months.

"I've got people in mind for the pitching and bench coach spots, but haven't reached out yet. No point stirring the pot without knowing what I can offer."

"That makes sense." Tessa nodded. "Quinn's going to walk through the budget so you can see exactly what we can allocate." She slipped her tablet into her purse. "I've got to head to the brewery, but you're in good hands."

We both looked at Quinn, who hadn't said a word since she first arrived. Mostly, she just watched me. Not in a flirtatious or unfriendly way, just...assessing. Like she was trying to figure me out, or decide if I was worth the investment she'd made.

This wasn't just about a scoreboard or filling a roster. It was about building something from the ground up. About legacy, and whether I was the guy to shape it.

I exhaled and shifted in my seat.

"Okay, let's get started," I said. "We've got a lot of work to do."

Quinn lifted her gaze, steady and confident.

"We do." Then she smirked. "Welcome home, Benny."

Chapter Two

Quinn

The words were barely out of my mouth before I wanted to reel them back in.

Welcome home, Benny.

Seriously? That's the best I could come up with? I'd tried to be clever and fun, but instead ended up sounding like a complete dork.

I've written lyrics people sing back at me in sold-out venues, and here I couldn't manage one normal sentence.

He gave a polite nod and moved on, while I was internally cringing hard enough to leave bruises.

I'd faced industry execs who tried to tear me down, stood on stages in front of tens of thousands, and kept my cool. But sitting across from Bennett Reed, every ounce of confidence I'd carried through boardrooms and stadiums melted like ice in the sun.

Old habits die hard, I guess. Because no matter how much I'd grown up or how many records I'd sold, being here, face to face with Benny, made me feel fifteen again. Like I was at my locker with Erin whispering, "Just go say hi," while he laughed with his friends across the hall. My heart sped up, half-hoping he'd notice me and half-terrified he actually would.

I never said hi. I went home and wrote a song instead—the one that became my first hit.

People have been asking for years who it's about, and I've always given a vague PR answer. The mystery has sparked endless conversations over the past twenty-five years about who it might be. Only Erin knows the truth.

Tessa glanced at her watch and let out a small sigh.

"Well, I should get back to the brewery," she said. "You two can dive into the numbers and we'll talk later."

And then she was gone, leaving me alone with him. My brain stuttered. Half of what Tessa had said barely registered, and I had to shove away the lingering pull of him to focus. I retrieved my notebook from my purse and flipped it open to a page of neat columns and numbers, gathering my thoughts before diving in.

"I haven't seen a paper notebook at a meeting in forever."

I looked up and caught him leaning back, eyebrow raised.

"Tactile approach," I said, tapping the page with my pen. "Writing things down helps me process and retain information better, especially numbers. It's old-school, I guess, but it works for me."

He nodded, a slow smile tugging at the corner of his mouth.

"Well, whatever works."

I took a slow breath, turned the notebook toward him, and found my professional voice.

"Okay, here's the working budget for the year. The big-ticket items are the scoreboard and video boards. Both systems are outdated, and replacing them will give us sharper replays, rotating sponsor spots, and more interactive features for fans."

"Timeline?" he asked.

"They're coming next week to discuss setup. Then the plan is to start prep work asap and kick off the full install in mid-November."

He nodded and pointed to the staffing columns.

"What's the situation here?"

I slid my pen along the paper.

"Here's a list of the coaching positions from last year. For the people staying, these are their actual contract numbers. I researched average salaries and came up with a range for the open roles." I angled the notebook more so he could see clearly. "If any of these seem off, let me know, and I'll update them. We built a little wiggle room into the budget."

Benny leaned in, scanning the page. I half-expected him to question every number, but he didn't. A small thrill ran through me. The meeting had started off rocky, but I'd found my stride. My teenage self—awkward, unsure, and barely able to say hi—would be proud. Especially since Benny looked like an older, broader version of the boy I used to daydream about. And now he carried a calm, effortless confidence built by years as a professional athlete.

"Those numbers look good," he said, his steel-blue eyes locking on mine again. "Do I need to clear anything before making offers?"

I shook my head.

"As long as it's within the ranges we discussed, you're good to go."

"Perfect." He leaned back in his chair. "I'll hit up the guys I've got in mind and get things rolling."

Some of the tension left my shoulders. Seeing him relax

made the whole meeting feel easier. For a second, I imagined him in the office, sending those offers, moving the team forward. Then I shook my head, forcing my focus back to the numbers in front of me.

Flipping to the next page, I walked him through the projections for travel and equipment. Benny leaned in, scanning the numbers with that calm, assessing stare. I glanced up and my heart skipped before I forced my eyes back to the page. Not that I'd let him know that.

Once I went over everything, I closed the notebook and rested my hands on top of it.

"Any questions?"

He studied me for a moment, then asked, "Why did you invest in this team?"

Part of me wanted to rattle off a corporate answer, but that wouldn't be the truth. It's more sentimental than that, and there's no reason not to share.

"This team was Mr. Bergmann's dream, and he poured everything into making it happen," I said. "He's one of the people who helped me realize my own, so there's no way I'm letting what he built slip away. The stadium and the team may look different now, but they're still part of my story. If I can keep them alive, why wouldn't I?"

He held my gaze for several seconds, as if he was gauging the truth of my words.

Whatever he saw must have satisfied him, because he gave a small nod before folding his arms on the table.

"I'm just gonna ask—this isn't about padding the numbers or boosting attendance to make the team look better for a sale, right?"

"What? No. Absolutely not." I shook my head. "That's not the plan at all."

He held my gaze for a beat, then sat back.

"Just making sure we're on the same page. My contract is for five years, and I expect to manage the Lagerheads at least that long."

"That's exactly what we're looking for," I said.

"Good. Now we can really build something."

The way he said it—so sure, so matter-of-fact—sent a swell of relief through me. Maybe I wasn't crazy to think this could work.

"That covers everything on my end," I said. "Unless there's something else you want to go over?"

Benny's eyes flicked to the notebook one last time, then back up at me.

"Nope. We're good."

"I'll be managing the budget until we hire someone, so if you have any financial questions, don't hesitate to ask. And if there's anything specific you need that's not listed, let me know and I'll do my best to make it work."

"Good to know," he said, then glanced at his watch. "I promised my sister I'd pick up my niece and nephew from school, so I better get going."

I slid my notebook into my bag, standing as he did the same.

We left the conference room and walked toward the elevator. He pressed the button and glanced my way.

"I appreciate the walk-through," he said.

"Anytime."

We stepped into the elevator and the doors slid shut behind us. "Sailing" by Christopher Cross filled the small space. Nothing like yacht rock to make an already awkward elevator ride feel like a bad prom slow dance.

In the tight space, I was suddenly aware of every inch between us. I tucked a piece of hair behind my ear, like that would somehow make me look less flustered.

When the doors opened, he stepped back, letting me walk out first. His stride stayed right with mine, and as we neared the front door, he moved ahead, holding it open. I glanced back as I passed and said, "Thanks."

"You're welcome," he replied, his voice even, casual.

We walked across the parking lot in the crisp air. I noticed the way he moved, the sound of his shoes on the pavement, the calm that hung between us. I slid into my car, and he into his. For a beat, the simple act of leaving felt heavier than usual, as if the moment itself was holding its breath.

I started the engine but didn't pull out right away. Instead, I watched him drive out of the parking lot as my mind drifted back to the only time we'd ever spoken in high school. I wondered if he remembered too.

Shaking the thought off before it could pull me back there, I reminded myself that was a lifetime ago, and this was now. I was an investor, not a kid at my first keg party. And if he didn't remember...well, that's probably for the best.

Chapter Three

Benny

Picking up Grace and Charlie from school was like being mobbed by puppies—loud, fast, and impossible not to grin at. Grace spotted me first, her face lighting up as she bolted across the lawn before I even made it to the sidewalk. Charlie was right behind her, lanky legs pumping like he was running out a play at first base.

I got tackled by both of them at once. Not that their combined weight could actually take me down, but they gave it a hell of a try.

"Uncle Benny!" Grace squealed. "Can we get ice cream?"

"Can we get chicken fingers and fries?" Charlie asked at the same time, as he shoved his glasses up his nose.

They'd figured out early on that *Uncle Benny* was code for *automatic yes*. I might've been the one holding the keys, but those two were the real drivers. With an arm slung around each of their shoulders, I steered them toward the car.

"Alright, we'll go to the diner and you can have chicken first and ice cream for dessert. Deal?"

They cheered and ran the rest of the way to the car, scrambling into the back seat and buckling themselves in. As I slid behind the wheel, they immediately started talking over each other. Grace was already weighing ice cream flavors.

"Maybe chocolate...no, cookie dough—oh! Mint chip!" she said.

Charlie gave a running commentary on the virtues of each kind of fry—curly, waffle, or seasoned—like he was defending a thesis.

By the time Grace tossed strawberry into the ice cream mix and Charlie wrapped up his fry dissertation, we were halfway to the diner and my phone buzzed with Cat's name.

"Hey, how was pickup?"

"Went well," I said, guessing she was calling to make sure I hadn't forgotten to get them.

Grace leaned forward in her seat and yelled, "We're going for ice cream!"

"Food first, Grace," I corrected. "Ice cream's for dessert."

Charlie cheered behind me, and Grace huffed but went back to her flavor debate.

"Since you saved me by picking them up, I'll deal with the sugar high," Cat said with a chuckle. "Seriously, I can't thank you enough. You're a lifesaver."

"Don't mention it," I said.

With her usual sitter sick, I was glad I could help.

We pulled into the diner, the kids practically bouncing in their seats, talking about the chicken fingers, fries, and mountain of ice cream they were going to demolish.

I requested a table out of the way. After being cooped up in school all day, I couldn't expect the kids to be quiet, and I didn't want to disturb anyone. Luckily, it was that sweet spot between the lunch and dinner rush, so the place was pretty empty.

The server showed up a few minutes after we slid into the booth. The kids each ordered chicken fingers and fries, and thankfully the food came quickly. Grace tore through hers like she hadn't eaten in days, while Charlie picked at his fries one at a time like he was rating them.

As promised, once they cleared their plates, I let them have ice cream. Grace switched her order to cookies and cream at the last minute, while Charlie stuck with classic vanilla. I steered them toward bowls instead of cones, hoping to avoid sticky hands. My plan didn't work perfectly, but thankfully the server brought over some wet wipes, and I managed to get them—mostly Charlie—cleaned up enough so they wouldn't leave messy fingerprints all over my Jeep's interior.

We stopped at the park on the way home so they could burn off some of their sugar-fueled energy. Grace and Charlie immediately challenged me to a race across the field. I let them go, jogging a few steps behind, watching them squeal and shout, dodging a stray soccer ball. Once they stopped running, we made good use of that ball, kicking it around. Grace was all giggles every time I let her score a goal, while Charlie chased the ball like a whirlwind, tripping over it more than once and laughing so hard he could barely stand.

The light started to fade, so I called them in before we lost the ball for good. They jogged to my side, still laughing, cheeks flushed, hair sticking to their foreheads.

"Let's get you home."

Their shoes crunched over the gravel as we made our way back to the Jeep. By the time we pulled into the driveway, the backseat had gone from chaos to sleepy mumbling about Mario Kart and who "definitely didn't cheat." I had no idea how anyone *could* cheat at Mario Kart, but apparently, it was serious business.

When we walked into the house, Cat was in the kitchen, juggling a cup of coffee and some paperwork.

"Mom! Uncle Benny played soccer with us and I scored so many goals!"

Charlie ran in right behind her.

"And I beat him running!"

Cat laughed and pulled them both into a hug.

"Sounds like you had fun with Uncle Benny," she said, ruffling their hair, her relief clear. She glanced at me, a small smile tugging at her lips. "Thanks again."

"Don't mention it," I said. "If you need, I can grab them the rest of the week if your sitter will still be out."

"Are you sure?"

"Yep."

"That would be amazing." Her eyes softened. "She's definitely out tomorrow, and honestly, I'd love to tell her to take the rest of the week off so whatever she's got doesn't hang around or hit the rest of us."

"I've got you covered."

The kids lit up when I mentioned I could watch them for the rest of the week.

"Really?" Grace squealed.

Charlie bounced on his toes, chanting, "All week, all week!" like it was the best news he'd ever heard.

"Alright, I'm going to talk to Uncle Benny," Cat said. "You two can go play a little Mario Kart before bath time."

They dashed to the living room, voices tumbling over each other, already planning who would pick which character.

Cat sat at the kitchen table and after grabbing a bottle of water from the refrigerator, I settled across from her.

"So, how'd your meeting with Tessa go?" she asked.

"I think it went really well."

"You *think*?"

I leaned back, stretching my legs out.

"Yeah. They have some good plans for the team," I said. "The budget's tight, but realistic. They're already thinking about staffing, player development, and ways to get more fans in the seats."

"Wait!" Cat raised an eyebrow. "Who's they?"

"Tessa has an investor—Quinn Logan." I shrugged. "And it seems like she's pretty involved beyond writing checks."

Cat didn't look shocked.

"Quinn, huh? Makes sense."

"Why does it make sense?"

"She's always been quietly generous. Helping people behind the scenes, supporting causes that mattered to her, and making sure her name stayed out of it."

"If they never put it out, how do you know?"

"The people she helped made it known, never her," she said. "And I've learned a lot since coming back here and working in family law. She's been keeping a ton of local organizations afloat." Cat shrugged, a mix of admiration and disbelief in her expression. "She's invested in the community for the long haul, so it makes sense that she'd want to see the Lagerheads succeed."

I had a million questions, but before I could ask even one, the kids started bickering in the next room.

"Sounds like it's time to get them settled down before bed."

"I'll head home and let you handle the chaos," I said.

"Gee, thanks," she said, sticking out her tongue at me.

I walked into the living room and leaned down to give Grace and Charlie each a hug.

"See you tomorrow."

"Good night, Uncle Benny!" Charlie said.

"Bye, Uncle Benny!" Grace added as she wrapped her arms around my neck.

"Alright, you two, go get cleaned up," Cat said. "Decide who's going first. I want to hear water running in thirty seconds."

Both immediately pointed at each other, then burst out laughing before racing toward the stairs.

With a quick goodbye, I headed out the door, slid into my Jeep, and headed home. By the time I hit the couch, the day had caught up to me. But instead of zoning out watching TV, I grabbed my laptop.

I knew Quinn as the girl reporters always asked me about, the one who left Waypoint and made it big, not as some stealth philanthropist quietly pumping life into the town while no one was looking.

I typed "Quinn Logan charity" into Google.

Turns out that what Cat mentioned barely scratched the surface.

Between the gossip about her dating life and articles covering her retirement, there were write-ups about her philanthropy. Stuff like endowments to children's hospitals, surprise grants to indie music programs, and relief funds after natural disasters. She'd donated more money than some companies netted in a year.

And tucked in there were the local stories—Waypoint Public Library talking about her funding their new children's wing. The Harbor Fund crediting her for the latest round of microloans to female entrepreneurs. Even the town paper ran a piece about the community center, saying she was the reason they'd been able to keep their after-school programs running.

Then I found the interviews. Not the big glossy spreads —these were smaller, more personal, the kind you do when you actually want to be honest. She talked about struggling in school. Feeling invisible. Nerdy. Out of place. Like she never quite fit.

That was so far from my own high school experience, it might as well have been another planet. I was a three-sport athlete and friends with half the school. In a town like Waypoint, that made you kind of a big deal.

But she hadn't been part of it. Not really. And still, she was quietly pouring money into the same town that hadn't made space for her.

Why? Why give back to a place that probably made her feel small?

Did she forgive it? Did she love it anyway? Did she want to change it into something better than it had been for her?

And with this investment in the Lagerheads, was she planning to stick around, sit in the stands, and watch the team fight its way back to glory? Or was it just another cause to support?

I shook my head to clear it.

Still, my finger hovered over the mouse, almost afraid to click the next article. Somewhere beneath all the headlines, philanthropy, and perfect public image, there was a real person. And for some reason, I wanted to see her up close.

Chapter Four

Quinn

We'd just finished dinner, and I leaned back in my chair, letting Erin's kitchen and her family's presence settle around me like a warm blanket. Liam had been talking about football, Rosie about dance class, and the two of them had gone back and forth sharing stories from school. Erin and her husband Steve followed every twist and turn of the kids' stories, asking questions and laughing along. I joined in when I could, but mostly just enjoyed being part of their world.

Erin glanced at the clock.

"Okay, you two, it's homework time."

Rosie groaned.

"But Nini's here."

I smiled, remembering the first time Liam had called me that in his little toddler voice. Somehow the nickname had stuck, and I couldn't help but love it.

Erin shook her head, laughing.

"Nini being here isn't the special occasion it used to be since she lives in town. You see her all the time now," she said. "Besides, you hung out with her after school, which is why you didn't get your homework done earlier. Go finish up so you can shower and have some screen time before bed."

The kids grumbled good-naturedly and went off to grab their backpacks.

Erin stood to clear the table, and I rose to help her.

"Dishes and homework checks are on me." Steve said, stepping between us with a grin. "You two go relax."

Erin smiled at Steve and gave him a quick peck on the cheek.

"I knew there was a reason I married you," she said, her eyes twinkling. "Thanks for holding down the fort. I'll pay you back later," she added with a wink.

"Oh, I'll hold you to that," he said, giving her a quick kiss. "Now go on ladies, I've got this."

I followed Erin down to the family room in the basement. She grabbed a bottle of shiraz from the bar, popped the cork, and poured two generous glasses while I got comfortable on the couch.

"Here you go," she said as she handed me one.

"Thanks."

Before sitting, she lit the candle on the coffee table, the soft glow making the space feel even cozier.

"To surviving another crazy evening," Erin said, raising her glass.

"To chaos managed," I replied, clinking my glass gently against hers. I took a sip, letting the rich, velvety wine settle on my palate.

She sat cross-legged against the arm of the couch, giving me her "I'm all ears" look.

"So, how'd it go with Benny?"

I'm sure it had been killing her to wait until we were alone to ask.

"It went well," I said. "They were both already there when I arrived. Tessa introduced us, then filled him in on the general plan for the team and my role in all of it."

"Did he recognize you?"

"He said it was nice to see me again, but I don't think he had a clue."

"Seriously?"

"Why are you surprised? He didn't know who I was in high school."

"Maybe not back then, but Quinn," she said, pointing her wine glass at me, a smirk tugging at her lips, "unless someone's been living in an ice cave since 2001, *everyone* knows who you are. You're an international pop star, not some random investor from Waypoint."

"Well, he didn't look like he recognized me." I shrugged and took a sip of wine. "Maybe being in the MLB is the same as living in an ice cave."

"Maybe," she said with a chuckle. "Now get back to the meeting. I want the details."

"Tessa went over a few things, then had to run to a meeting at the brewery, so it ended up being just the two of us going over the numbers. He didn't complain about the budgets, so I'll call that a win."

"Aside from all the business stuff, how was it?"

I leaned back and crossed my legs, mirroring her position.

"Honestly, I was nervous at first. I mean, it's Benny. Seeing him again after all these years made me feel like a nerdy teenager all over again. But I focused on business and got through the budgets and projections, all professional and precise. Adult Quinn was in full force."

I took a slow sip of wine, waiting for her to respond. I didn't have to wait long.

"Adult Quinn?" she chuckled.

"Yeah, she shows up sometimes," I said with a grin.

"But I'm not surprised you kept your shit together. You started facing down music executives before you were out of high school. If you could handle those sharks in thousand-dollar suits trying to lowball you, one old crush wasn't going to rattle you for long."

"I kept reminding myself of all those meetings with the record executives," I said. "Although none of them were as hot as Benny Reed."

"He still looks good?"

"Oh yeah. Maybe hotter. And he smells amazing." Just thinking about him made my cheeks warm. I shrugged, trying to keep my voice casual. "But once I settled in, I treated it like any other business meeting."

Erin finished her wine and leaned forward to place the empty glass on the coffee table. Instead of settling back into place, she rested her elbows on her knees and looked me directly in the eye.

"Let's forget about the business part of the meeting and focus on the fact that just talking about Benny Reed still makes you blush."

"That's crazy."

"Quinn, your face is so red right now, you look sunburned."

"I'm drinking wine."

I held up my glass hoping my show and tell would convince her the red liquid—not Benny—is the reason my cheeks are pink.

"We've been friends since pre-school, so don't even try to pretend," she said. "And admit it—you *are* the person who just saw your high school crush and got all fluttery."

"I never said I got *fluttery*."

"You didn't have to." She grabbed the wine bottle and filled her glass, then topped off mine before sinking back into the couch. "But seriously, you're both single and back in town. If you're still attracted to him, why not ask him out for a drink sometime?"

I choked on the sip I'd just taken and, once I caught my breath, shook my head.

"That's totally ridiculous."

"Why?"

"Because..." I gestured, hoping my hands could explain since the words weren't coming. Her raised eyebrow said they didn't. "He's Bennett Reed."

"And you're Quinn Logan," she said. "Do I need to go through everything you've accomplished?"

"Please don't."

"This isn't high school and you're not the nerdy girl crushing on the jock. You're on a level playing field now." She chuckled. "Actually, you're way out of his league."

I took a slow breath and let it out.

"When I was out in the world, touring and living my life, I felt confident and capable, like I had everything under control. I knew who I was and what I could do. But being back in Waypoint...sometimes it hits me out of nowhere and suddenly, I'm that awkward, self-conscious teenager again, the one who worried too much about what everyone thought, who second-guessed every word. It's like stepping back into a high school hallway full of ghosts I thought I'd left behind."

"I get that," she said, giving me a knowing look. "You left and didn't really come back much, so you never got the chance to shake all that off."

"Yeah. I thought I'd grown past it, but apparently teenage me just took a long nap."

Erin laughed.

"Maybe she just needed the right reason to wake up," Erin said with a grin. "Look at Steve and me. He was one of the golden boys in high school, and we barely spoke back then. Now—" She waved a hand around the room. "Here we are, married with kids. Sometimes life's weird like that."

"You and Steve are the exception." I sighed. "Besides, I told you after I broke up with Mick that I'm done with men. Remember?"

"Little Lord Insecure just couldn't handle your success." She shook her head, equal parts exasperated and amused. "Which is crazy, because you were successful when he met you. Instead of supporting and celebrating what you'd built, he tried to knock you down to make himself look bigger." She flicked her hand like swatting away a fly. "Good riddance."

I let out a short laugh, swirling the wine in my glass.

"Yeah, but he was just the latest in a long line of disappointments. Honestly, I'm happy with my life the way it is now," I said. "After being on the road half my life, then retiring and seeing my mom through chemo, it's just nice to have my own space and not have to answer to anyone but myself."

Erin tilted her head, considering.

"I get that, but you're too young to close up shop."

"Close up shop?" I snorted, the sound louder than I intended.

She twirled her finger in the direction of my lap.

"Yeah, your va-jay-jay called and said she doesn't want to be retired."

"You're cuckoo for Cocoa Puffs, you know that?"

"Maybe, but I'm also right." She leaned closer, resting her elbow on the back of the couch. "Content is great,

Quinn, but it doesn't mean you can't make room for a little excitement."

I took a slow sip of wine, letting her words sink in. She had a point, though I wasn't ready to admit it out loud. Erin took my quiet as her cue to keep going.

"You could at least entertain the idea. You'll be spending a lot of time together so there'll be ample opportunity to make something happen. Your teenage self will thank you."

I smiled, though a quiet thrill fluttered in my chest. My heart was doing a little dance my mind was determined to ignore.

"Maybe." I shrugged. "But for now, I'm happy just talking to you and drinking wine in your cozy basement."

"I can live with *maybe*." She stretched her legs out, the picture of comfort. "I just want you to find a guy who loves, appreciates, and supports you the way you deserve."

"And you think Benny Reed is that guy?" I smirked. "He still has that cocky swagger. Back in high school, it was...well, kind of hot. But now his smugness would drive me completely nuts."

Erin tilted her head, a sly smile tugging at her lips.

"Even in high school, he couldn't have been all bad. Remember that keg party?"

"Ugh. I try not to," I groaned, covering my face with one hand. "And thankfully, he doesn't seem to remember it."

She leaned forward, her eyes sparkling with mischief.

"Do you still have his sweatshirt?"

"I probably do," I admitted, twisting the stem of my glass. "I never gave it back, so I'm guessing it's in my closet at my mom's house. And before your smirk gets bigger—it's not like I sleep in it or anything."

"You would have gotten rid of it a long time ago if it didn't mean something to you."

She's not wrong. And maybe she's right about opening myself up, too.

I bit back a laugh.

Being open was one thing.

Believing Benny Reed would ever look at me that way was another.

Chapter Five

Benny

I set the last dish onto the stack in the cupboard and broke down the box, pressing the cardboard flat before sliding it onto the pile by the back door. Another one done. The kitchen was finally in order, though a few boxes sat in the dining room waiting to be unpacked.

The place wasn't bad considering I bought it sight unseen. It had an open floor plan, a fireplace, and a deck that put buying a grill on my to-do list. The creaky floor reminded me of the house I grew up in, and the quiet screamed small town—no neighbors through the walls or constant rush of cars outside.

It felt good. It also felt temporary. Like the team, the place was half-settled, waiting for me to finish the job. Another day or two and it'd be squared away, which meant it was time to start doing the same with the staff. I glanced at the clock. Now was as good a time as any to text Dane Mercer.

> Hey, it's been a while. You got a few minutes to talk? Figured we could catch up and talk coaching.

Three dots appeared almost immediately.

> Coaching as in Little League? Or something with a paycheck?

> Paycheck. With the Lagerheads.

> You've got my attention.

> Zoom in 20?

> Send the link.

I headed to the dining room table, where my laptop sat in a nest of cords and unopened mail. After sending a meeting link, I killed time in my inbox, mostly deleting ads and spam. As I cleared out newsletters I don't remember subscribing to and travel deals for vacations I'd never take, I found myself thinking about Dane. His name had been circling my brain since the day I agreed to manage the Lagerheads. We'd logged a few seasons together in both Double- and Triple-A—me behind the plate, him on the mound. I went up to the majors first, and he followed the next year. After that, we faced each other across the field instead of sharing a dugout.

He'd retired two seasons ago, and as far as I knew, wasn't doing much of anything. But Dane's a baseball guy, same as me, and he couldn't stay away from the game forever.

I logged into Zoom and waited for him to join. Right at

nine, his face filled my screen. His hair was a little longer than the last time I saw him, but his eyes were just as sharp. The scar across his eyebrow caught the light, a reminder of the comebacker that grazed him in Reading back in Double-A.

"Benny Reed," Dane said with a grin. "You still look like you could squat behind the plate tomorrow."

"Yeah, right." I shook my head. "My knees would explode by the second inning."

"Fair." He chuckled. "But you haven't changed much."

"You have," I said. "It's different seeing you without the high-and-tight."

"Perks of not having to jam a hat on every day." Dane ran a hand through his hair, then added, "Congratulations, by the way. How's it feel being the guy in charge now?"

"Strange," I admitted. "And busy. Which is why I wanted to talk to you. I need a pitching coach."

He blinked, then laughed. "Wait—you mean—"

"I mean you," I cut him off. "You're at the top of my list. You've got the eye, the brain, and the feel for the game."

Dane scratched his jaw.

"That's flattering, but I thought I was done with buses and rosin bags."

"Sure. But you're not done with the game," I said. "You were always half a coach anyway. Remember Triple-A? You'd watch a guy pitch and tell him his release was drifting or that his arm slot was dropping when he got tired."

His mouth tugged into a grin.

"What I remember most about Triple-A is how we spent half our time arguing about pitches."

"You shook me off six straight times once," I said. "Finally threw the change up I wanted for strike three."

"Best pitch of my life."

"Best argument of mine," I shot back.

He chuckled, and for a second it felt like we were back in the clubhouse. Then he leaned forward, all business.

"So what's the staff look like?" he asked.

"Still forming," I said. "Tessa Bergmann is looking for a GM. For now, it's just me, a few open spots, and a blank slate. Which means I get to shape this thing from the ground up."

"And you want me to be your guy?"

"I know you should be my guy," I said. "You've got credibility with players, you know the grind, and unless you've got a wife and kids you haven't mentioned, there's nothing tying you to the Pacific Northwest."

"Nope," he said. "You already know my story—divorced ages ago, no kids. It's just me and a Ficus that's somehow thriving better than my love life."

"Hey, at least something's thriving," I said with a grin. "But I think Waypoint would be a good move for you. The stadium's quiet now, but you can feel it waiting. The town's small, but the people care."

He nodded slowly.

"I'm definitely intrigued."

"Glad to hear it."

Dane scratched his eyebrow scar, and I knew he was winding up for something.

"If you're really building this from scratch, I assume you'll be looking for a hitting coach."

"Working on it," I said.

"Add one more name. Marin Hollis."

"How do I know that name?"

"She's Brooke's sister. Used to come to a lot of games back in the day."

"Your ex-sister-in-law?"

"Yeah, I got her in the divorce," he said with a chuckle. "She's the sharpest hitting mind I know. Show her a few swings, and she'll see what's off and fix it fast. Mechanics just make sense to her, and she can explain them in a way that sticks."

I raised a brow.

"You're serious?"

Dane didn't flinch.

"Dead serious."

I leaned back, thinking it through.

"You think she can handle a major-league clubhouse?"

"Handle it? She'll run it," he said.

"I'm not doubting you, I just haven't seen a lot of women in dugouts."

"Then maybe it's about damn time," he said.

"Maybe you're right." I nodded, slowly. "Send me her info."

Chapter Six

Quinn

The Malt & Maiden was the kind of place that never tried too hard, mostly because it didn't have to. Everyone in Waypoint just called it The Maiden, as if it were an old friend instead of a tavern with time-worn tables and a fireplace that had been burning for generations. The air always smelled faintly of hops, fried food, and nostalgia.

I spotted Tessa sitting at a small table near the hearth, a short glass in front of her, the amber liquid catching the firelight. She looked up from her phone as I approached.

"You beat me here," I said as I slipped out of my sweater.

She smiled, the kind that held equal parts fatigue and satisfaction.

"Yeah, I snuck out of the office when no one was looking. I had to save what's left of my sanity."

I settled into the chair across from her.

"Fall into winter production keeping you on your toes?"

"You know it," she said with a nod. "The overlap's always brutal."

"My mom used to say those were the weeks no one at the brewery slept."

Tessa nodded. "And since my dad always had final approval on everything, everyone feels like they need mine. No one wants to make a decision without checking first. Not even my sisters."

"That's got to be exhausting," I said.

"It is." She picked up her drink. "They mean well, but it's like being haunted by approval-seeking ghosts."

I watched her swirl the contents of her glass, the ice clinking softly.

"What are you drinking?"

"Old fashioned with muddled orange and cherry." Her mouth curved into a smile. "My dad always said the fruit made it taste like the end of a long day done right. He wasn't wrong."

The drink looked rich and inviting, the kind of thing that promised warmth and danger in equal measure.

"Looks delicious," I said. "But bourbon and I broke up years ago. It was a toxic relationship. Anything more than a whiff, and I started telling people I love them."

Tessa snorted into her glass.

"We've all got that one ex in a bottle. Mine's gin. It makes me think I can dance."

Before I could respond, the server appeared beside our table.

"Can I get you something to drink?"

"Glass of red, please," I said. "Something dry."

"Cab okay?"

"Perfect."

"You got it."

When she left, I turned back to Tessa.

"Thanks for taking time to meet. Sometimes having a

conversation is easier than going back and forth in email or text."

"Are you kidding?" Tessa said, smiling over the rim of her glass. "I should be thanking you. It's nice to talk about the team without a spreadsheet open in front of me, or three people waiting for my signature on something."

I laughed softly.

"You mean this doesn't count as work?"

"Technically it does," she said with a mock sigh, "but this version comes with cocktails and good food." Her expression softened as she set her glass down. "Seriously, though, I appreciate you being flexible. Between the brewery and the team, my days get away from me faster than I can catch them. By the time I get home, I feel like my brain's been put through a grain mill."

"I get that," I said. "And honestly, I don't mind evening meetings. The Maiden beats a conference room any day."

"That's true," she said. "And it's nice to just slow down for a minute."

The server returned with my wine, setting it down before asking if we were ready to order. Tessa went with a burger and fries, and I chose fish and chips. Once she walked away, the quiet between us settled comfortably, filled with the soft murmur of conversation from nearby tables.

"I didn't mean to add to your workload by investing in the Lagerheads," I said. "But when my mom mentioned you and your sisters were considering selling, I felt like I had to do something."

"Honestly, we were overwhelmed. Between the brewery, the team, and the outdated stadium, it felt like too much. Selling seemed like the simplest option."

"It would've broken my heart to see the Lagerheads end

up in someone else's hands. Your dad put so much into building the franchise, it deserved a chance to thrive, not fade out."

Tessa studied me for a long moment, and I wondered if I'd overstepped. Then she smiled faintly.

"You sound like my dad when he used to talk about the team," she said softly. "He really did love it. Maybe too much, honestly."

"Too much?"

She nodded, tracing the rim of her glass with her finger.

"After he died, I went through his old files—loan documents, league correspondence, contracts. It was like piecing together a puzzle of what he had to do to move the Lagerheads up from minor league to major."

I stayed quiet, sensing there was more.

"Player salaries had to increase. Travel went from regional bus rides to cross-country flights. We needed new staff, more scouts, better medical facilities. Then the league required stadium upgrades—luxury seating, press boxes, locker room expansions, turf maintenance. The works."

"That's a lot."

My team had flagged the financial issues as soon as I said I wanted to invest. I knew they existed—I just hadn't asked for the full story behind them. The decision had already been made.

"Exactly," she said. "And Dad thought he could handle it all through optimism and hometown pride. He signed off on long-term loans, expecting ticket sales and sponsorships to cover the difference. But when attendance dipped after a few losing seasons, that gap just kept widening."

"And then things just snowballed."

She nodded and sighed.

"But he built something special, even if it stretched too

far. And now you're here to help make sure it doesn't fall apart."

"I didn't mean to bulldoze my way in when I offered to invest," I said. "I just wanted to help keep his vision alive, and I guess hang on to a little piece of my own history while I was at it."

"You didn't bulldoze anything, Quinn. You showed up with a plan when the rest of us were drowning. If anything, you gave us space to breathe." She smiled. "And I appreciate that you've been so hands-on. It's made my life a little easier."

Before I could respond, the server returned with our food, the warm scent of fried batter and charred onions drifting between us as she set down our plates. We thanked her, and when she walked away, I glanced across the table at Tessa.

Her words had caught me off guard in the best way. We weren't friends—at least, not yet—but in that moment, it felt like maybe this new chapter in Waypoint had room for more than I thought.

Chapter Seven

Benny

The construction crews were gone for the weekend, but the place still smelled like sawdust and fresh paint. Dust motes drifted through the light cutting across the half-finished clubhouse. Metal studs framed what would soon be lockers, piles of lumber stacked where couches would go.

I could picture it all, but for now it was just a promise.

Dane Mercer walked beside me, hands in his jacket pockets, scanning everything with a pitcher's focus. A step behind us, Marin Hollis took it all in, her ponytail swinging as her gaze tracked the space. The woman didn't just look, she assessed. You could practically see the gears turning as she did.

"This'll clean up nice," Dane said, voice bouncing off concrete.

"Eventually," I said. "Right now it's like walking through a blueprint."

Marin crouched near the taped-off floor where the locker row would start.

"Good sightline from here to the entrance," she said. "If you want to keep eyes on players coming and going."

"Always do," I said. "Helps when you're trying to read a mood before it walks through the door."

She smirked.

"Spoken like a catcher."

I shrugged. "Old habits."

The three of us stepped into the adjoining hallway that would become the training area. The faint tang of plaster and paint hung in the air.

"Hydro's over there," I said, nodding toward the wall. "Strength and conditioning will be through that set of doors."

Marin glanced around. "It's bigger than I expected."

She wasn't wrong, but it'd feel smaller once the players and all the equipment took it over.

We followed the hallway toward a stretch of framed drywall.

"Coaches' offices will line this wall," I said, gesturing toward the framed-out section. "Each of you'll have your own. They won't be fancy, but they'll be functional and private."

"Nice," Marin said, glancing around like she was already picturing it.

"I like the setup," Dane said.

"Once the cables and drywall go in, it'll start looking like a real operation. Until then, you're borrowing my temporary space upstairs."

Dane grinned.

"Can't wait to see how a big-league temporary office looks."

"Don't get your hopes up," I said. "It's got four walls and bad lighting, but the coffee's close."

We left the clubhouse, our footsteps echoing in the quiet. "The hallway to the elevator was lined with paint cans, coiled cords, and a ladder leaning against the wall. Everything waiting for Monday's crew to return.

I hit the up button, and the light flickered once before the doors slid open. The elevator hummed softly as it carried us up to the front-office level. When the doors opened, the change was instant. The walls were clean, lined with framed photos of past seasons, and the carpet looked like it had never seen a speck of dust. Up here, baseball was paperwork and polish instead of dirt and noise.

My temporary office sat near the end of the hallway, wedged between operations and media relations. It wasn't much—just a standard-issue space with a solid desk, a couple of chairs, and a couch under the window that was surprisingly comfortable.

I moved behind the desk and sat, and they followed my lead—Dane taking the chair closest to the door, Marin the one beside him.

"Not bad," Dane said, taking a look around.

"It's functional." I glanced at Marin. "Dane said you've coached before?"

She nodded.

"Yeah. both baseball and softball—travel teams, hitting clinics, a couple years at a $D3$ program. I played $D1$ softball, but baseball's where I started, until I had to switch."

"You've been around the game your whole life, then."

"Pretty much," she said. "Just never thought I'd end up here."

"Not many get the chance," I said. "Dane speaks highly of you. That goes a long way with me."

Marin glanced at him, a small, genuine smile forming.

"He's been in my corner a long time, and I'm grateful for that."

"She's earned it," Dane said.

I believed him. The way she carried herself, it wasn't hard to see why.

It wasn't technically official, but in baseball, a handshake and a walk through the clubhouse meant almost as much as ink. As far as I was concerned, they were my first hires.

There was still plenty to sort out—contracts, titles, logistics—but the foundation was there.

I glanced at my watch.

"Let's head to the conference room," I said. "We're meeting Tessa Bergmann there."

I stood, and they followed. Dane rolled his shoulders like he was loosening up between innings, while Marin slipped her hands into her jacket pockets as we headed down the hall.

Tessa was already there when we arrived, sitting at the head of the table glaring at her laptop. She looked up when we walked in, offering a quick smile.

"Tessa, this is Dane Mercer and Marin Hollis," I said. "Our pitching and hitting coaches."

She stood to shake their hands.

"Nice to meet you both. I've heard good things."

"Likewise," Dane said.

Marin smiled. "Thanks for having us."

"Thank you for coming." Tessa glanced at her computer. "I need to run and grab my charger, but I'll be right back." She walked to the door, then paused. "Go ahead and grab a seat. Oh—and Quinn's able to join us."

Dane dropped into a chair, leaning back like he owned the place already. Marin sat next to him, but she wasn't focused on the room. Her gaze stayed fixed on the door Tessa had just walked through.

Marin's head turned sharply toward me.

"Wait," she said. "Did she say Quinn? As in Quinn Logan?"

"That's the one," I said.

She blinked.

"*The* Quinn Logan?"

"That's usually how it works when there's only one," Dane said.

She ignored him completely, eyes wide, shaking her head in disbelief. "I knew she was from Waypoint, but I didn't think I'd ever actually be in the same room as her." Her eyes lit up. "I had her songs on every pregame playlist. Her music was the theme of my twenty-first birthday. My roommates and I once drove six hours to see her live."

I leaned back in my chair. "You gonna be able to keep it together?" I asked, only half joking.

"Barely," she muttered, though she was smiling. "I didn't even know she was involved with the team."

"Most people don't," I said.

"Okay, that's wild." Marin shook her head. "I don't usually get starstruck, but come on—it's *Quinn Logan*."

"Relax," I said, fighting a grin. "She's not showing up with a microphone. Just a notebook."

Dane chuckled, and Marin gave him a mock glare, but the blush in her cheeks gave her away.

I'd seen plenty of players lose their composure in the box, but watching one of my new coaches try to get hers back in a conference room was a first.

A second later, soft footsteps sounded in the hall. Marin straightened like she'd been caught doing something she shouldn't, her expression hovering somewhere between professional and panic.

The door opened, and Quinn stepped inside with that quiet ease that came from someone who'd learned how to make any room feel smaller. She wore jeans, white sneakers, and a black sweater, her hair pulled into a loose knot that had probably taken two seconds but somehow looked perfect anyway. A hint of nervous energy flickered behind her smile, but she carried it well.

Her gaze found mine and the corners of her mouth lifted, just enough to say she was glad to see me. Something settled in my chest.

"Hey," she said softly.

"Hey," I answered, my voice coming out lower than I intended.

The air between us held still, just long enough for it to mean something. Before it got too heavy, Tessa breezed back into the room, laptop charger in hand. She caught sight of Quinn and smiled.

"Oh, good, you're here," she said as she took her seat at the head of the table. "Have you met our new coaches?"

"Not yet."

I stood, remembering my manners.

"Quinn, this is Dane Mercer, our new pitching coach."

Dane stood, polite and steady.

"Nice to meet you."

"You too," Quinn said, shaking his hand.

"And this is Marin Hollis, our hitting coach."

Marin half-stood, half-froze, her eyes wide. Then she blinked, trying—and failing—to stay professional.

"Wow. Sorry, this is just...surreal." Then she repeated what she'd just said to Dane and me a few minutes earlier, stumbling through a rush of disbelief and fandom.

Quinn laughed, easy and kind.

"I hope it was worth the drive."

"It was," Marin said, nodding so hard she looked like a bobblehead.

Quinn's eyes sparkled as she looked back at me.

"I heartily approve of your coaching choices," she said, her tone all mock-serious. "Anyone with taste that impeccable clearly knows what they're doing."

I couldn't help but smile. "I'll try to live up to the standard."

"Good," she murmured, settling into the chair next to me.

A faint trace of her perfume drifted over. And just like that, staying focused on the meeting got a whole lot harder.

Chapter Eight

Quinn

This wasn't really a meeting, but more of a casual get-to-know-you thing. There was no agenda, spreadsheets, or negotiations. Just introductions and conversation.

Tessa and I were there to make it official in spirit, even if the contracts weren't signed yet. The team lawyers were trading edits with Dane and Marin's reps, ironing out the details that came with every MLB hire. But according to Benny, they were fully on board. Which was exciting, because they seemed like a good fit to me.

We talked easily about our plans for the Lagerheads, local coffee shops, and hiking trails nearby. Dane had the quiet steadiness of someone still adjusting to normal life after years in the majors. He didn't say much, but when he did, it came with the kind of thoughtfulness you only learned from being part of a team for a long time. Marin, on the other hand, was a mix of enthusiasm and control. She listened more than she talked, but when she did, her thoughts came out sharp and sure. You didn't have to know baseball to see she belonged here.

Thankfully, it didn't take long for the wide-eyed, starstruck look she'd gotten when I first walked in to fade. I'd gotten used to that reaction years ago, but it never stopped feeling strange. Underneath it all, I was still just a dork from Waypoint, trying to make sense of the world one step at a time and trying not to trip.

"So, what's Waypoint like?" Marin asked. "Any areas I should avoid looking at for rentals?"

"There are some sections better than others, but nothing you'd call terrible," Tessa said. "It just depends on what want."

"If you want quiet, stay west of Main," I added. "Closer to the brewery gets a little louder on weekends, but you'll never run out of good food or live music."

"Good to know."

Tessa pulled out her phone.

"I'll text you the name of a realtor I've worked with. She's great, and knows which landlords actually fix things when they break."

"That'd be great, thank you," Marin said.

"We can explore tomorrow and get a feel for the town," Dane said, stretching his shoulders. "Right now, I'm too tired to be driving around."

"I forgot you were up before the sun to catch your flight," Benny said. "Go check into the hotel. I figured we'd grab dinner around seven-thirty, so you've got time to relax beforehand."

"Perfect," Dane said.

Benny glanced between Tessa and me.

"You two should come. I was thinking Roma since we won't need a reservation."

"Pasta and wine? I'm in," Tessa said with a grin.

"Sounds good," I added.

"Great." Benny said to me. "I have two quick budget questions. I'll text them to you. Unless you've got your notebook with you," he added with a grin.

"Actually, I do," I said, tapping my purse. "So we can talk now if you'd like."

"Perfect."

Dane pushed to his feet, stretching once.

"Then we'll get out of your hair. I think we're both ready to crash for a bit before dinner."

"Yeah, it's been a long day of travel," Marin said. "I'll feel human again after a shower and some rest."

Tessa stood and grabbed her bag. "I'll walk you out," she said to Dane and Marin, then she looked at Benny and me. "See you later."

"See you later."

The three of them walked out of the room, their voices trailing down the hall. Then it was just Benny and me.

I pulled my notebook from my purse and set it on the table. I'd tabbed the pages—because of course I had—so I knew exactly where to flip to.

Benny leaned over the table, one palm down on the wood as he looked. "You color-coded this since I last saw it."

"Welcome to my coping mechanism," I said. "Blue is fixed costs, green is flexible, yellow is wiggle room. If there's a pink dot, it means I had coffee and optimism at the same time."

His mouth curved. "Dangerous combination."

"Per my mother, yes," I said with a smile.

I answered his questions about staff-line-item ranges I'd suggested and how the scoreboard payment milestones were tied to installation phases. He listened like a man who'd learned patience one inning at a time—focused, alert, and still in body but not in mind.

When I finished, he said, "That helps. Thank you."

"Anytime." I closed the notebook and slid it back into my purse.

For a second, neither of us moved, suspended in that quiet in-between where business ended and something else might start.

"Shall we?"

He nodded toward the door.

"Right," I said, pushing my chair back to stand.

We left the room, walking side by side through the quiet office level. When we reached the elevator, Benny hit the down button, and the doors opened with a soft sigh. He gestured for me to go first, then stepped in.

The doors slid shut, and the car moved maybe two feet before a dull clang sounded above us and the motion stopped dead. A single, half-hearted ding followed—less "arriving at your floor" and more "I tried my best."

I stared at the panel like it might offer an explanation.

"Um."

Benny pressed one button, then another.

"Well," he said dryly, "that was a new sound."

The lights flickered once but stayed on—a dim, steady, the kind of glow that made everything feel too quiet. He exhaled through his nose, calm but assessing, like he was running through options the same way he probably used to on the field.

He hit the red emergency call button. A few seconds later, the tiny speaker crackled to life.

"Building security," a voice said, distant and tinny. "Are you stuck in an elevator?"

Benny leaned toward the panel.

"Sure looks that way," he said.

"All right, sir," the voice replied, calm but slightly

distorted through the speaker. "I'll notify maintenance right away. Please don't try to force the doors. How many people are in there with you?"

"Just one," Benny said.

"Is anyone hurt?"

"No," he answered.

"Good. Then sit tight. Maintenance will be there within the hour."

The speaker clicked off, leaving only the quiet hum of the fan.

Benny looked at me and exhaled a slow breath through his nose. "Guess we're not going anywhere for a bit."

"Guess not."

He pushed off the wall and sank to the floor, stretching one leg out and resting his forearm on his bent knee.

"Might as well get comfortable," he said.

I hesitated for a second, then slid down the opposite wall. The space between us felt smaller sitting like this, our legs only a couple of feet apart.

"Well," I said, tucking a strand of hair behind my ear. "This is officially the most unexpected part of my day."

He chuckled softly.

"Can't say it's how I pictured mine either."

"I like Dane and Marin."

"Yeah, I think they'll work out well." He rubbed the back of his neck. "I'm glad Dane recommended her. She's not someone I would've normally looked at."

"Because she's a woman?" I asked, feigning a gasp.

"Partly," he admitted, a half-smile tugging at his mouth. "But mostly because her résumé isn't what I'd usually go for. Most of her experience is in travel ball and D3 college— not exactly the traditional path to the majors."

"Then why'd you hire her?"

"Because I trust Dane. And after talking to her, I believe him when he says she's the best."

"She comes across calm and collected," I said. "Like nothing shakes her."

"That was true until you walked in."

"She was sweet."

Silence stretched for a beat before he spoke again.

"I take it that happens a lot."

"More than I ever knew how to handle," I admitted. "And it still feels strange. Underneath all of it, I'm just me."

"You ever miss it? The stage, the spotlight?"

"Sometimes," I said honestly. "I loved my fans and performing for them. I loved the feeling of a song connecting with a stadium full of people. The way a show can feel like everyone's heartbeat syncing." I scratched lightly at my wrist, searching for the right words. "But the noise, the scrutiny, the feeling that every breath had to be on display wore me down, and I needed a break."

"Everyone thinks they want the spotlight until they realize how hot it gets." His eyes met mine. "Still...walking away takes guts."

I huffed out a small laugh.

"Or weak knees." His brow lifted, amused. "I'm serious," I said, smiling despite myself. "Those final tour workouts nearly killed me. Dancing in heels under stage lights at forty? That's an Olympic sport."

He laughed quietly, the sound low and easy. For a moment, it felt lighter between us, like the conversation had traded its weight for something simpler.

"Is that why you came back here? For a break?"

"Partly," I said. "But mostly because of my mom. She was diagnosed with breast cancer right at the end of my final tour. I asked her to move to L.A. for treatment, but she wanted to stay here. So I came home."

Benny's expression softened.

"How's she doing now?"

"She's good," I said, smiling. "Her scans have been clean for over a year now. She's back to her usual routines and spending time with her friends."

The quiet that followed wasn't heavy, just the kind that let you exhale and made small talk unnecessary. It stretched, full of something unspoken. Then Benny looked over, his voice easy.

"You know, sitting here, it's hard to picture you as the same person who used to be on all those magazine covers."

"That girl had a whole team behind her," I said with a small laugh. "The lighting, the styling, the editing—none of it ever felt like me. I've always been the same person underneath it all. I just look a little more like myself now."

"Looks good on you," he said. "The real version."

The words landed softly but lingered. His gaze held, not sharp, just...intent. Curious. Like he was trying to see all the parts of me I kept tucked away.

"Thanks," I managed, though my voice came out a little thinner than I meant it to.

The air felt warmer, or maybe that was just proximity—two people sitting on the floor, knees a foot apart, sharing too much space and not enough air.

He leaned back against the wall, eyes still on me.

"You make it easy to forget you used to fill stadiums," he said.

"Good. I just want to be plain old Quinn."

His mouth curved, slow and sure.

"There's nothing plain about you, Quinn."

The air between us thickened. My heart did an

unhelpful fluttery thing, and I tried to steady my breath. He didn't look away, and I didn't want him to.

"Benny—" I started, but whatever I meant to say vanished the second his knee brushed mine. Funny how something so insignificant could change the entire temperature of a room. Or, in this case, an elevator."

He leaned in, close enough that I could catch the warmth of his skin and the faint, clean scent of his cologne. His gaze flicked to my mouth, then back to my eyes, and for a beat the world felt balanced on that breath between maybe and almost.

"Quinn," he said, my name coming out rough, like gravel and hesitation all at once.

The sound of it was enough to undo me a little. I shifted forward just a fraction, and for a heartbeat, the world went perfectly still. Then the elevator jolted hard. A metallic thunk echoed through the car as the lights flickered back to full brightness.

The jolt sent me off balance, and I caught myself against the wall. Benny blinked, then let out a short laugh.

"Perfect timing," he said.

"Yeah." My voice came out breathier than I wanted. "Impeccable."

Wait until I tell Erin the elevator cockblocked me out of kissing Benny Reed.

Chapter Nine

Benny

Roma was the kind of place where you didn't have to rush. It moved at a slow rhythm, like a long seventh inning stretch. Forks clinked, someone laughed near the bar, and Sinatra played low through the speakers, smooth and familiar.

Garlic and Italian herbs hung in the air, mixed with the kind of warmth that came from simmering tomato sauce and bread fresh out of the oven. I got there first and claimed a corner table near the window, where I could see the whole room without feeling too exposed."

I'd just started looking through the menu when the noise shifted enough to catch my attention. Quinn stood just inside the door, scanning the crowd until her eyes found mine. She smiled, and something in my chest loosened.

As she crossed the room, I caught myself noticing the little things—the way her hair fell forward when she moved, how she pushed it back without even thinking, the quick, half-wave she gave when she got closer. She'd probably call herself awkward, but to me, it just looked like Quinn being Quinn.

I stood as she approached, the way my mom drilled into me years ago.

"Hey," she said when she reached the table.

"Hey yourself."

"I forgot how cozy this place is," she said, glancing around before taking the seat across from me.

"Yeah," I said. "Roma's kind of the definition of reliable—same lights, red candles and smell of garlic that clings to your clothes after you leave."

She laughed quietly.

"Exactly. My parents used to bring me here all the time when I was a kid. We'd always sit in that corner booth over there." She nodded toward the back of the restaurant. "It felt so fancy back then."

"Still does," I said, glancing around. "Just in a small-town kind of way."

"Yeah. I guess it does."

Her smile softened, nostalgia flickering across her face.

"What's that smile for?"

"My parents used to let me order Shirley Temples and pretend I was a grown-up for the night."

I couldn't help but smile, picturing tiny Quinn in that corner booth, all bright eyes, drinking sugar water, thinking the world was hers.

"Let me guess. Extra cherries."

Her laugh was soft, the kind that stuck with you.

Before she could answer, the server stopped by our table.

"Can I get you something to drink while you wait for the rest of your party?"

Quinn shook her head lightly, still smiling.

"Water's good for now, thanks."

"Same," I said.

The server nodded and walked off. For a moment, neither of us said anything. The sounds of the restaurant filled the space instead—the clatter of plates, the low murmur of conversation, Sinatra giving way to Dean Martin crooning about getting kicked in the head by love.

A couple of people passed our table, their eyes flicking toward her. I noticed it before she did. Or maybe she noticed and just didn't react.

"You know, if the whole town didn't already know you're involved with the Lagerheads, they will after tonight."

Her eyes flicked up, amused.

"It was bound to happen eventually."

"Yeah," I said, letting a grin tug at the corner of my mouth. "But I didn't think it'd start with people rubber-necking over their pasta."

That made her laugh, quiet but genuine.

The server came back with our waters, setting them down with the kind of practiced ease that came from years of balancing trays.

"Here you go," she said with a smile. "I'll give you a few minutes before I check back."

"Thanks," Quinn said, wrapping her hands around her glass.

Before I could say anything else, I noticed Tessa, Dane, and Marin weaving through the tables toward us. I stood as they approached.

"Hey, you two," Tessa said, slipping out of her coat.

Marin took a quick look around before pulling out a chair and sitting next to Quinn.

"It smells incredible in here."

"Seriously," Dane said. "I wasn't even hungry until I walked through the door."

I sat back down once they were all seated.

"How's the hotel?" I asked, shifting my gaze between Dane and Marin. "You get settled in okay?"

Dane nodded.

"It's nice. Quiet."

"The bed's ridiculously comfortable," Marin said. "Although, I was so tired, I could've slept on a bed of nails."

"That's travel for you," Tessa said. "At least you'll get some real rest tonight."

"Here's hoping," Marin said with a faint smile.

The server reappeared with water for the three of them, setting the glasses down one by one.

"Can I get you started with any drinks?"

After a quick debate, Dane and I ordered a pitcher of Bergmann Lager to share and the ladies went with a bottle of red wine.

"I'll be right back with those and some bread," the server said.

When she left, conversation hovered for a beat before finding its rhythm again. Dane rested an elbow on the table, glancing over at Tessa.

"I'm impressed with everything you've got planned for the stadium.

Tessa smiled, half-proud, half-exhausted. "Yeah, there's a lot happening."

"Any concerns about the short timeline?"

"Well, we're not touching the seating or structure, just the clubhouse and the boards." She took a sip of water and continued. "We brought in a firm that really knows stadium work, and they've been great. It's a tight schedule, but they're moving fast and tackling everything in phases."

"It sounds like a huge coordination effort," Marin said.

"It definitely is," Tessa said with a small laugh. "My dad built the place solid, it just needed some modernization." She smiled at Quinn. "And luckily, we've got someone on the team with a good eye for design."

Quinn's her mouth curved, more wry than proud. "I never thought my experience designing stages would come in handy in baseball, but here we are."

Tessa's expression softened. "You've been invaluable. I couldn't do it without you."

I wasn't sure if she meant financially or otherwise, but it didn't really matter. From what I'd seen, Quinn wasn't just signing checks, she was helping manage the whole thing. That notebook of hers was packed with project details, budgets, and notes I couldn't begin to decode.

"Since we're talking about the stadium..." Tessa glanced between Quinn and me. "I'm so sorry about the elevator."

"There's no reason for you to be sorry," Quinn said. "It wasn't your fault."

"What happened?" Dane asked.

"Quinn and I got stuck in the elevator when we were leaving the stadium earlier," I said.

Marin's eyes rounded. "Oh, I would've lost it. You'd have had to peel me off the ceiling."

Quinn laughed. "It wasn't that bad. We were out in less than an hour."

"Still, trapped in a metal box?" Marin shook her head. "Nope."

"Remind me to never ride in an elevator with you just in case," Dane said with a smirk.

Marin elbowed him, and everyone laughed, the sound tapering off as the clink of glasses and the low music took over again.

"So, what's good here?" Dane asked, flipping open his menu.

"Everything," Tessa said with a grin. "I usually stick with the homemade pasta unless one of the specials catches my attention."

Marin nodded, scanning the page. "Homemade pasta's hard to beat."

The table went quiet as everyone looked over their menus. I picked mine up too, though I couldn't have said what was on it. All I could see was the inside of that elevator, the soft glow of the overhead light, and Quinn sitting inches away.

And then we'd almost—

Yeah. Almost.

I glanced up and found her watching me. Her expression was calm, maybe even curious, but there was a flicker in her eyes. Something that said she remembered it, too.

Maybe she was wondering the same thing I was...what would've happened if we hadn't been interrupted?

The server came back with bread and drinks, breaking the moment. After we placed our orders, conversation sparked again, but I barely heard it. My mind was still in that elevator, stuck in the moment right before almost.

Chapter Ten

Quinn

My phone buzzed against the nightstand, dragging me out of the kind of half-sleep where your brain won't shut up. I'd woken up more than once, stuck halfway between dreaming and that elevator, like my brain hadn't gotten the memo that the day was over. Forty-five minutes between floors, one almost-kiss, and now my brain was apparently screening the extended edition.

I groaned, rolled over, and grabbed my phone from the nightstand. Eight missed texts, three emails from Tessa about design revisions, and one message from my mother.

> Call me before noon or I'm assuming you've joined a cult.

I typed back a reply.

> Not a cult. Just sleeping in. Coffee first.

Mom's response was instant.

I've got a fresh pot and cinnamon rolls in
the oven.

She knew my weaknesses too well. Only the promise of caffeine and sugar could lure me out of bed after a restless night.

I dragged myself upright, ran a brush through my hair, and traded pajamas for leggings and a hoodie. It wasn't exactly brunch attire, but my mom wasn't picky.

Her house was five minutes away and smelled like nostalgia. Mom was in the kitchen when I walked in, pulling a tray of cinnamon rolls from the oven like some kind of domestic sorceress.

"Well, look who decided to join the land of the living," she said, setting down the pan and turning toward me with a knowing smile. "Late night?"

"No, I just didn't sleep well," I said, sliding onto a stool at the island. "My brain wouldn't shut up."

"Ah," she said, grabbing two mugs from the cabinet.

"What does that mean?"

She gave me a look over her shoulder.

"I've seen you sleep in the middle of airports and through hotel fire alarms. When you're tired, you're out cold. So, if you were tossing and turning, something's up."

She poured coffee into a mug and passed it to me.

"You really missed your calling as a therapist."

"Please. I'd get fired for telling people the truth." She leaned against the island, eyes bright. "Now what's keeping you up at night?"

"Nothing dramatic," I said, wrapping my hands around the mug. "Just project things. Design things. Baseball-adjacent things."

Mom's mouth curved, the kind of knowing smile that made me instantly regret talking.

"Are the baseball-adjacent things the reason you're blushing?"

"I'm not blushing."

"You're absolutely blushing."

I held up my mug

"It's the steam."

She didn't answer, just turned back to the counter, picked up the bowl of cream cheese icing, and started spreading it over the cinnamon rolls like she had all the time in the world. The smell of warm sugar filled the kitchen, and my stomach made a traitorous noise.

Without looking at me, she said, "You know, people usually deflect when there's something worth deflecting."

She finished icing one, slid it onto a plate, and handed it to me. Then she plated another for herself, wiped her hands on a towel, and came to sit beside me at the island. The chair creaked softly as she settled in, like even it knew what was coming.

"I'm not deflecting," I said around a bite of cinnamon roll that was way too good to be eaten mid-interrogation.

"Sure you're not." She took a slow sip of coffee, eyes glinting over the rim of her mug. "So, what's got you losing sleep, if it's not whatever's happening in your baseball-adjacent world?"

"Mom."

"*Quinn.*"

Her tone softened, but her expression stayed expectant. I sighed, setting my fork down. Might as well tell her because she wasn't going to relent.

"Fine. Benny and I got stuck in the elevator at the stadium yesterday."

Her eyebrows lifted.

"Oh?"

"For forty-five minutes."

Her mouth curved into a grin.

"My God, I raised a rom-com heroine."

"It was an elevator malfunction, not a meet-cute."

She laughed, shaking her head.

"Forty-five minutes trapped with your teenage crush, who still looks like that, and you're telling me nothing happened?"

"Nothing happened."

"But you wanted it to."

"Mom."

"*Quinn.*"

I groaned.

"Can we not do this before I finish my coffee?"

"Sweetheart, I've been your mother for forty-one years. I know that tone."

"What tone?"

"The one you get when you're trying to convince yourself something was *no big deal* when it's absolutely a big deal."

I stabbed at my cinnamon roll with my fork.

"It wasn't."

"Mmm hmm," she said, all disbelief and mom judgment rolled into two syllables. "So, what did you do for forty-five minutes?"

"Talked."

"About what?"

"I don't know—things."

"Things," she repeated, her smile turning sly. "Did any of those things include gazing longingly while the elevator lights flickered romantically?"

"Seriously?"

She rested her elbows on the island and leaned toward me, eyes sparkling with mischief.

"I'm guessing there was a moment." I hesitated, which was apparently as good as confessing. Her grin widened. "Oh, there was definitely a moment."

I nodded, exhaling.

"There was a moment."

Her voice softened.

"What happened?"

I traced a line through the icing on my plate with my fork.

"Nothing. Not really. We were sitting there, talking, and then the vibe just sort of...shifted."

"Shifted how?"

"The air changed," I said, feeling ridiculous even as the words left my mouth. "He was sitting across from me, I looked up, and suddenly it felt like we weren't just waiting to be rescued anymore. He looked at me, and it was—" I broke off, shaking my head. "You know that feeling when everything slows down and you can practically hear your heartbeat in your ears?"

Her lips curved.

"Yeah," she said softly.

"We just looked at each other, and things between us felt so real."

"So...what happened?"

"We leaned in, but before our lips touched, the elevator jolted back to life and ruined the whole thing."

She smiled into her coffee.

"Well, that's one way to kill the mood."

"Yeah," I said, half laughing, half groaning. "And when the doors opened, we both jumped up like nothing had happened. I think I actually said, 'Well, that was fun,' which ranks high on my personal list of most humiliating sentences."

She didn't say anything right away, just watched me with that quiet kind of understanding that never needed words.

Finally, she set her mug down and said, "Maybe it didn't ruin anything. Maybe it just pressed pause."

"It's complicated," I said. "I'm trying to keep things professional."

"Of course you are," she snorted. "Which explains why you've been replaying it all night and came here for caffeine therapy."

"You're impossible."

"I prefer insightful."

I tried to look annoyed, but she was right. She was *always* right.

"He's nice," I said finally, keeping my voice even. "Funny. Grounded. Not what I expected."

Her expression softened.

"And how does he look at you?"

"What do you mean?"

"I've seen people look at you your whole life—on red carpets, in interviews, even in grocery stores. They see the version of you they think they know. But if this man looks at you like he actually sees you, that's not nothing."

"It was just one of those weird, suspended moments. Nothing more."

"Honey, moments like that are never *nothing*."

I stared down at the swirl in my mug, pretending to study it. But even as I drained the last sip, my mind wandered back to dinner—the way Benny's laugh rumbled low, how he'd looked at me across the table. The same look from that elevator. The one that made everything around us go quiet for a second too long.

I told myself it was nothing.

But my stomach still flipped like I'd wandered into a slow-burn rom-com—the kind where the heroine definitely knows better, but falls anyway.

Chapter Eleven

Benny

The dining room gleamed the way old money does—quietly.

Soft gold wallpaper, heavy drapes, and polished silver caught the chandelier's light.

The kind of timeless décor that never needed changing because it wasn't allowed to go out of style.

Antique rugs that had probably come over on a ship. Oil paintings of people we weren't related to. Heavy crystal on the sideboard that never moved, even when the table did. It didn't look new, but it didn't look old either—just settled, like everything in this house had already earned the right to stay.

Grace and Charlie were the only bright, loud things in the room. They were arguing over napkin rings at the far end of the table.

"Mine's shinier," Grace said.

"They're the same!" Charlie countered.

Cat stifled a laugh beside me. Mom didn't.

"Children," Mom said, not raising her voice but ending the argument anyway.

Dad sliced the roast at the head of the table, posture straight, movements precise.

"Still got it," he murmured, like anyone had questioned his carving credentials.

We all sat. The chandelier light glinted off crystal water glasses. The air smelled like rosemary and expectation.

Dad passed the platter to Mom, who served portions with practiced care. Plates made their way around the table, and for a few minutes, the only sounds were the soft scrape of silverware and the clink of china.

Mom dabbed the corner of her mouth with her napkin, her voice softening as she looked down the table.

"So, Charlie, how was school this week?"

"Pretty good! We made scarecrows in art class. Mine's named Frank. He's missing an arm, but my teacher said it gives him character."

Dad chuckled. "Sounds like Frank's been through some things."

Mom smiled, her voice warm in a way I didn't remember from when I was a kid.

"I'm sure he looks very handsome."

Charlie beamed.

"He's kind of lopsided, but I think he'd still scare crows."

"A lopsided scarecrow probably scares more crows," Dad said.

That got Charlie grinning wide, and Mom laughed. Even Cat chuckled, and Grace joined in too.

The sound of it hit me weird as it filled the room like it belonged there. I couldn't remember ever laughing at this table when I was a kid. It was...nice. And maybe a little unsettling, like walking through a house you used to live in and realizing the furniture's all been moved.

Mom turned toward Grace, still smiling.

"And how about you, sweetheart? How was your week?"

Grace sat a little taller.

"Good! We're having a talent show. Me and Sami are doing a dance to "Messy in the Best Way." It's our favorite Quinn Logan song! We copied some moves from the video, but we made up the rest."

"That sounds lovely. I'm sure you'll be wonderful." She glanced toward Dad. "We can't wait to see the show."

"She's been practicing in the living room every night." Cat grinned. "I think I could do half the routine in my sleep."

Charlie groaned.

"She makes me be a backup dancer."

"Every star needs a supporting act," Dad said with a chuckle.

Grace giggled, Charlie rolled his eyes, and for a second the whole thing felt like a real family dinner—comfortable, loud, a little chaotic.

Then Mom set her wineglass down and smoothed her napkin, the move that always meant she was about to pivot. Her gaze shifted to me, polite but deliberate.

"I saw Ava Corbyn at church last Sunday," she said. "She asked about you."

A low sound left my throat—maybe a grunt, maybe acknowledgment. Either way, it wasn't encouragement.

Mom carried on like I'd said *please, tell me more.*

"She's divorced now, poor thing—but still just as lovely as ever. You should give her a call sometime."

I set my fork down, slow enough not to make a sound.

"Pretty sure Ava and I ran out of things to talk about twenty years ago."

Mom tilted her head, that gentle smile never slipping.

"You two were such a handsome couple back then."

"*Back then* is the key part of that sentence."

She sighed softly, disappointment wrapped in civility.

"I just thought you might like to reconnect. She's always been such a sweet girl."

If she knew half the things that *sweet girl* and I got up to the summer before senior year, she'd probably have a stroke.

"Mom," I said, keeping my voice even. "Please don't play matchmaker. I'm good."

Across the table, Cat caught my eye, her silent version of *let it go.*

And then, because timing was his superpower, Dad spoke up.

"Speaking of reconnecting, I heard you had dinner with Quinn Logan the other night."

Grace froze mid-bite. "*The* Quinn Logan? Like, "Messy in the Best Way" Quinn Logan?"

Her excitement pulled a small smile out of me before I could stop it.

"That's the one. It was a business dinner. Tessa and two of my new coaches were there too."

Cat looked down the table at Grace.

"You know Uncle Benny and I went to school with Quinn."

"That's *so* cool." She hesitated, eyes bright. "Maybe I can meet her sometime?"

"We'll see, kiddo," I said with a smile.

She grinned, clearly taking that as a yes.

"I've heard whispers that she's involved with the team." Dad leaned back in his chair. "So, it's true, then?"

"She is, yeah. But it's not public knowledge."

He huffed, the sound halfway between a laugh and a warning.

"After that dinner, I'd say it is." He picked up his wineglass, swirling it once before taking a slow sip. "You should be careful, Benny. The team needs to stand on its own merit, not on some celebrity name attached to it."

There it was—concern disguised as advice, with just enough judgment baked in to hit its mark. I didn't respond. Instead, I focused on my plate, cutting another piece of roast that suddenly tasted like cardboard.

Across the table, Cat shifted the conversation toward the kids. I could feel Dad's eyes on me while I chewed, that familiar weight across the table, like he was just waiting for the right opening.

"You know," he said, when he finally got it. "I still think you retired too early. You had more years in you."

There it was. Right on schedule.

"My knees didn't agree."

Dad gave a short scoff, half laugh, half disbelief.

"That's what physical therapy and cortisone shots are for. You could've pushed through it if you'd wanted it badly enough."

I bit back the urge to point out that two decades of crouching behind the plate *was* pushing through it, that I'd already traded enough cartilage for a career. But there was no point.

It took getting out of Waypoint to see it clearly. The way Dad's approval had always come with conditions. The way Mom's pride depended on performance. Growing up, I mistook that for motivation. Maybe it was, at first. Without it, I might not have worked as hard, pushed as far, made it to the majors.

But now, I wasn't sure if I'd chased greatness because I

loved the game, or because it was the only way I knew to earn their love in the first place.

And that was the thing about Dad—me playing in the majors had meant something to him.

That was prestige.

That made him a man whose son's name got printed in newspapers and flashed across highlight reels.

That earned him nods at the country club and polite envy from colleagues.

A player could make him proud. A manager only reminded him that the glory days were over.

It was never really about me. It was about what reflected best on John Reed.

And maybe, for the first time, I was okay with that.

Because I was finally building something that was mine, not theirs.

Chapter Twelve

Quinn

Tessa warned me to bring patience and caffeine, but nothing could've prepared me for this much optimism before noon.

The screen at the front of the conference room glowed with a color-blocked PowerPoint deck. Nora Blake, the marketing manager for the Lagerheads, stood beside the screen with her laptop open. Her hair was pulled into one of those effortless knots that only women who actually have their lives together can pull off.

"The projections are trending higher than last year," she said. "Renovation buzz is driving solid pre-sales, but if we want a sellout crowd for Opening Day, we need to go bigger."

Across the table, Kelsey Hartman, the marketing assistant, shifted her gaze between Nora and her iPad, the tip of her stylus gliding across the screen as she took notes. Beside her, Luke Farnham, the team's events coordinator, scrolled through his own copy of the deck on his tablet, nodding along.

"We've got giveaways, theme nights, and community

tie-ins on the calendar, but Opening Day needs something bigger. Something emotional. People buy tickets because they want to feel part of something."

Across from me, Tessa sipped her coffee like she'd been through this rodeo before. Probably because she had.

Nora clicked to the next slide, showing the stadium's renderings. "The upgrades are beautiful, but we all know shiny seats only go so far."

"We could feature longtime season-ticket holders," Luke said. "Do some spotlights on

fans who've been coming forever—season ticket holders, multi-generation families, that kind of thing."

"Good," Nora said. "Community ties, nostalgia, home-grown pride. Those are the emotions that sell tickets."

"I like that," Tessa said. "Make sure that goes in the social plan."

"Got it," Kelsey said.

Nora nodded, but her expression said she wasn't done.

"Those are good ideas, but we need something that gets people talking before they even think about buying tickets. Here's one idea," she said smoothly. "A full-circle moment for the new era of Bergmann Stadium."

She clicked to the next slide, and there was my name, lined up with phrases like *heritage* and *community impact*, which was funny considering I used to sing the anthem here for free hot dogs and a photo op.

Nora's gaze landed on me, and suddenly the room felt smaller.

"You used to sing the anthem here all the time, Quinn. Having you back on the field feels like the perfect way to connect the new era with the old."

The slide changed, and I was suddenly staring at twelve-year-old me—in all my bedazzled jean jacket glory, high ponytail bouncing, gripping a microphone like my life depended on it. Nothing like being ambushed by your own origin story before lunch.

Before I could figure out how to respond, the conference room door opened and Benny stepped in.

"Sorry I'm late," he said, sliding into the open seat across from me. "I had a call with a potential first base coach that ran long." He glanced at Tessa, then me. "I'll fill you in later."

"Sounds good." Tessa said, then gestured toward Nora. "Go ahead."

Across the table, Nora gestured toward the screen.

"As I was saying, having Quinn perform the national anthem would give us a great full-circle story to tell. She started here, and now she's back as part of the team's new chapter. It's nostalgic, local, and emotional. All the things that sell tickets." She glanced at Tessa. "We could build a social campaign around it—old footage, fan memories, a throwback clip of her singing, then a modern teaser leading into Opening Day."

Tessa nodded slowly, thoughtful. "There's potential there. It ties into the community angle we've been pushing."

It made sense—nostalgia sold.

So did my name supposedly, though I'd never say that out loud.

Still, the idea of standing in front of a packed stadium again made my stomach twist. I hadn't sung in public since my final tour, and the thought of doing it here—where everything started—felt less like a homecoming and more like poking a bruise just to see if it still hurt.

I forced a smile and pretended to study the slide, mentally scrolling through ways to say *thank you, but abso-*

lutely not without sounding ungrateful—or worse, like a diva.

Before I came up with anything better than a noncommittal nod, Benny's low voice cut through the air.

"Or it turns Opening Day into a publicity stunt."

The silence stretched just long enough for me to wonder if fake fainting would get me out of here.

He leaned back in his chair, calm as ever, but there was an edge under the even tone.

"People should be in the seats to watch baseball, not a reunion tour," he said. "I get the nostalgia thing, but if people are showing up for Quinn Logan instead of the Lagerheads, we've missed the point."

I bit the inside of my cheek hard enough to taste metal. Nothing like being accused of stealing the spotlight before you've even agreed to the gig.

Tessa's mug paused halfway to her lips. "It's just the national anthem, Benny."

"You really think that?" Benny's mouth curved into an almost-smile that carried more edge than humor. "The second her name hits a press release, this isn't about baseball anymore."

It wasn't the words so much as the way he said *her name* —like he was spitting out something bitter.

Nora's polite smile didn't falter.

"The anthem isn't about performance—it's about pride. Nostalgia builds emotion, and emotion fills seats."

He leveled her with a steady look.

"Emotion doesn't win games," he said. "Our focus should be baseball, not turning Opening Day into a media event. If we win, the seats will fill."

Nora's hand tightened around the clicker, her knuckles whitening against the black remote.

"Let's put a pin in that for now," she said, her tone even. "We still need to cover in-game promotions and community events."

She clicked forward, moving on like the air hadn't just dropped ten degrees. For the next twenty minutes, the discussion circled through giveaways, sponsorships, and fan-experience ideas—safe territory everyone could agree on. Tessa kept things moving, asking the occasional question, nodding in the right places.

I kept my expression polite and professional, even as I cringed at the thought of standing on the field, singing in front of thousands of people. It wasn't that I didn't want to help. I did. But writing checks to support the Lagerheads was one thing. Getting back on stage for it might be taking team spirit a little too far.

While Luke outlined ideas for youth clinics, I doodled in the margin of my notebook. By the time I realized what I was doing, it was filled with a variety of hearts, flowers, and stars. I'd have to rewrite my notes later to keep things neat.

Once Luke wrapped his portion, Nora stepped back in and moved through the remaining slides. Thank-yous, deadlines, next steps—the kind of tidy wrap-up that made people feel like progress had been made, even though a lot was still up in the air.

I slid my notebook into my purse and offered quick smiles to Tessa, Nora, Luke, and Kelsey as they gathered their things.

"Thanks, everyone."

Then I turned toward the door without so much as glancing at Benny. If he didn't notice, fine. If he did, even better.

I'd almost made it to the elevators when footsteps fell into rhythm behind me.

"Quinn," Benny said, his voice steady but low. "Got a minute?"

Years of training, of smiling through exhaustion, swallowing my feelings, and keeping my expression pleasant no matter what, told me to stop, turn, and make nice. Instead, I hit the elevator button and kept my eyes on the numbers above the door.

"Sorry," I said, cool and clipped. "I can't right now."

I didn't explain why or make up an excuse. The truth was, I didn't trust myself not to say something I'd regret.

The elevator doors slid open with a soft chime. I stepped inside and turned to face him, forcing a smile that didn't reach my eyes.

Same elevator as last week, different kind of tension.

"Have a good day, Coach."

The elevator doors met in the middle, shutting him out, and I let my smile drop.

The second her name hits a press release...

Her.

He'd tossed that word out like I was a problem to manage, not a person he talked to every day.

God knows people in the music industry had treated me like that.

I just didn't think he would.

Chapter Thirteen

Benny

The smell of Chinese takeout filled the truck as I turned into Cat's driveway. Grace had her forehead pressed against the window, humming a song under her breath. Charlie leaned forward, eyeing the paper bags buckled into the passenger seat.

"Why does the food get to sit up front?"

"So the car doesn't get covered in soy sauce and lo mein," I said.

"I only did that one time."

"That was one time too many."

Grace laughed, already unbuckling.

"That was epic."

"Messy's not epic," I said, as I turned off the engine.

We piled out of the Jeep, and the kids bolted for the front door, bickering over who got to punch in the code like it was a race to defuse a bomb.

Grace won by a step, her finger jabbing the keypad before Charlie could reach it. The lock gave its soft click, and she threw the door open with a triumphant grin.

I followed them inside, balancing the takeout bag in one

hand while Charlie trailed after his sister, still muttering about unfair starts. The familiar scent of vanilla candles and detergent hit as soon as we stepped into the living room.

Cat had been working more hours than usual lately, and a comfortable kind of chaos had taken over her house—laundry folded but not yet put away, a stack of unopened mail on the counter, and a vase of flowers that had started to give up.

"Wash your hands before you touch anything," I said automatically, which earned me matching eye-rolls.

They did it anyway, splashing water all over the counter in the process.

I grabbed a stack of plates from the cabinet and started unpacking the food—dumplings, fried rice, lo mein, pepper steak, orange chicken, and the broccoli in garlic sauce I'd ordered for the illusion of balance.

Grace hopped onto a stool on the other side of the island, eyes bright.

"You got two orders of dumplings!"

"Of course I did," I said. "I learned my lesson last time when I didn't get any because you two ate them all."

Charlie grinned and climbed onto the chair next to her. "That's because you were too slow."

"Or too polite," I said. "Neither of which works in this house."

I grabbed a serving spoon and added a little of every-thing to two plates, making sure the portions were even—especially the dumplings. The last thing I needed was to listen to them whining about who got more.

After handing them each a plate, I filled one for myself and dragged a chair around to sit across from them. Charlie chewed on a dumpling while picking every pea out of his fried rice, and Grace poured enough soy sauce to flood a small pond. To each their own.

"How's the dance for the talent show coming along?" I asked Grace as I dug into my food.

"So good! We came up with this cool spin part." She climbed down from her chair. "Watch!"

Before I could tell her to finish eating first, she twirled across the kitchen. Then she dropped into a pose with one arm raised and a dramatic hair flip for good measure.

Charlie clapped like she'd just nailed the Olympic floor routine.

"Nice work," I said, even though my jaw tightened halfway through. Hearing her sing Quinn's song didn't exactly help my mood.

Grace twirled again, humming the song under her breath, and I couldn't help picturing Quinn in that meeting —composed, unreadable, giving nothing away. Then later, the flat "I can't right now," before she'd walked off like I wasn't worth the conversation. I'd only wanted a few minutes to talk about the damn budget.

Right then, the door from the garage opened, and Cat stepped into the kitchen.

"I wasn't expecting dinner and a dance recital," she said.

She dropped her bag on the counter, kissed the top of Grace's head, and ruffled Charlie's hair before glancing over at me. Her smile softened, but her brow creased just a little.

"Please tell me you two were good for your uncle."

"We were good," Grace said.

"Uncle Benny took us to the park and pushed us on really high on the swings," Charlie said around a bite of lo mein.

Grace twisted on her stool to face Cat.

"And Charlie almost fell off."

Cat's eyes widened as they flicked to me.

"I was fine," Charlie said quickly, beating me to it.

"Thankfully," Cat said. "I'm too tired for an ER visit."

She loaded up a plate, then slid onto the stool next to Grace.

The kids filled Cat in on their day, all the highs, lows, and end-of-the-world playground politics. She took it in stride, reacting like it all made perfect sense, while I just sat back and tried to remember if school had always been that dramatic.

By the time they were done recounting every tiny detail, Grace pushed back her stool. "Can we watch TV?"

"For a little while," Cat said. "But I don't want to hear any fighting over what to watch."

"We won't fight," Charlie said quickly, which usually meant they would.

They both dropped their plates in the sink and their laughter echoed as they ran down the hall. Then the sound of the TV kicked on.

Cat sighed—more amused than exasperated—and turned her attention back to me.

"Carrie texted earlier. She's finally feeling a hundred percent again, so she'll be back next week." A small smile tugged at her mouth. "Which means you're officially off the hook."

"I love hanging out with them." I leaned back in my chair. "I can help out anytime—at least until the season starts."

"You know I'll take you up on that." Cat studied me for a beat. "You okay?"

"Yeah. Why?"

"You seem aggravated," she said. "I figured the kids

drove you nuts, but that doesn't seem to be the case. Unless there's something you're not telling me."

"No, they were fine."

"Then what is it?"

"What do you mean?"

"You're doing that thing."

"What thing?"

She pointed her fork at me and twirled it in tiny circles.

"The tight-jaw, something's-bothering-me-but-I'm-too-proud-to-say-it thing."

"I'm not doing a thing," I said, though I had to consciously unclench my jaw, proving her point.

"So what's got you grinding your teeth?"

"It's nothing."

"Nothing looks an awful lot like you're about to bench someone."

That got a laugh out of me, quiet but real.

"It's stupid."

Cat leaned her elbows on the counter, giving me that look that said she could sit there all night if she had to.

I rubbed a hand over the back of my neck.

"I wanted to talk to Quinn after the marketing meeting today, and she blew me off."

"Blew you off?"

"Yeah," I said. "I caught her after the meeting, asked if we could go over some numbers, and she said she couldn't. Then she got on the elevator and left."

She tilted her head, her expression somewhere between curious and amused.

"And that annoyed you because...?"

I hesitated. It sounded ridiculous even in my own head, but I said it anyway.

"I'm trying to get my coaches in place and I need to clear the budget."

"Was her tone more like 'I'm busy right now' or 'go away forever'?"

I exhaled, dragging a hand through my hair.

"She was short. Clipped. Like she didn't want to talk to me at all."

"Did something happen in the meeting?"

"Nothing I can think of," I said. "They were throwing around marketing ideas, and I said one of them was stupid."

Cat's eyes narrowed.

"What was the idea?"

I frowned, running back through the conversation.

"Somebody said Quinn should sing the national anthem on Opening Day. I said it was a bad idea."

She stared at me like I'd just told her I'd insulted Santa in front of a bunch of kids.

"You said *what?*"

"I said it was a bad idea. People come to see baseball, not a concert. It turns Opening Day into a publicity stunt."

Cat blinked, then let out a laugh that was equal parts disbelief and exasperation.

"You said that *in front of her?*"

"Well, yeah, but—"

"*Benny.*"

"It's not like I said she can't sing. I just meant the focus should be on baseball."

She gave me the kind of look that could curdle milk.

"You told a Grammy-winning pop star she'd make Opening Day feel like a publicity stunt."

"I didn't tell *her* anything," I said. "I made a point about priorities."

Cat pressed a hand to her forehead.

"You have *got* to be kidding me."

"What? I wasn't wrong."

"You don't see it, do you?" She rolled her eyes. "The woman used to sing the national anthem there when she was twelve. It's like a full-circle hometown story, and you basically told her she'd ruin Opening Day."

"I didn't mean it like that."

"Intent doesn't matter, genius. *Tone* does. And I'm guessing your tone was about as warm as a postgame press conference after a loss."

I dragged a hand down my face.

"So, what—you think she's mad at me?"

"I think she's human," Cat said. "You embarrassed her in a room full of people. If someone did that to you in a meeting, you'd still be stewing about it two weeks later."

She wasn't wrong. I didn't like being called out, especially not in front of other people.

"So what do I do?"

"You apologize."

"Apologize?"

"Yes, apologize," she said, like it was the most obvious thing in the world. "Not one of your 'my bad, didn't mean it' half-assed versions either. A real one."

I hated that she was right. Even more than I hated admitting it.

"Fine. I'll apologize."

"Good. Do it soon, before she convinces herself you're a total jackass."

I scrubbed a hand over my face, the weight of it settling heavier than I wanted to admit.

Too late for that, probably.

Chapter Fourteen

Quinn

The timer on the oven dinged just as I wiped my hands on a dish towel.

I opened the oven and pulled out the bubbling pan of mac and cheese, setting it on a trivet to rest before serving. The panko coating on top was perfectly golden, the edges crisped just enough to promise that satisfying crunch when you break through the surface.

Over the years, cooking had become my therapy. No cameras, no critics, no one weighing in on every decision. Just food that didn't talk back and a rhythm that was entirely mine. After a day like today, I needed that kind of peace.

Music pulsed through the kitchen. I'd put my favorite disco playlist on before I started pulling ingredients from the fridge, my guilty pleasure on nights when I needed to shake off everything else. You can't be sad when you're singing along with Donna Summer, Gloria Gaynor, or the Bee Gees.

I dredged chicken strips through flour, egg wash, and breadcrumbs, laying them carefully in a pan of hot avocado oil. The sizzle joined the beat, and I found myself swaying my hips, singing along to "Hot Stuff" as golden bubbles formed around the edges of the chicken.

That's when I heard the knock at the front door—sharp, unexpected, and perfectly offbeat as it sliced through the chorus. I stiffened, caught off guard by the sound. Nobody just dropped by out here. That was kind of the appeal.

I wiped my hands on the dish towel as I walked through the living room. When I opened the door, I froze.

Benny Reed stood on my porch, hands in his pockets like this was perfectly normal. It wasn't. Not him, not here, not standing on my pastel Welcome-ish doormat like he belonged there.

"Hey," he said, voice low. "Can we talk?"

Something in his tone had me stepping aside before I could decide if that was a good idea.

"Sure."

"It smells good in here," he said as I closed the door behind him.

The words had barely left his mouth before I remembered the chicken.

"Shit."

I spun and bolted for the kitchen, disco still pulsing from the speaker. The oil hissed as I flipped a piece over. Thankfully, nothing was burnt, just more golden than I prefer. I moved them to the cooling rack I'd repurposed as a chicken strip drainer.

"It smells even better in here," Benny said from behind me, his voice warm enough to compete with the stovetop heat.

I glanced over my shoulder.

"Sorry. I had to rescue the chicken before it crossed over to the dark side."

A small smile tugged at his mouth. "Glad I showed up in time for the rescue mission."

"Yeah," I said, turning off the burner. "Timing's everything, right?"

The words came out sharper than I intended. Because really, what was he doing here? He didn't strike me as the kind of guy who dropped by for social calls.

"Hopefully my good timing will make up for my bad manners earlier."

I raised an eyebrow. *Nice try.* He probably thought that grin of his came with diplomatic immunity.

"Did you have dinner yet?" I asked before I could stop myself. My brain was screaming *don't feed the man who insulted you in a meeting,* but my stomach was louder. "Because I'm starving, and I was taught not to eat in front of people."

"I did, actually." He glanced toward the stove again, and his voice dipped a little lower. "But I could eat again."

"Okay then," I said, a little too briskly. "Have a seat."

Reaching for two plates, I moved before my brain could override the decision.

He shrugged out of his jacket, draping it over the back of the chair before sitting, then pushed his sleeves to his elbows. I looked away before my brain started writing a song about his forearms.

Focus, Quinn. Food. You like food.

Once he was settled, I slid his plate across the table and took the seat opposite him.

He picked up his fork.

"This looks amazing."

"Thanks," I said, cutting into a piece of chicken. "It's my favorite meal when the day's been...a lot."

He took a bite, closed his eyes, and let out a low groan that might've been illegal in several states.

"This is really good."

That sound did inconvenient things to my insides. Heat climbed my neck before I could stop it, and I pushed my chair back and stood a little too fast.

"What do you want to drink?" I asked as I opened the refrigerator. "I've got, uh, water, iced tea, ginger ale, wine, beer..."

"Water."

After grabbing two bottles, I closed the fridge door.

"Would you like a glass and ice?"

"The bottle is good."

He took the bottle I offered and twisted the cap off, drinking slowly as he watched me over the top like he was still trying to read me. The silence stretched and I took a bite of mac and cheese, chewing slowly, letting the cheesy warmth take the edge off the quiet.

"So," I said after a beat, "how'd you know where I live? And, more importantly, why are you here?"

He gave a small shrug.

"Small town," he said, rolling his shoulders slightly. "And I, uh...talked to my sister earlier. She told me I owe you an apology."

That caught me off guard.

"An apology?"

"For what I said in the meeting. Or maybe how I said it."

I stayed quiet, waiting for him to explain.

"I was trying to make a point about keeping Opening Day focused on baseball, not turning it into a publicity thing. But Cat said it probably came out like I was accusing *you* of being the publicity thing."

A small laugh escaped me before I could help it.

"She's not wrong."

"Yeah," he said with a wry grin. "She tends not to be."

Our eyes met, something unspoken flickering between us before his grin faded and his tone lost its edge.

"I wasn't trying to make it personal," he said. "You didn't deserve that. I just meant...you don't have to sing to make the team matter."

Something about the honesty in his voice, without the PR gloss or defensive edge, hit deeper than I wanted it to. His words hadn't been cruel, just blunt. But blunt still stings.

"I didn't even agree to sing," I said, keeping my tone light. "But the way you said I shouldn't felt like a slap." He cringed, then nodded slowly. "It seemed like you thought I was just waiting to get back on stage to relive my glory days. And that's just not true."

"It's not about that," he said. "It's about focus. I'm working to rebuild the team's identity. I'd rather people talk about the lineup than the pregame entertainment."

My quiet laugh didn't sound very amused.

"I get it. I do. Having me around is unfortunately going to be a distraction, and not the kind you can game plan for. I can't help that."

"That's the problem," he said quietly. "Everything about this team has been noise for the past few years. I'm just trying to keep the focus on the field for once." His gaze stayed steady on mine. "Your involvement is a good thing, Quinn. We can't control how people react to that." He paused, holding my gaze. "I handled what they said in that meeting all wrong, and I'm sorry."

Something in his tone knocked the wind out of me a little. He wasn't spinning it or trying to win points. He was just being honest. And that shouldn't have mattered as much as it did.

"Apology accepted," I said quietly. "Just try not to insult anyone's childhood nostalgia next time, okay?"

That earned a real laugh.

"Deal."

Silence settled again, no longer neutral but alive somehow. Every clink of silverware sounded too loud, every small movement tugging at the edges of something I didn't want to name. I kept my focus on the food, pretending it was the reason my pulse had picked up instead of the man sitting across from me.

When we were both done, I stood and gathered the plates, grateful for something to do that involved motion instead of thinking. Benny rose too, the soft scrape of his chair on the floor sending a ripple through the stillness as he followed me to the sink.

"Thanks for dinner," he said, leaning his hip against the counter next to me. "And for accepting my apology."

"You're welcome." The words came out quieter than I intended, something in his voice knocking loose a piece of my composure. I cleared my throat, trying to shake it off. "And thanks for making it."

When I looked up, he was closer than I realized—close enough that I could see flecks of gold in his steel-blue eyes. Probably because I'd never let myself look this long. The realization hit harder than it should've, curling low in my stomach and scattering whatever I'd planned to say next.

He didn't move, just stood there watching me, quiet and steady. The space between us felt smaller with every breath, charged with something that didn't belong in a kitchen but didn't feel wrong either.

"Quinn," he said softly, voice low enough to vibrate through me.

I should have said something clever. Maybe told him this was a bad idea. But my brain short-circuited the second his hand came up, brushing a piece of hair from my face.

The touch was barely there, but it sent a ripple through me all the same. My breath caught. His fingers lingered just long enough to tuck the strand behind my ear, tracing the edge of my jaw before falling away.

Backing off would've been the smart move. Instead, I stayed exactly where I was, caught somewhere between reason and want.

He bent his head toward me and hesitated, like he was giving me one last out. Maybe I should've taken it, but then his gaze dropped to my mouth, and whatever air was left between us vanished.

The first brush of his lips was tentative, testing, as if he expected me to pull away. When I didn't, the second was firmer, more certain, sending heat spiraling straight through me. His hand slid to the back of my neck, steady but gentle, and the room seemed to shrink until all that existed was the pulse pounding in my ears and the taste of him—warm, unexpected, and wrong in all the right ways.

Then his mouth opened against mine, and everything shifted. The kiss deepened, his tongue tracing the seam of my lips and when I parted for him, the sound that escaped me was something between a gasp and a surrender. He took his time, exploring with maddening patience, the slow slide of his tongue against mine both languid and deliberate.

The heat between us intensified, each stroke sending fresh waves of warmth pooling low in my stomach. His fingers tightened at my nape, angling my head just so, and I felt the scratch of his beard with every shift, every tilt, grounding and intoxicating all at once. Our tongues tangled, the kiss growing messier, more urgent, all pretense of control slipping away.

When he finally pulled back—just enough to let us breathe—his lips were still barely a whisper from mine. My heart hammered so loudly I was sure he could hear it.

"That probably wasn't a good idea," I whispered, breathless. "Considering we work together."

His mouth curved, slow and dangerous. "Some of my worst ideas turned out to be my best ones."

I laughed softly, shaking my head, though my pulse refused to slow.

Because whatever this was, it had nothing to do with the starry-eyed girl who used to crush on Waypoint's golden boy.

This was about now. About the man standing in my kitchen, looking at me like he wanted to kiss me again.

And God help me—I wanted him to.

Chapter Fifteen

Benny

Sleep didn't stand a chance.

Every time I closed my eyes, I saw the way Quinn looked at me right before I kissed her. The kind of look that makes a guy forget logic, timing, and the dozen reasons why he shouldn't be standing that close to someone he works with.

After tossing and turning for hours, I gave up on pretending. I showered, dressed, and drove to the stadium. The construction crew hadn't shown up yet, but the lights over the field burned through the dark like a promise. Or maybe a warning.

By the time I parked near the office entrance, the horizon had started to lighten from dark blue to pale gray. Inside, the air was still and cool, tinged with the sterile scent of disinfectant from freshly cleaned offices, softened by traces of coffee and paper.

"Morning," Dave, the night security guard, said from behind the desk. He had a coffee mug in one hand and a crossword folded in front of him.

"Morning," I said, scanning my ID badge.

"Early start today."

"Yeah, I couldn't sleep."

He huffed a small laugh.

"Ah, one of those nights."

"Yeah."

"There's fresh coffee in the break room if you need it."

"Thanks, I appreciate it," I said, then continued toward the elevator, my footsteps echoing in the empty corridor.

The brushed metal doors opened with a hiss that sounded louder in the quiet, and I stepped inside, pressing the button for the third floor.

As the car hummed to life, the steady vibration under my feet did nothing to help me *not* think about Quinn. Ever since the day we'd gotten stuck between floors, stepping into this elevator was enough to put her right back in my head. Forty-five minutes of flickering lights, nervous laughter, and her perfume threading through the metallic air—not to mention the almost kiss before the power kicked back on.

But there was nothing *almost* about last night's kisses. By the time the elevator reached the third floor, I'd replayed them at least half a dozen times. When the doors hissed open, I stepped out into the quiet corridor and started toward my office.

Inside, everything was how I'd left it, papers spread across the desk in what looked like chaos but made sense to me. I dropped my bag, shrugged out of my jacket, and sat down. Player evaluations, scouting notes, offseason plans— all stacked in a way that probably looked random but wasn't. I sorted through a few pages, trying to focus, but everything blurred together. My head wasn't in it, no matter how much I wanted it to be.

Every time I blinked, I wasn't seeing stats or names. I was back in Quinn's kitchen surrounded by the smell of baked cheese, with disco playing in the background. The way she'd looked at me when I apologized—surprised and maybe a little hurt—stuck with me. Cat had been right.

And the apology had made things better. Until it didn't. Because then I kissed her.

It hadn't been impulsive so much as inevitable. Sparks had been flying between us since the elevator. One second she was standing there, close enough that I could feel her breath, and the next, logic didn't stand a chance.

I exhaled, scrubbing a hand down my face.

Apologizing had been the right call. Kissing her had not, but damned if I could bring myself to regret it.

Didn't change the fact that it couldn't happen again.

My rookie-year manager used to say, *"Don't screw the crew."*

But Quinn wasn't just crew. She was signing the paychecks.

Managing the Lagerheads might have fallen into my lap, but that didn't mean I wasn't taking it seriously. I knew how rare this shot was…taking a team that had been a punch line for years and turning it into something worth watching again.

Tessa trusted me with that, and she wanted someone who could make the tough calls. Someone who'd give a damn about every name on the roster and every dollar spent on getting them ready to win.

That was supposed to be me.

It *would* be me.

If I could keep my focus where it belonged…on the team, not Quinn Logan.

Unfortunately, that would be tricky. Quinn was nothing like I'd imagined she'd be. She wasn't just a glossy, untouchable pop star adored by millions. She wasn't even the hometown girl everyone talked about like she'd walked on water. She was grounded, sharp, and seemed genuinely invested in making this team successful. And she listened. Really listened.

It didn't hurt that she made the best damn mac and cheese I've ever tasted, either.

There was just something about her that pulled my attention. The way she carried herself like she'd seen every kind of storm and decided to dance through the rain anyway. The way she looked at you like she expected an honest answer, not a performance. Hell, maybe that's what threw me off most—she wasn't performing.

And now I'd gone and kissed her.

A brilliant move from the guy who swore he'd keep his head down and focus.

Footsteps and chatter filtered through the hall signaling the day was officially starting.

I checked the clock and blinked. How had two hours gone by?

So much for productivity.

If only thinking about Quinn qualified as work.

I pushed away from the desk and reached for my mug.

Caffeine was the bare minimum requirement for surviving the rest of the day. Especially when it started with a meeting that included both Tessa and Quinn.

Chapter Sixteen

Quinn

"I need details. All of them. Right now."

That was the first thing out of Erin's mouth as soon as I opened the door. She didn't even say hello, just walked in like a woman possessed, her purse swinging from her shoulder and determination written all over her face.

"Hi to you, too."

"Don't give me that. You don't text 'I kissed Benny Reed' and expect me to wait calmly like a normal person." She tossed her coat onto the arm of the couch. "It's bad enough that twenty-four hours have gone by and I *still* don't have details."

"I texted you last night," I reminded her, shutting the door behind us. "It's not my fault you didn't see it until this morning."

Erin waved that off like it was a technicality.

"Right now, I need details." She spun to face me. "You kissed him? Like a real kiss—tongue, chemistry, the whole deal?"

"Yeah. Real kiss. Hands-in-hair, knees-wobbly, totally-lost-track-of-time kind of kiss."

Erin shrieked, slapping both palms down on the counter like I'd just handed her a winning lottery ticket.

"Shut up. You're lying. Are you lying? You're not lying."

We were acting like fifteen-year-old girls at a sleepover, not women firmly planted in our fourth decade of life. But I didn't care. It felt good to have someone to gush with.

I held my hand up as if I was taking an oath.

"Swear on my first guitar."

Erin clutched her chest.

"If you're swearing on Millie, I know you're serious."

I laughed and turned toward the kitchen.

"Come on. I'll fill you in over dinner. I'm starving."

"Wait, what? You're going to make me wait while you reheat food?"

"I can multi-task," I said, opening the fridge and pulling out the leftover mac and cheese and chicken strips. "I haven't eaten since breakfast. My stomach was in knots after seeing him this morning."

Erin followed me like a loyal bloodhound on the scent of drama.

"*Hold up.* What happened when you saw him?"

"I'll get to that. But if I don't eat something in the next sixty seconds, I'm going to start gnawing on the corner of a cabinet."

She dropped onto a stool at the island, elbows on the counter, chin in her hands.

"Fine. But I expect a full play-by-play with absolutely no strategic withholding."

I popped the first plate in the microwave.

"So, I was cooking dinner..." I gestured toward the leftovers. "...and listening to my disco playlist. Donna Summer was playing, and I was singing along like an idiot when I heard a knock on my door."

Erin grinned. "And it was Benny Reed, looking all regretful and hot?"

"Pretty much," I said, pulling the first plate out and sliding in the second. "He said he came to apologize. Apparently his sister told him he'd been an ass."

"Interesting," Erin muttered.

"He looked so uncomfortable standing there, I just let him in. And of course, I'd left the chicken frying on the stove, so I ran back to the kitchen, trying not to burn dinner and also trying not to look like I was completely unraveling."

"I would *pay money* to see you trying to play it cool."

"Obviously I failed spectacularly. My name and cool will never share a sentence. You know that." I set the plates on the counter and handed her one. "I asked if he wanted dinner—because manners—and he said yes. Then we talked, and he was actually nice. Like, *surprisingly* nice," I said, taking a bite of mac and cheese. "He said he wasn't trying to make it about me. That he just wants to make sure focus stays on the team."

"And you believed him."

"What he said made sense, and he both looked and sounded sincere." I shrugged. "Either he was sincere or he's a hell of an actor."

"Okay, so how do we go from apology to kiss?"

I pressed my lips together to keep from smiling, but it didn't work.

"After we ate, I started cleaning up. He followed me to the sink, leaned his hip against the counter and thanked me —for dinner, and for accepting his apology." I paused, and Erin leaned closer like she was afraid she might miss it. "I said, 'You're welcome,' and when I looked up, he was just *there*. Close. Watching me like…" I waved my hands around, as I searched for a way to describe it. "…like he was trying to memorize me."

Erin let out a low, dramatic gasp.

"Get to the kiss."

"He said my name," I said softly, the memory blooming warm and bright in my chest. "And then he brushed a piece of hair from my face. Just lightly. Tucked it behind my ear and let his fingers trail along my jaw before he pulled away."

"Oh *my God*, Quinn," she screeched.

"I should've said something. Something clever or maybe logical. But then he leaned in—and he *hesitated*. Like he was giving me one last out."

Her voice was a whisper now. "You didn't want to."

"Nope. The second his lips touched mine, my brain flat-lined. It was soft at first, like he was checking if I was okay with it. Then it changed. He kissed me like he'd been thinking about it for a long time. Like he wanted to take his time and get it *exactly* right." I squeezed my thighs together at the memory. "His hand was on the back of my neck, warm and solid," I said. "He angled my head just so and kissed me like he knew what he was doing. And when I opened for him and he deepened it, I swear I forgot what year it was. It was soft and unhurried, but underneath it there was this heat, like if we weren't standing in my kitchen, he would've kissed me until the world stopped turning."

Erin's fork clattered against the table.

"I need a fan. And a therapist. And possibly a defib-rillator."

"It was a hell of a kiss."

Erin sat back, eyes still wide.

"So, what happened this morning when you saw him?"

I sighed, half laugh, half groan.

"He acted like it never happened. It was just business as usual—cool, calm, and completely unbothered," I said. "Meanwhile, I sat across the table from him mentally replaying the kitchen make-out and obsessing over how his beard felt scraping against my skin in the best possible way."

Erin scowled.

"Classic male panic," she said, waving her fork.

"It doesn't matter." I shrugged, stabbing another bite of mac and cheese. "We should probably keep things professional anyway. Otherwise it could get complicated."

"*Complicated*," she echoed. "That's code for *really hot, but ill-advised,* isn't it?"

"Basically."

"So nothing you haven't done before."

I tossed my napkin at her. It missed its mark and landed on the floor.

"You're impossible."

"I'm delightful," she said with a cheeky grin. "So what's the plan?"

"Pretend it didn't happen," I said. "If he can ignore it, I can too."

"Sure." She flashed a cat-that-ate-the-canary grin. "Until the next time you're alone in a room together again."

I could play it cool, be sensible, and follow all the professional rules. But God help me, I wasn't sure I wanted to ignore it at all.

Chapter Seventeen

Benny

The air in Scottsdale was warm and dry, not oppressive like it got in the summer. Just enough heat to make you roll your sleeves up, not break a sweat. It was the kind of weather that made people fall in love with the desert.

I wasn't in town long. Just a couple nights before heading back to Waypoint. If it had been anyone else, this would've been a phone call. But Lou wasn't just anyone.

I hadn't seen him in person since his wife's funeral two years ago. That day had been all noise and condolences—too many people, too many memories, and not enough words that actually mattered.

Lou was one of the good ones. The kind of manager who didn't just teach you how to play the game, but how to hold your head up when it kicked your ass. He'd taken me under his wing back in Triple-A, pushing when I needed it, backing off when I didn't. Not many coaches got that balance right. Coming here, to Scottsdale, wasn't about a job pitch. It was about showing up. The way he'd always done for me.

I headed up the walkway and the front door cracked open before I could knock.

"Thought I heard a car," Lou said, pushing it wide with a grin. "You're five minutes early. That means I've trained you right."

"You gave me enough speeches about punctuality. Guess something had to stick."

He stepped out to meet me, pulling me into a solid, two-pat hug that still carried traces of Old Spice and laundry detergent. He looked fit, tan, and was standing straight as ever. If I didn't know better, I'd think he was still coaching full-time.

"You look good."

"I keep myself busy," he said with a shrug, stepping back and gesturing for me to follow him inside.

Inside, the house was exactly like it had been the last time I was here—neat, quiet, lived-in. Family photos filled the spaces I could see. Not staged, just part of the place.

"You want something to drink?" he asked, already heading toward the kitchen. "I've got a fresh batch of iced tea in the fridge."

"Sounds good," I said, following him through to the kitchen.

Lou poured two tall glasses, handed me one, then nodded toward the back door.

"Come on. Let's sit out back."

The patio opened to a wide stretch of yard framed by desert landscaping—gravel beds, bursts of green from low succulents, a few tall palms swaying lazily in the heat. To one side, an outdoor kitchen sat under a slatted pergola—grill, mini-fridge, the works. His pool sparkled like it'd been skimmed five minutes ago. Knowing Lou, it probably had.

We sat in a pair of cushioned wicker chairs and placed our iced teas on the glass-topped table between us.

Like always, the talk turned to baseball—the offseason moves, the guys making headlines, the ones getting written off too soon. Lou still had that sharp, measured way of seeing the game, pulling out details most people missed. Listening to him, I could almost hear the dugout again, the low hum of a night game settling in. For a second, I was twenty-two again, chasing a shot at the big leagues under his watch.

Lou took a sip of iced tea, then glanced my way.

"So, how's it going with the Lagerheads?"

"Better than I expected, honestly." Lou gave me a look that said, *go on.* "You know how it is, moving to a new team. There's always a little chaos before things settle. But so far, they've let me run things the way I want. No one is breathing down my neck, or second-guessing every call." I rolled the glass between my palms. "After Walter Bergmann died, half the organization scattered. We're light on staff, but his daughter Tessa is looking to me to help fill the gaps. It's early, but it feels right. Like I actually get to build something instead of just steering what's already there."

Lou nodded. "That's how it should be. And they hired you for a reason. The best thing they can do is stay out of your way."

"Yeah," I said, a corner of my mouth lifting. "And since you brought it up...I wanted to talk to you about something." One of his brows lifted. "We're looking for a bench coach."

Lou nodded slowly, gaze drifting toward the pool. "Can't say anyone jumps to mind right off, but I'll think about it and let you know."

"I appreciate that," I said. "But I already have someone in mind."

His eyes shifted back to me and he studied me for a long moment, then gave a low chuckle and shook his head. The kind of reaction that said he figured out why I'd shown up—and he wasn't sure whether to laugh or give me hell for it.

"And you thought of me."

"I did."

He leaned back, the wicker creaking under him. For a second, all I heard was the steady buzz of cicadas and the soft splash of water against tile.

"You always did know how to flatter a man."

"That wasn't flattery," I said. "We're building something real back in Waypoint, and I need someone who understands what that takes. Someone I can trust, who knows the game, and who'll tell me when I'm being an idiot."

Lou didn't say anything right away. He just took another sip of tea, set his glass down, and sighed.

"I live here."

"I know."

"This house was Marlene's dream. She followed me through every city I played and coached in. I told her that when I retired, she could choose where we settled. She picked here."

"I remember," I said quietly.

"She died two years ago, and I've kept everything just the way she liked it." He looked around. "The yard. The pool. I even cook the meals she used to make. Figured I'd honor her by keeping it all running."

"You've done that," I said. "This place is beautiful."

"I'm busy Benny. Just not doing anything." He looked back at me. "You understand?"

"I do."

And I did. I saw it in his eyes. The loneliness under the surface. The hunger he was trying to satisfy with routine.

"I do miss the dugout," he admitted. "The smell of the grass. The weight of a season. The grind. Shit, even the bad days meant something."

"Then come back."

He shook his head.

"Missing it might not be enough." He ran a hand over his face, rubbing his jaw. "I don't know if I have it in me anymore."

"You do," I said. "And I don't need a hype man. I need someone in my corner who knows what this job really takes. I'm not asking for nostalgia, Lou. I'm asking because you're one of the best baseball minds I've ever been around."

Lou's gaze drifted toward the water, jaw working like he was chewing on words that wouldn't come. The pool filter clicked on, a soft whir against the quiet. Finally, he said, "What would I do with the house?"

And even though that's what he said, what he really meant was, *Can I leave her?*

"You don't have to let go of her to come back to the game. She'd want you to be where you're needed. You know that."

He drained his iced tea like it was a shot of whiskey and set the glass down.

"It's been a long time since I sat in a dugout."

"That doesn't matter with someone like you," I said. "This team needs someone who remembers how to shape players without burning them out. A coach who knows when to press and when to back off. That was always your gift."

He stood then, walking to the edge of the patio, looking

out over the pool like it might hold the answer. After a long silence, he said, "Let me think about it."

I stood, too.

"That's all I'm asking."

He turned to face me.

"You're not the kid I managed anymore."

"No," I said. "But I remember what it felt like to play for you. And I want my guys to experience that too."

Chapter Eighteen

Quinn

By the time Tessa and I wrapped our "quick" recap, my notebook looked like it had been in a bar fight—highlighter bruises and sticky-note bandages everywhere.

"Okay," Tessa said, blowing out a slow breath as she closed her laptop. "We've got the stadium walk-through with the construction manager on Wednesday. Benny should be back by then."

"Back?" I asked, in what I hoped was a normal, totally-not-invested tone.

Tessa nodded.

"He's in Scottsdale meeting with a potential bench coach."

"Oh." I adjusted the pen on top of my notebook like that was suddenly the most important task in the world. "I didn't realize he was out of town."

Not that I should've. It wasn't like Benny Reed owed me his travel itinerary. Still, finding out from Tessa instead of him left a weird little hitch in my chest. I told myself it was professional curiosity.

Sure, Quinn. Let's go with that.

Tessa slid her laptop into her bag, then hesitated, fiddling with the zipper pull before looping it over her shoulder. Then she nodded, like she'd just made a decision.

"Listen," she said, not quite looking at me. "I'm meeting Margot and Sylvie at The Maiden. Would you like to come along?"

I blinked.

"With your sisters?"

"Unless there are other Margots and Sylvies who text me fifty times a day," she said with a hesitant chuckle, like she thought I was going to say no. "It'd be nice. If you want to, I mean."

"I don't want to intrude," I said automatically, because some part of me was still twelve and performing for hot dogs.

"It wouldn't be an intrusion," she said, the hesitation slipping from her voice. "Just a drink or two and enough greasy food to make a nutritionist cry."

The invite hung there, simple and kind, and I realized I wanted to go. My circle's pretty small these days, mostly by choice. When I was younger, I was the geeky outcast. Then I got famous and trusted everyone, which was obviously a terrible plan. Turns out not all smiles mean friendship, especially when there's money or headlines involved.

Since then, I've been careful. Maybe too careful. But Tessa wasn't like that. We weren't friends back in the day, but there's no reason we couldn't be now. Maybe it was time to stop acting like every new connection came with strings attached.

"Okay," I said.

Her mouth curved into a smile.

"Good. I was hoping you'd say yes."

We left the stadium and split off in the parking lot. The drive to The Maiden was short—past the river, the old post office, and the mural that still made me smile every time I saw it. Small-town charm was in my blood, whether I wanted to admit it or not.

I parked behind Tessa in front of the pub and we walked in together. We spotted Margot and Sylvie at a high-top near the back. I hadn't seen either of them in years, but they were instantly familiar. Sylvie was waving both arms over her head like a ground crew marshalling us in, her bracelets jingling even over the din of the restaurant. Margot lifted her glass with a grin that looked almost exactly like Tessa's.

"Look who I found wandering around the stadium," Tessa said as we slid onto stools. "She's joining the Bergmann sister circus tonight, so be on your best behavior."

"She had me at greasy food," I said. "You two are a bonus."

"I've heard that before," Sylvie said, eyes bright. She hadn't changed much—still all motion and sparkle, the kind of person who seemed to generate her own spotlight. Her energy was a little chaotic in the best way. The room tilted toward her without her even trying.

Margot arched her brow. "She wasn't just talking about you, Syl."

Laughter rippled around the table, and just like that, I didn't feel like the odd one out.

A server came by to drop off waters for Tessa and me, took our drink orders, and disappeared back into the crowd. The easy energy around the table softened when she left. Margot angled toward me, her smile gentle.

"It's really good to see you, Quinn. How's your mom?"

"She's doing well. Thankfully her last scan was clean."

"That's great news." Her smile softened. "The brewery isn't the same without her keeping us all in line."

"Now she keeps her garden in line and bakes like she's training for the Great British Bake Off," I said with a small laugh.

Margot's grin widened.

"Well, if she ever gets tired of gardening and baking, she's always welcome back at the brewery. It's been...spirited lately."

"Controlled chaos," Tessa said, but her tone made it sound like wishful thinking. "But between the team, the renovations, and the brewery, I need either a clone or a time machine."

"I vote for the time machine," Sylvie said. "One Tessa's enough for the tri-state area."

"Speak for yourself," Margot said. "I'd hire the second one to keep *you* on schedule."

The teasing kept going, easy and familiar, the kind that only comes from years of shared history. I found myself smiling, the sound of their laughter easing a tension I hadn't realized I'd been carrying all day.

"You know," I said. "If you really need help, I can ask my mom if she'd want to fill in for a while."

Tessa's eyes lit up like I'd just offered her a golden ticket.

"Do you think she would? I mean, even part-time would be amazing."

"I think she'd love it," I said. "She's been restless ever since she ran out of things to alphabetize at home."

That got a laugh from all three sisters, the sound bright and easy.

"Then consider this our official cry for help," Tessa said, smiling.

The server swung by to take our orders—burgers, flatbreads, fries for the table, and something Sylvie insisted counted as a salad only because it involved arugula. By the time she walked off, the conversation had drifted to the Lagerheads.

"So, how's the team shaping up?" Margot asked, glancing between Tessa and me.

"Good," I said. "The stadium construction is on track and Benny's been scouting both players and coaches nonstop."

Margot shook her head.

"I still can't believe he agreed to coach in Waypoint."

"Why?" I asked.

"Back in high school, he couldn't wait to get out of here," she said.

"Well, he got out. Maybe he just decided it's not as bad as he remembered." I shrugged. "Or maybe coming home feels different once you've seen everything else."

Sylvie leaned forward, chin in her hand.

"Is that why you're staying?"

I blinked, caught off guard.

"Why I'm staying?"

She shrugged, like it was the most casual question in the world.

"Yeah. You could live anywhere, but you're here."

I could feel all three of them watching me, curious but kind.

"I came back for my mom," I said. "And because people here mostly let me live my life." I smiled, trying to keep it light.

"Do you like being back in town?" Margot asked.

"Honestly?" I traced the rim of my glass with my finger. "It's been good. Weird sometimes, but good. I forgot how quiet it gets at night. How people wave even if they don't know you."

"I'm pretty sure everyone everywhere knows you," Sylvie said with a chuckle.

"Maybe." I shrugged. "But at least here, they're polite enough to pretend otherwise. It's like living in a fishbowl where nobody taps the glass."

That got a round of laughter, breaking whatever hint of awkwardness had crept in.

I took a drink to reset. Even after two decades in the spotlight, fame still felt like an outfit I borrowed and never quite grew into, so any reference to it still made me feel like a fraud.

The server returned with our food and we dug in, the table filling with the kind of easy chatter that comes from shared history—even if some of it wasn't mine. Between bites, Sylvie detailed her latest marketing campaign and Margot talked about a new hop supplier and said things like "alpha acid" in a way that made me want to take notes. Then conversation shifted to social media.

Sylvie lit up.

"Oh! Did you see that reel about the guy who trained his dog to run the bases after every home game?"

I shook my head. "But full disclosure—I'm not on social media."

Sylvie blinked.

"Like...not at all?"

"I don't even lurk," I said. "I used to, but it wasn't good for my mental health."

The air at the table shifted—lighter, not heavier. Understanding, not pity.

"Yeah," she said quietly. "I can't even imagine what your comments look like."

"Most of them were great," I said, because that was also true. "But the loud ones were...loud. And addictive in the way jumping into a bonfire would be if pain came with a dopamine hit."

Sylvie winced like I'd described a physical injury.

"Fair."

"I have someone in my business manager's office running the accounts now," I said. "She posts dates and good news. I send photos sometimes, but never look. I know it makes me sound like a dinosaur, but protecting my brain has been better for me than scrolling."

"Protecting your brain is the move," Tessa said, almost absently, like she was talking to herself as much as to me.

"You're allowed to have boundaries," Margot added, nudging a basket of fries toward me like it was a peace offering. "Also, for what it's worth, I think it's kind of badass."

We clinked glasses to celebrate boundaries and fries— maybe the two best things I'd added to my life lately.

Not everything needed strategy or spin.

Sometimes it could just be fries, sisters, and the kind of noise that felt a lot like belonging.

Chapter Nineteen

Benny

I parked in the lot like I always did—far enough from the pickup line chaos to save my sanity. SUVs idled at odd angles, parents waved like air-traffic controllers, and kids darted through gaps in the chaos as if reflective backpacks were force fields. It didn't take long to spot Grace barreling toward me, ponytail flying, with Charlie right behind her.

Grace reached me first, skidding to a stop just before impact. "Uncle Benny!"

I caught her shoulder before she could crash into me.

"Easy there, speed racer."

Charlie arrived a few seconds later, adjusting his glasses again.

"How was school?" I asked.

"Good." She grinned. "Can we get milkshakes?"

"You two ever say hi like normal people?"

"Hi, Uncle Benny," Grace said sweetly. "Can we get milkshakes?"

"Better," I said, fighting a smile. "Let's go."

They hopped into the back seats, and once I watched

them click their seatbelts into place, I closed the door, then climbed behind the wheel.

"So, about those milkshakes," Grace said as I pulled out of the lot.

"Your mom said no going out to eat because you have the Halloween pizza party at your dance school tonight."

"Oh right."

"But milkshakes aren't dinner," Charlie said with all the wisdom of a seven-year-old.

"Can't argue with that," I said.

We swung by the diner, but this time we grabbed stools at the counter instead of a booth since it was just a quick stop.

Grace went with strawberry, Charlie picked chocolate, and I just asked for water.

"Grandma and Grandpa are taking us to the pumpkin patch this weekend," Grace said, as the server walked away.

"Grandpa said he'll do the corn maze with me," Charlie added with a big grin. "Mom and Grace never want to go in."

"That's because it's creepy and I don't want to get lost in there."

"We'll be safe with Grandpa. He won't get lost."

I smiled, even though something about it tugged in a quiet spot I didn't usually notice. I didn't remember ever doing stuff like that growing up—no hayrides, pumpkin patches, or matching flannel photos. My parents hadn't been the type for that. But they were clearly making up for it now, and I couldn't be mad about it.

The server returned, sliding the milkshakes in front of them, piled high with whipped cream and a cherry. Charlie went straight for his straw, but Grace scooped off the whipped cream with her spoon first.

While they worked through their milkshakes, the kids hopped from one topic to another—carving pumpkins, baking the seeds, costume debates, school gossip, and their excitement over the homecoming bonfire next week.

After their glasses were empty, we hung out for a little while, talking about the pumpkin patch and whose milkshake was better. I didn't rush them. Some moments were worth letting stretch.

Eventually, I dropped a few bills on the counter, thanked the server, and waited while they slipped into their coats before we headed for the door. Outside, the air had cooled fast, and a mix of fryer grease and fall leaves hung in the air. The kids climbed into the Jeep, still talking over each other about whose pumpkin would look better.

As I started the engine, I caught sight of the empty front seat out of the corner of my eye. I glanced over, looking for my laptop bag, but it wasn't there. I checked the floor. Nothing.

I looked at the kids through the rearview mirror.

"You guys see my bag back there?"

They both leaned forward, scanning the floor around their feet.

"Nope," Grace said.

Charlie shook his head. "Uh-uh."

"Perfect," I muttered, though it was anything but.

"What's wrong?" Charlie asked.

"I left my laptop at the stadium," I said. "We'll have to swing by and grab it."

For a second, I thought about leaving it, but there's a bunch of stuff I planned on getting through tonight. So unless I wanted to start the morning behind, I'd better stop.

The late-afternoon light stretched long across the

asphalt as I pulled into the stadium lot and parked in my usual spot.

"Come on." I turned off the engine. "We'll run in quick."

Grace's eyes went wide.

"We get to go *inside?*"

"Yep." I said. "But don't be too excited. I'm in a temporary office so there's really nothing in it."

She hopped out of the Jeep first, spinning once in the cool breeze. Charlie followed, crunching through a few scattered leaves.

"This is *so* cool," she said.

They both looked at the entrance like it led to Narnia.

"Haven't you two been to the stadium before?" I asked.

"Yeah," Charlie said, "but only through the big gate."

"Well," I said, pulling the door open, "welcome to the thrilling world of back hallways."

The metal door clanked shut behind us as we passed the empty security desk. Gary must've been doing a walk-through or taking a bathroom break.

We took the elevator to the third floor and were walking toward my office when Grace stopped suddenly.

"Uncle Benny," she whispered, tugging on my sleeve. "Is that *her?*"

I followed her gaze toward the glass conference room. Quinn sat at the table, hair pulled into a messy bun, glasses perched on her nose as she flipped through her notebook. The light from the high windows hit her hair just right making it shine gold where the sun caught it and auburn in the shadows.

"Yeah," I said. "That's her."

Grace's hand flew to her mouth. "Really?"

Her voice wasn't loud, but it was enough. Quinn looked up, spotted us, and smiled.

"Hey," she said. "Didn't expect to see you back today."

I stepped into the conference room, resting a hand on each kid's shoulder.

"I forgot my laptop," I said. "These two came along for the ride."

"You're *Quinn Logan!*" Grace blurted.

Quinn laughed softly. "Last I checked."

"This is my niece, Grace, and my nephew, Charlie," I said. "Guys, this is Quinn."

Charlie tilted his head. "You look different than in your videos."

"That's because I'm not wearing sequins," Quinn said with a grin.

Grace giggled, her awe melting into a smile.

Quinn glanced at me.

"I didn't see you earlier, so I was going to text and ask how your call went."

"With Tony Rivas?" I said. "Seemed to go well. He knows his stuff, so hopefully we'll have the bullpen coach spot confirmed in the next few days."

Quinn smiled.

"We're getting there. Slowly, but surely."

I huffed a quiet laugh.

Grace stood there, half-turned toward Quinn, eyes wide and bright, like she was afraid to blink and miss something."

Quinn must have noticed too, because her smile softened as she turned to them.

"So, are you two happy your uncle's back in Waypoint?"

Grace nodded instantly.

"Yes!"

"Me too!" Charlie said. "He just took us to get milkshakes."

Quinn laughed quietly.

"Sounds like he's doing something right, then."

I shook my head, but I couldn't stop the smile tugging at my mouth.

"Alright, you two," I said, nodding toward the hallway. "Come on, let's go grab my laptop so we can get you home."

Grace hesitated, shifting her weight from one foot to the other.

"Can I stay here while you get it?"

She hit me with those big eyes that always meant I was about to give her anything she wanted. Charlie hovered just behind her, clearly hoping I'd say yes without him needing to ask.

Before I could answer, Quinn smiled. "It's fine. The company will be nice."

"Okay, I'll be right back," I said. "Be on your best behavior."

I headed out of the room and turned toward my office. Glancing back, I saw that Grace was already talking, hands flying as fast as her words. Quinn leaned on the table, listening like it was the most important conversation she'd had all day.

Something about it stopped me for a second—the ease, the warmth. Grace didn't get shy often, but this was different. She was glowing. And Quinn wasn't just humoring her, she looked genuinely interested.

I shook it off and kept walking. My laptop bag sat right where I'd left it, slumped on the corner of the desk. I slung the strap over my shoulder and headed back.

By the time I reached the conference room again, Grace

was in the middle of an animated story about her dance routine for the school talent show.

"...and we practiced the turns, but Miss Angie says if we smile, the judges won't notice if we mess up."

"That's solid advice," Quinn said. "I can't wait to see it."

Grace's eyes went wide. "You're going to be there?"

Quinn nodded. "My friend Erin's daughter Rosie is performing too."

Grace looked equal parts thrilled and terrified. "Then I have to practice extra."

"You'll be great. Just don't forget to have fun."

"I'll try," Grace said, her grin returning.

Charlie had claimed a chair near the end of the table and was spinning in slow circles,.

"Alright, you two," I said, stepping back into the door-way. "We've gotta go before your mom gets home and wonders where you are."

Charlie hopped off his chair and waved to Quinn.

"It was nice meeting you," he said.

"You too, Charlie," Quinn said warmly.

Grace stood and hesitated for a second before throwing her arms around Quinn in a quick hug.

"Thanks for keeping me company," Quinn said when Grace pulled back.

"Thanks for letting them hang out," I said. "They'll be talking about this all night."

"Anytime," she said. "They're great kids."

"Yeah," I said quietly. "They are."

For a second, neither of us moved. The moment stretched until Grace's voice broke it.

"Bye, Quinn!" she said, waving as she started for the door.

Quinn waved back.

"Bye, Grace. Bye, Charlie."

"See you," I said, giving her a small nod before following the kids out.

We headed out, the kids unusually quiet, still caught somewhere between awe and disbelief. They climbed into the Jeep and buckled in without a word. A small miracle in itself.

I started the engine and eased out of the lot, headlights cutting across the empty asphalt.

Halfway down the street, Grace finally spoke, her voice a mix of wonder and accusation.

"I can't believe you *work* with Quinn Logan," she said. "Why didn't you tell me?"

"It wasn't really something I could talk about yet," I said. "Quinn being involved with the team's been kind of a secret."

"Well, it's the coolest secret ever."

"Glad you think so," I said, thinking about the way Quinn had smiled when Grace hugged her.

I told myself it didn't mean anything, but I didn't buy it for a second.

Chapter Twenty

Quinn

I didn't realize I was still smiling until the glass door closed and the conference room went quiet again.

Grace's hug had been quick—kid fast, all impulse and sincerity—but it lingered in the air like a chord that hadn't quite finished ringing. I rubbed at the spot on my arm where her cheek had landed and glanced down at my notebook. The page where I'd scribbled notes about community outreach and ticketing had morphed into an abstract of loops and arrows. Proof that even when I was supposed to be focused, my brain was busy trying to map out something I couldn't quite name yet.

I slid the tablet into my bag and sat for a beat longer than I needed to, letting the quiet settle before my mind wandered where it always seemed to lately.

Benny by himself was already potent in a way that got under your skin. But Benny with kids? That was downright dangerous.

He had a calm sort of authority, the kind that didn't need to say much to be felt, but he also knew when to let a moment stretch just because two kids were happy.

Grace and Charlie had lit up around him. He lit up right back.

Dangerous, my brain said, and not in the tabloid way. In the way that sneaks up on you, like sunlight shifting across a room until you realize you're warm.

I stood and rolled my shoulders, shook out the stiffness, then gathered my bag and headed for the elevator. Thankfully the ride down was uneventful. I doubted I'd ever step into one again without that flicker of panic. By the time the doors opened, I'd forced a breath and found my footing again.

The security desk was empty, so I made a mental note to ask Tessa about bringing on another guard so we can stagger coverage, even in the off-season.

Outside, the sky was slipping toward that purple-gray where the streetlights blink on and the whole town looks like someone dimmed the track lights for ambiance.

I could've gone straight home. Instead, I texted Erin.

> You home? I have something for Rosie.

The three dots popped up almost immediately.

> We're here! She's "rehearsing" to the song you told her to try last week. Brace yourself for jazz hands.

> Can't wait to see.

On impulse I added...

> I met the cutest nine-year-old named Grace who's dancing to "Messy in the Best Way" in the talent show.

Grace Turner...Benny's niece?

That's the one.

Can't wait to hear how you met her.

Before I could answer, Dad's picture filled the screen—baseball cap, sunglasses, and the ocean behind him. Leave it to him to call just as my thoughts started circling back to things I shouldn't unpack in a parking lot. I hit accept and put him on speaker.

"Hey, Superstar," he said. "You busy?"

"No, I'm just leaving the stadium and heading to Erin's. I have rhinestone clips for Rosie."

"Rhinestones," he said, fond and mock-exasperated at once. "Go figure."

"Hey, you can take the girl off the stage..." I said. "How's the left coast?"

"Sunny and overpriced," he said. "The traffic sucks, but the view's not bad."

"Only you would call the Malibu oceanfront 'not bad.'"

"Hey, I'm keeping it humble," he said. "Can't let the Pacific get a big head."

"You're ridiculous," I said, but I was smiling.

"And how are you?"

People had called me a lot of things through the years—professional, resilient, a machine. But my parents' voices were the only steady ones that ever cut through all that noise. The ones that kept me sane when the rest of the world spun too fast.

"I'm good," I said. "I'm really enjoying working with the team. It's busy, but in a good way."

I gave him the CliffsNotes version—meetings, planning,

the usual spreadsheets and schedules. He'd understand. Running a team wasn't all that different from running a tour. It was just a different kind of circus.

"I bet your notebooks are full of numbers and notes," he said, then chuckled. "And doodles."

"You know me too well."

"You always had a good head for business," he said.

"Because you made sure I did," I said. "You never let me just pop on stage and sing without knowing what was happening behind the scenes."

"Damn right," he said. "I made sure you were paying attention, just in case I wasn't there to keep people from taking advantage of you."

I smiled as something in my chest tugged.

"Guess it worked. No one's managed to pull anything over on me." I chuckled. "Not in business, anyway."

"Hey, some of those guys had me fooled too. So don't feel bad," he said, his tone easy. then a beat of humor slipped back in. "Speaking of, is there anyone special I should know about?"

Heat crept up my neck before I could stop it. My mind flashed to Benny's hand at the back of my neck, the taste of him, the way the world had gone quiet.

"No one worth mentioning," I said, probably too quickly.

"Uh-huh," he said. "That quick answer tells me everything I need to know."

"It tells you nothing," I said, laughing. "Because there's nothing to tell."

"Whatever you say, baby girl." His tone softened. "Speaking of things to tell you...I was talking to your mom yesterday. She asked if I was coming to Waypoint for the holidays."

"You said yes, right?"

He nodded.

"And I don't have anything going on here I can't handle from Waypoint, so I figured I'd come out next week and stay through the new year. That is if you've got room for your old man."

"Always," I said, meaning it.

He grinned, and something inside me loosened. Once I started touring, family life was never what anyone would call traditional, but my parents had done their best to keep it as normal as possible. Especially in between tours.

Even when we were holed up in some rented house with gates and security, that stuff faded into the background. What I remembered most were the small things—messing around in the backyard, movie nights that went too late, and Sunday dinners that made wherever we were feel like home.

We talked a few more minutes, laughing about old tour stories and the time he accidentally left my costume trunk in Cleveland, before saying goodnight.

I stared at the blank screen for a second longer, still smiling. Then I reached out and shot Erin a text.

> Sorry. I got held up. On my way now.

After backing out of my spot, I shifted into drive and pulled out of the lot, headlights cutting across the dark asphalt. As I hit the main road, my dad's question about "anyone special" echoed louder than I wanted to admit. My parents had never stopped hoping I'd find a good guy and have a normal life...whatever that even meant for me.

But I wasn't so sure anymore. Through the years, I'd dated other singers, celebrities, and the occasional "normal" guy. They all swore they could handle the attention until it turned to them. Until they decided the glare of my life was too bright, or too much, or both.

It wasn't arrogance to think that if I started seeing someone, it would make news. It always did. Even here in Waypoint, where I'd almost convinced myself I was living in anonymity, privacy was a myth.

I wanted to believe Benny would be different. But wanting and knowing aren't the same thing.

Chapter Twenty-One

Benny

By the time I pulled into the parking lot at El Rincón, I was already questioning my decision to come.

It had seemed like a good idea yesterday when the guys invited me—grab dinner, catch up, have a few laughs. But after a day full of calls with prospective coaches, and a few too many updates from Tessa about next season's logistics, I was pretty much talked out. My enthusiasm had flatlined somewhere between leaving the stadium and pulling into the lot.

I sat there for a second, engine idling, staring at the string lights draped across the patio. The place hadn't changed since I was a kid. Same cracked stucco, faded sombrero sign above the door, smell of grilled onions and lime drifting into the parking lot. It was one of those small-town constants, like time had decided to stop here.

Inside, the Friday-night crowd buzzed with families in booths, couples sipping margaritas, and the faint thump of early-2000s pop through the speakers. I spotted them in the back corner with a half-empty pitcher in the middle of the table—Kevin Williams, Tommy Benson, and Ryan Bush. We'd been tight in high school, the kind of friends you saw every day until one day you just didn't.

Over the years, we'd kept in touch—group texts, the occasional beer when I was in town. They'd regularly come to my games, and I'd stood up in their weddings. It was always a little weird, though. Their lives had stayed in Waypoint. Mine hadn't.

"Look who finally decided to show up," Tommy said as I slid into the booth. He still had that grin that made you think he was about to start a story that ended with detention.

"Lost track of time," I said.

"You? Shocker," Kevin said, earning a few laughs from the table.

Ryan slid a mug toward me and filled it from the pitcher.

"To hometown legends who still answer our texts," Scott said, raising his glass.

We clinked mugs, and I took a drink. It tasted cold, crisp, and familiar.

Across the table, Ryan drained his and immediately refilled it. The guy who used to go by Ryan "Gets-All-The" Bush was now a happily married father of four daughters—living proof that the universe had a sense of humor.

The server swung by to drop off a basket of chips and salsa and take our orders. The guys didn't even look at their menus, but I glanced at mine long enough to pick something.

A few more jokes flew around, mostly at my expense. It felt like being seventeen again—loud, stupid, and harmless. Then Tommy's grin went sly.

"Speaking of local legends," he said, phone in hand. "Want to explain this?"

He flipped his phone toward me.

A blurry photo of Quinn and me at The Maiden filled the screen.

Pop Princess Quinn Logan Spotted Cozying Up to Former MLB Catcher Benny Reed

Fantastic.

Kevin laughed.

"Guess we know why you've been too busy to hang out."

"Come on," I said, waving it off. "You believe that crap?"

"I don't know," Ryan said, smirking. "It looks convincing. You two make a good pair."

"Yeah," Tommy added. "Baseball and pop go together like peanuts and Cracker Jack. America's favorite combo."

They all laughed. Just guys being guys. Still, it landed wrong.

"I don't go online much," I said. "And clearly, that's still the right choice."

"You can't blame 'em." Scott shrugged. "The woman's a walking headline. You have dinner with her and people are gonna talk."

"It was a business meeting," I said. "Tessa and a couple prospective coaches were there too."

"Sure," Ryan's grin made me want to throw my beer at him.

Tommy elbowed him.

"Remember when she used to sing at the talent shows? Who knew she'd end up being *Quinn Logan*?"

"Yeah," Scott said. "If we'd known she was gonna turn out that hot, maybe we would've paid attention back in school."

They all laughed, the kind of noise that belonged to another lifetime of high school jokes and bad beer. I used to love that sound. Now it just felt loud.

I didn't even think about it before I said, "She was always like that."

They looked at me, a little surprised.

"What, hot?" Ryan asked.

"No, *Quinn Logan*, talented and driven," I said, sharper than I meant. "The rest of us were just too dumb to see it."

I barely remembered her from school, but her rise to fame was well documented. I'd spent more time than I'd like to admit looking her up online the past few weeks.

The table went quiet for a second before Tommy lifted his beer.

"Damn, Reed. You sound almost offended."

"Just saying," I muttered. "She worked her ass off. It doesn't seem fair to act like it was some kind of fluke."

"Relax, man," Scott said with a chuckle. "We're just messing around."

I nodded, pretending that settled it, but the back of my neck felt tight. I took a long drink of beer I didn't even want.

They moved on to other topics—high school football, the best wings in town, who was opening what new business on Main Street. The usual small-town noise.

Eventually, the conversation drifted back my way. This time they asked how the Lagerheads were shaping up and what the new season might look like. I gave them the polished version we fed the press, the one with the edges sanded off.

But even as I talked, my mind kept drifting to Quinn.

To that photo. To the look on her face when she hugged Grace. The pull that had been between us for weeks. The kiss I still hadn't stopped thinking about. And now the headline.

I told myself it didn't matter. That it was just gossip.

Except I knew better.

For someone like Quinn, rumors weren't just noise, they were shadows that followed her everywhere.

The server showed up with food a few minutes later. She slid the plates between half-empty mugs and baskets of chips that had been picked down to the crumbs. The smell of grilled meat and peppers hit my nose, making my mouth water.

For a minute, nobody said a word. Forks scraped plates, and the only sound was chewing. I grabbed a few strips of steak and poblano, wrapped them in a warm tortilla, and took a big bite. The heat hit slow and lingered just long enough to make me reach for my beer.

Once our plates were half cleared, the conversation picked back up. It shifted to the glory days, as it always did when we got together. State championships, playing baseball in April snow flurries, and dugout antics that somehow never got us benched. Once they started filling in the details, I remembered most of it. But I've played a lot of baseball between then and now, and some of it blurs together.

When the stories finally ran out, Ryan flagged the server for the check. I reached for it out of habit, sliding my card in before anyone could argue.

"You don't have to pay every time we get together," Tommy said, shaking his head.

"I'll let you get the next one," I said.

Kevin grinned.

"We're holding you to that."

"Fair enough," I said, sliding out of the booth.

Outside, we lingered in the parking lot for a few minutes, not really saying anything that mattered. We were just dragging out the goodbye because that's what you do. Eventually, Ryan checked the time and said he should get going, and the rest of us followed his lead. Before we got into our trucks, we promised to do it again soon. I smiled through it, meaning it and not meaning it at the same time.

On the drive home, the streets were quiet. Storefronts dark, stoplights blinking yellow. Waypoint looked exactly how it always had, and somehow that made it feel different.

Maybe it was just me. Between the team and everything with Quinn, there was too much noise in my head to appreciate the quiet. I'd told myself I wanted to keep the focus on baseball, to keep Quinn separate. But the longer this went on, the more impossible that seemed.

And funny enough, it didn't bother me as much as it used to.

Chapter Twenty-Two

Quinn

I pulled the lasagna out of the oven, the heat rolling up my arms as I set the pan on the stovetop. The cheese on top was exactly how I wanted it—golden brown with a few darker, crisped patches, the edges bubbling where the sauce had pushed through. The whole kitchen smelled like tomatoes, garlic, and heaven.

"Thank God," my brother Miles said behind me. "I'm starving."

"It has to rest," I said, still admiring my masterpiece. "You know that."

"I *know* it but don't *understand* it."

"It's so the layers have a chance to set," Mom said as she finished slathering garlic butter on the loaf of crispy Italian bread I picked up from the bakery earlier.

"And also so you don't burn your tongue off," I added.

"I'm willing to take my chances."

"I want perfect layers of meat, cheese, and noodles, not a lava-hot pile of regret," she said, handing me the garlic bread. "It won't kill you to wait."

"It might." He let out a dramatic moan. "How long?"

"Fifteen to twenty minutes," I said as I slid the bread into the oven.

He groaned again.

Dad sipped his wine. "You sound like you're being tortured."

"I am. My sister's feeding me false hope."

"You'll survive," I muttered.

Mom handed him a stack of plates.

"Here. Set the table. It'll keep you from drooling over the lasagna."

He muttered something under his breath about "cruelty in the home," but he took the plates from her and walked over to the table.

I wiped my hands on a dish towel, stealing another glance at the lasagna. The edges were settling, the cheese smoothing out like it knew it was being admired. Fifteen minutes. Maybe more if Miles kept whining.

Mom went to the drawer and pulled out silverware and a stack of napkins, walking them over to Miles like she fully expected him to complain the entire way.

"Put these out too," she said.

"I'm being worked to death," he muttered.

Dad snorted quietly, taking another sip of wine as he leaned back against the counter. It was nice having him staying with me—a welcome addition to the quiet.

I grabbed the oven mitt again and pulled the garlic bread from the oven. It smelled buttery, toasty, and exactly right. After cutting it into thick slices, I tucked them into the woven basket I'd left on the counter earlier.

We carried everything over to the kitchen table—bread, salad, drinks, plates, the whole spread—and once the timer hit the magic number, I brought the lasagna over too. Miles sat so fast his chair scraped.

"Easy," Dad said. "Act like you've been fed before."

"No promises," Miles said.

I cut into the lasagna, easing the spatula under the first square, and lifted it out in one perfect piece. I set it on a plate and handed it to Mom.

She pointed at the cleanly defined layers.

"This is why we wait."

Miles rolled his eyes.

"It would taste the same either way."

"Blasphemy," Mom said.

Dad smirked.

"Son, you're outnumbered."

I cut slices for Dad and Miles, handing them their plates before sitting down with mine.

Conversation stopped for a few minutes. Just the sound of forks scraping and appreciative noises filling the room.

"This is amazing," Mom said once she swallowed. "Definitely better than I ever made."

I laughed. "Food always tastes better when someone else cooks."

"That can't be the only reason this tastes so good," she said, reaching for a piece of garlic bread.

Dad nodded his agreement and continued to eat. Miles was almost done with his slice like he expected it to vanish if he didn't eat fast. It felt good—easy, familiar, everyone in their usual roles and the kitchen warm in that way I'd missed.

Mom looked around the table. "Anyone have plans tomorrow or Sunday?"

Miles swallowed a too-big bite. "Chloe and I have a wedding to go to tomorrow."

From there, Mom got the who, what, where, and when out of him faster than a bloodhound reporter.

Once she was satisfied she had all the details, she smiled. "She's such a sweetheart. I really like her. Tell her we missed her tonight."

"So do I," Miles said. "And I will."

His girlfriend had been invited to dinner, but she had to work.

Dad wiped his mouth with his napkin. "I'm planning on doing absolutely nothing, and I'm thrilled about it."

"I'm heading to Erin's tomorrow. Rosie and a couple of her friends are doing a dress performance of their dance before the talent show," I said. "If you're not doing anything, you can come along."

"I'd love to, but I'm having lunch with my ladies, and we're hitting the outlets before the Christmas madness kicks in."

"That sounds fun. You'll see the official show next week anyway," I said. "And I met Benny Reed's niece Grace a couple weeks ago. She's doing a dance to 'Messy in the Best Way' and she lit up when she found out I'd be there to see it."

"Oh, that's sweet. How old is she?"

"I didn't ask, but I'm guessing around Rosie's age."

Mom nodded, but before saying anything else, her gaze drifted toward Dad.

She pointed her fork at him. "What's with that face?"

He straightened a little. "This is just my normal face."

"No, it's definitely not," Mom said with a snort. "It's your *I-have-something-to-tell-you* face."

Dad lifted his wine like it might shield him. "It's nothing."

Mom gave him a look that probably would make James Bond spill all his secrets.

As the silence stretched, Miles and I shifted our eyes

back and forth between them like we were watching a tennis match.

Finally Dad blew out a breath and answered. "Since you mentioned Benny Reed," he said to me. "Julia reached out earlier."

Julia. My manager-slash-buffer to the outside world. If she's putting something on Dad's radar, it usually wasn't great.

"About?"

"There's some chatter online about you and Benny being on a date. There was a picture of you two having dinner," he said. "Julia said it's nothing serious, but she wanted me to be aware since it's local."

"Great."

Mom's eyebrows shot up.

"Were you on a date?"

"No." I shook my head. "It was a business dinner. Tessa and two potential coaches were there, too."

The kiss flashed in my mind before I could shove it back down. The way the world narrowed to the space between us. The way it felt like a line crossed and something started at the same time.

I took a sip of water, hoping my face didn't give any of that away. My mom's face-reading abilities aren't limited to my dad. She can read Miles and me like we have closed captions on our foreheads.

"Quinn..." Dad shifted in his chair, clearly debating how much to say. "...do you think we should hire security again?"

"No," I said. "I feel safe in Waypoint. Really safe."

Dad's brow creased. "But if this draws people here—"

"I'm not ignoring the possibility of that, but I really don't want to go back to being followed everywhere," I said.

"If something weird happens, we'll deal with it. But I don't want to bring people into my space unless I have to."

Dad rubbed his jaw, the way he always did when he wanted to argue but couldn't justify it.

"Okay," he said finally. "But if anything feels off—*anything*—you let me know and we'll take care of it. Immediately."

"I will," I said. And I meant it.

We fell back into an easy rhythm after that. Mom served the apple pie she'd brought, the buttery crust flaking just right as she plated slices while Dad added scoops of vanilla ice cream.

As we ate, Miles grumbled about having to wear real shoes to tomorrow's wedding, earning himself a chorus of eye rolls.

I tried not to let what my dad said ruin the relaxed rhythm of the night, but inside, something stirred, soft, steady, impossible to ignore.

Waypoint had become a safe place.

The first time in years I could walk around town and just...exist.

And I wasn't sure what scared me more—the idea that chaos might follow me or the truth that I cared way too much about what Benny Reed would think if he ever saw that headline.

Chapter Twenty-Three

Benny

Rain hammered the windshield in loud, steady bursts as I pulled into Cat's driveway. The front door flew open before I even came to a full stop.

Grace shot out like she'd been fired from a confetti cannon—pink raincoat flapping, her sparkly costume peeking with every bounce of her run. I barely had time to put the Jeep in park before I was out the door and into the rain.

"Hey, slow down," I called, my hair already dripping as I jogged toward her.

She didn't slow. If anything, she sped up, her grin big enough to light up the whole damn street.

"You look ready for the big stage," I said, pulling open the door for her.

Her eyes sparkled as she climbed into the back seat.

"I am."

By the time she clicked her seatbelt in place, Cat and Charlie were making their way down the walkway under an umbrella that was doing the bare minimum. Cat had one arm hooked around Charlie's shoulders, shielding him as best she could, but the rain sheeted off the sides, soaking them anyway.

"Hop in bud," I said to Charlie as they reached the Jeep.

He climbed in beside Grace, shaking a little rain off his sleeves.

Cat climbed into the passenger seat and shut the door fast to keep the rain out.

I closed the back door, jogged around to the driver's side, and climbed in, my pants sticking to my legs, hair dripping onto my collar. At least my shirt was mostly dry under my jacket.

"All set?" I asked as I started the engine.

Grace and Charlie answered in perfect unison.

"Yep!"

"Thanks again for driving," Cat said, as I pulled out of the driveway. "Parking's going to be a disaster."

"I'll drop you three at the door then go hunt for a spot."

"Mom and Dad texted and they're still planning on coming," she said, adjusting the vents toward her damp jacket.

I nodded. Some things didn't need commentary with the kids listening.

We hit another patch of heavy rain halfway to the high school. The kind that blurred the world into streaks of streetlights and wet pavement. I glanced in the rearview and caught Grace swaying a little in her seat, humming "Messy in the Best Way" like she couldn't contain the nerves buzzing through her. Beside her, Charlie traced slow patterns in the fogged-up window, following the paths the raindrops carved.

I made a mental note to clean the fingerprints off. Again.

Cat glanced over at me.

"You okay? You've been quiet."

I shrugged. "Long day."

Between calls with potential coaches, roster discussions, construction timelines, and the general chaos that came with trying to rebuild a team from the ground up, my brain felt like an overstuffed filing cabinet. Closed, full, and one hard tug away from spilling everything.

But that wasn't the real reason I'd been so preoccupied.

Quinn had gotten into my head this week, more than I wanted to admit. We'd kept things strictly professional, exchanged quick hellos in hallways or meeting rooms, both of us pretending nothing had shifted.

Except it had.

Because every time she was near, something in the air crackled like a live wire. My attention dragged to her without permission. My thoughts drifted back to her even when I was supposed to be focused on anything else.

And I wasn't about to explain any of that to my sister.

We reached the drop-off circle in front of the high school. A line of cars snaked around the curve, hazard lights blinking through the rain. When our turn came, I eased under the overhang, close enough that they wouldn't have to make a run for it.

"Go," I said, throwing the Jeep into park. "I'll find a spot and meet you inside."

They piled out of the car and Cat herded both kids toward the doors, the rain still blowing sideways even under the cover.

I pulled away from the curb and into the lot. Cars crawled through the rows in a slow parade, everyone hunting for the same miracle spot. I trailed them for a few passes just in case, but there wasn't a single space anywhere.

So I headed toward the far edge of the lot and backed into a spot. Ten feet or a hundred yards...made no difference. I was going to get soaked no matter where I parked.

Jogging through the rain, I cut across the slick sidewalk, already soaked by the time I grabbed the school's front door and pulled it open. Warm air rushed out and hit me with the familiar mix of floor wax, disinfectant, and whatever brand of industrial soap every school seemed to use. It was the exact same smell it had twenty-odd years ago.

I walked farther inside, wiping a hand over the back of my neck, trying to keep the water from running straight down my spine. The main hallway stretched in front of me, the same scratched tile floors and cinderblock walls I remembered. It felt smaller now, like someone had taken the building and shrunk it in the wash.

The trophy cases lined the first long stretch of corridor, their glass fronts gleaming beneath the fluorescent lights. Same old displays—school records, science fair ribbons, art pieces behind curling construction paper borders, sports trophies polished within an inch of their lives. Waypoint High might've been small, but the kids here had always punched above their weight.

I kept moving toward the auditorium. A volunteer near the doors handed me a program without breaking their rhythm.

"Thanks," I murmured, shaking a little more rain from my hair.

I stepped inside and paused just long enough to scan the room. Families filled rows, kids bounced in their seats, and parents juggled coats and umbrellas. Cat had texted me exactly where she and the kids were sitting, so I wasn't looking for them.

Which meant there was only one person I could've been looking for. But I didn't see her.

A flick of disappointment hit anyway, sharp and stupid.

Before I could look again, Cat spotted me and waved. I headed down the aisle and slid into the empty end seat. Our parents sat on her other side, with Charlie tucked in beside them.

"You made it," she said. "I was afraid you'd float away."

"Came close." I brushed a hand through my damp hair as I leaned forward to see my parents better. "Mom. Dad."

My mom offered a small smile. "Glad you made it."

Dad looked up just long enough to meet my eyes, gave a quick nod, then refocused on Charlie beside him. Charlie was completely zoned out, absorbed in whatever game he was playing on my dad's phone.

Typical. The kid could block out an earthquake if he had a screen in front of him.

Cat nudged my arm. "The show's starting soon. Grace is second to last, so we have a while."

I nodded, letting my eyes drift over the crowd again—casual, or as casual as I could fake. Parents settling in, toddlers climbing over laps, a few teachers shuffling programs.

And then I saw her.

A tight little pull hit low in my chest. Nothing huge. Just...there.

Before I could look away, her head turned like she felt me watching her. Her gaze moved across the room, skimming past people until it landed on me.

Her mouth curved, barely there but unmistakable. Not a smile exactly. More of a quiet nod to whatever this was between us.

The lights blinked twice, and the noise in the room cut in half. A teacher walked onto the stage, and tapped the microphone.

"Find your seats, folks. We're ready to begin."

Chapter Twenty-Four

Quinn

Applause rolled through the auditorium like a soft wave. The kids onstage stepped forward in one uneven line to take their bow. Most of their costumes were sparkly and a little disheveled, askew in the way only elementary school performances could manage. Rosie was toward the middle, hands clasped with her two friends, grinning like she'd just won a Tony.

It was adorable.

The moment held for another beat before finally tapering off, like no one in the room wanted the moment to end. The kids scattered offstage in a burst of energy, teachers calling after them as if they could possibly herd that much excitement into a straight line.

Seconds later, chairs creaked, programs were folded, and the whole auditorium shifted at once—parents gathering coats, kids bouncing in the aisles, everyone trying to get somewhere.

"She did amazing," Erin said, loud enough to be heard over the noise.

Scott nodded. "Best one up there."

Erin elbowed him. "You can't say that."

"It's not bragging if it's true," he said.

"Her turn at the end was *perfect* tonight," I said.

"It was," Erin said. "She's been practicing it nonstop. I swear she did it down the cereal aisle yesterday."

We stayed seated for a few more minutes, letting the crowd funnel toward the doors. No point diving into the chaos of half the auditorium trying to leave at the same time.

While Erin promised Liam they'd be heading out soon, I looked around, telling myself I wasn't searching for anyone in particular. But when I spotted *not anyone in particular* slipping out of the auditorium, my traitorous heart fluttered anyway.

Once the initial rush eased into something less like a stampede and more like normal human movement, Erin grabbed her purse and nudged my arm.

"You ready?" she asked.

"Absolutely," I said, pushing up from the seat.

We filed out of the aisle behind Scott and Liam and joined the steady shuffle toward the exit. Once we reached the foyer, the crowd spread out into small clusters of parents and kids reuniting.

"I'll grab Rosie," Scott said. "Art room, right?"

Erin nodded. "Yep. We'll wait here."

He gave Liam's hair a quick ruffle before making his way through the crowd toward the hallway.

Erin nudged my arm. "That's where it all began," she said, nodding toward the framed display on the wall.

I followed her gaze and...yeah. There it was. A framed poster from my first tour still hung in the foyer like a time capsule nobody asked to preserve. Seventeen-year-old me stared back, eyeliner too heavy, bangs too blunt, wearing a smile I'd practiced in a bathroom mirror.

It felt like a lifetime ago.

And also like yesterday.

"You okay?" Erin asked quietly.

I nodded, but my throat tightened a little.

"I went straight from the middle of junior year to tours, interviews, recording studios..." I exhaled. "Sometimes it feels like part of me got stuck. Like everyone else graduated and grew up, and I just stayed the girl on that poster way too long."

Erin's expression softened in that I-see-you way only she could manage.

I forced myself to look away before I spiraled and my gaze caught the display case we were standing next to. A picture of eighteen-year-old Benny in a crisp jersey from draft day. He looked young, cocky, and stupidly handsome, even in faded print.

Of course he did.

As if the universe wanted to rub it in, movement across the foyer caught my eye.

Benny—very real, very present, and still very handsome—stood near the opposite set of doors, laughing at something Charlie said.

I forced my attention back to Erin, but the universe apparently wasn't finished messing with me. Because just then, I spotted Cat weaving through the foyer crowd with Grace at her side—grinning, animated, bouncing with the kind of post-performance energy only ten-year-olds can generate.

They were heading straight toward Benny and Charlie.

Erin followed my line of sight and smirked.

"Oh? Interesting direction you're staring in."

"I wasn't staring," I lied instantly. Badly.

Her eyebrows lifted in the *sure, Jan* way only best friends can achieve.

"I want to go tell Grace how amazing her dance was."

"Mmm-hm." Erin crossed her arms. "Is Grace the *only* person in that family you're hoping to see?"

Of course not.

But what I said out loud was, "I see Benny almost every day at the stadium."

Erin made a noise that translated directly to *you are so full of shit*, but she let it go, mostly because Scott reappeared then with Rosie in tow. Rosie launched straight into a rapid-fire recap of who tripped, who almost fell, how good the lights looked, and exactly how much glitter was on her costume.

We all listened, chimed in, and fussed over her until she darted off to talk to one of her friends.

"Go," Erin said. "Before they leave."

I took a steadying breath and walked toward them.

A few people glanced at me as I moved through the foyer—those quick double-takes that always looked like *wait...is that—?* But nobody approached, or called my name. Waypoint wasn't like that. They stared long enough to confirm their suspicions, then politely pretended they hadn't.

I was halfway there when someone across the foyer called Benny's name. He glanced over, lifted a hand in acknowledgment, and headed in their direction.

Honestly? Probably for the best.

I'd felt him in the auditorium the entire show. A warm, steady awareness in the back of my mind I couldn't shake. I wasn't sure I was ready to be right next to him while my pulse tried to stage a full-scale riot.

"Grace!" I called when I was just a few steps away.

She spun, eyes widening.

"Quinn!" And then she launched herself at me like a pint-sized missile. I caught her easily, laughing as she squeezed me around the ribs.

"You were incredible," I said, pulling back to look at her. "Truly. I loved how you hit every beat, and your arms were perfect. And your ending?" I brought my fingertips to my lips in a chef's kiss. "Perfect."

Grace beamed so hard I thought she might float away.

"Really?" she asked, bouncing once on her toes. "You really liked the ending?"

"I loved it," I said. "Honestly? I think your version is even better than the original choreography."

She spun toward her mom.

"Mom! Did you hear what she said?"

Cat laughed. "I sure did." Then she looked at me and offered her hand.

"I'm Grace's mom, by the way. Cat Reed."

"Quinn," I said, shaking it. "You were a year behind me, right?"

Cat's brows lifted. "Yeah. I was."

We hadn't been friends or anything back then, but I definitely knew who she was. Cat had always been sweet and a little bookish—definitely closer to my social orbit than Benny's.

Grace bounced on her toes, already half-turned toward the hallway.

"Can I find Hailey?" she asked, eyes wide with the kind of hope no adult could ever say no to. "I want her to meet you."

"Sure," I said.

Cat nodded with a smile. "Go ahead. We're not staying

long because Charlie went home with Grandma and Grandpa and we have to pick him up."

Grace ran off, her excitement trailing behind her in a glittery blur.

And just like that, I was standing there with Cat and Benny.

"She's a great kid," I said to Cat.

"Thanks." She tucked a piece of damp hair behind her ear. "She was over the moon when she found out you were coming tonight," she said warmly. "She must've practiced that dance a hundred times this week."

I smiled. "It showed. She nailed it."

Before Cat could answer, Grace came bounding back through the foyer with a girl at her side—pony-tail swinging, sparkly leggings, the whole ten-year-old powerhouse vibe.

"This is Hailey!" Grace announced, practically vibrating. "Hailey, this is Quinn."

Hailey's eyes went cartoon-wide. "Hi," she whispered, then immediately blushed so hard I wondered if she might combust.

"Hi, Hailey. You two were wonderful up there."

Grace elbowed her friend. "I told you she'd say that."

Hailey grinned shyly. "Thank you."

Grace immediately launched into a breathless recap of everything that happened backstage. At first, Hailey stood there staring at me wide-eyed, clearly a little starstruck. But eventually the awe melted, and she jumped in with her own additions, talking just as fast, her hands flying everywhere.

I let them talk, smiling through all of it. Kids that age were pure, unfiltered joy, and these two were...honestly, adorable.

Cat watched them with a soft expression, the kind of

look that said she could listen to Grace tell stories like this all night.

As the foyer started to clear a bit, Cat checked her watch and winced. "Alright, girls, say your goodbyes.

They groaned in unison but threw their arms around me anyway—Grace with her usual full-body enthusiasm and Hailey with a shy squeeze that still managed to be earnest.

"Bye, Quinn!" Grace said, practically skipping even as she stood still.

"Bye," Hailey echoed, softer but beaming.

"You were both incredible tonight."

I turned back to find Erin waiting a few feet away with Rosie and Liam, all bundled and ready.

"You heading out?" she asked.

"Yeah," I said, readjusting my purse strap.

"Scott's pulling the car around," she said. "Do you want us to drive you down to yours?"

I shook my head. "I can walk. It looks like the rain finally eased up."

We walked outside and I hugged Rosie then Liam and said goodbye just as Scott pulled up to the curb.

"Text me when you get home," Erin said.

"Okay, Mom," I said with a chuckle.

She smiled and opened the back door. I waved to Scott and headed down the hill toward the lot.

The air was cool and damp, but the downpour had faded to a light drizzle, more mist than rain. The parking lot glowed with red brake lights, puddles reflecting headlights like little pieces of scattered sky.

I'd barely made it ten steps when I heard a familiar voice behind me.

"Quinn."

I turned.

Benny was striding toward me, hands in his jacket pockets. He looked way too casual for someone who made my whole night tilt with his mere presence.

"Mind a little company?" he asked.

The question was simple, but something in his voice wasn't.

A tiny spark zipped down my spine—annoyingly warm, annoyingly welcome.

"Sure," I said, tucking my hands into my pockets as we fell into step.

We walked a few quiet steps, the kind that didn't feel awkward, just...aware.

Benny cleared his throat.

"You made Grace's whole night, you know. The praise... being here..." He huffed out a soft laugh. "I'm probably going to hear all about it when I pick her up from school tomorrow."

I looked over. "Do you pick them up a lot?"

"A couple days a week," he said, shrugging like it was nothing. "Just to fill in when Cat's sitter has classes or can't cover."

"That's really nice," I said.

It was actually more than nice.

He didn't do the thing men sometimes did—talk about helping with kids like it was some grand heroic act. He said it casually, like it was the most natural part of his week. Like showing up mattered. Like Grace and Charlie mattered.

"I like spending time with them. And once the season starts, time gets tight." He rubbed a hand over the back of his neck. "So I'm doing as much as I can now."

My heart pulled—slow, warm, traitorous.

Of course a man this confident and put-together also

had this soft, grounded part of him. A part I'd only glimpsed but felt like I could fall for if I wasn't careful.

I nodded toward the second row.

"That's me."

Instead of saying goodbye, he walked me to my car. We stopped beside the driver's side door. The mist swirled in the streetlight, gentle and silver.

For a second we just stood there. The space between us was small enough that I could feel the leftover heat of him from sitting in the auditorium.

"It was good seeing you tonight," he said quietly.

"You too," I breathed, because anything else felt dangerous.

His gaze flicked to my mouth for the briefest, most reckless second.

And then—

"See you tomorrow," he said.

Not a question. Not even really a goodbye. A promise.

He stepped back, hands still in his pockets, and headed toward the back of the lot, slow enough that I knew he was waiting until I was safely inside.

I opened the door and settled in behind the wheel, watched him go, pulse fluttering like I was fifteen again.

Except I wasn't a kid anymore.

Which somehow made it both worse and better.

Chapter Twenty-Five

Benny

I didn't actually plan on coming to The Maiden tonight. When the guys texted—*You in for a drink tonight?*—I'd answered *maybe*. Which, from me, translates to *probably not*.

But then this afternoon, right after our meeting ended, Tessa and Quinn started firming up their plans to go out with Margot, Sylvie, and Erin.

And suddenly *probably not* turned into *I'll meet you there*.

I'm not proud of it, but here I was, walking through the door anyway.

The place was packed and music vibrated through the floorboards. A local cover band was onstage, blasting "Mr. Brightside" like it was 2004. People were singing along, the whole room electric in that small-town, everyone-knows-everyone way.

I found Kevin, Tommy, and Ryan staked out at a tall table near the back with a bucket of Bergmann Lager between them.

Kevin looked up first and let out a low whistle. "Look who actually followed through on a maybe."

"Yeah, normally when I say maybe, it's a definite no," Tommy said.

I chuckled and grabbed a bottle from the bucket.

If they only knew what actually brought me here.

The last notes died out and the next song's opening riff hit. The pub erupted in a cheer, then immediately quieted, everyone leaning in like they'd trained for the exact moment to jump in.

The singer finally stepped up to the mic—and the crowd was ready.

Show me, show me, show me how you do that trick...

Ryan tipped his beer toward the stage.

"That song makes me feel like I'm seventeen again."

"Ah yes, the glory days. Back when you had a full head of hair," Kevin said.

"And before the dad-bod kicked in," Tommy added.

Ryan patted his stomach like it was an old friend.

"I support Waypoint athletics by eating at the concession stand."

"Meanwhile, Mr. Three-Percent Body Fat over here managed to avoid the concession stands in MLB stadiums across the country," Tommy said, pointing at me.

"Five percent," I corrected. "And if a cheese product comes in a fifty-gallon drum, I'm not putting it in my body."

That earned a round of snorts, and the guys joined the band and half the room in belting out the chorus. They weren't on key. They weren't even close. But it didn't matter. Everyone knew the words, and no one cared about perfection. It was loud, nostalgic, and a little sloppy around the edges. Like this town.

I took a drink and looked around, telling myself I wasn't searching for anyone in particular. But I knew better. I'd just set my bottle down on the table when I spotted her.

Quinn and the other ladies were crammed around a high-top across the room, belting out the lyrics with zero shame. Erin, Tessa, Margot, and Sylvie were full-send dramatic about it, singing into their forks like they were headlining a tour.

Quinn was right there with them, singing into her fork mic like she was onstage and not in a corner of The Maiden. She wasn't trying to be funny or beautiful, but she was both.

A couple of phones were up, people recording the band or maybe the crowd singing along. I hoped none of those cameras caught her. Not because she didn't look good, but because she deserved to have one night where it wasn't anyone else's business.

The last chord of The Cure faded out to a messy, happy cheer, the kind only half-drunk bar singers can manage. The frontman leaned into the mic, a little out of breath.

"We're gonna take a break after this next one," he said. "But we need your help on a very specific part. You'll know it when it hits."

That got a laugh.

Then the band slipped into a steady, bouncy intro, and the whole place recognized it before the vocal even landed. The other half figured it out a second later and groaned in good humor.

"Sweet Caroline."

No chaos this time. No surprise. Just inevitability.

People braced for it—shoulders squared, beers raised, waiting for that moment.

Ryan cracked his knuckles like he was warming up to

pitch. Kevin shook out his arms like he was preparing for a sprint. Tommy started stretching his neck.

This song will always remind me of playing in Boston. The fans there didn't sing it, they attacked it regardless of who was winning.

It didn't take long for the first cue to come...

Bah! Bah! Baaaah!

A beat later came the answer, even louder...

SO GOOD! SO GOOD! SO GOOD!

It was more enthusiastic yelling than singing, but no one cared.

I didn't plan on joining in. My mouth just did it anyway, pure muscle memory.

The band dragged out the ending like they were milking applause, then cut the sound all at once. The room gave them one last cheer, and the singer shouted something about grabbing a drink and tipping the staff before they took their break.

Without the music, the noise shifted. Where the guitars had been, chatter swelled in. louder than you'd think talking could be. Glass clinks, laughter, orders shouted to the bartenders. The energy didn't disappear, it just changed shape.

A couple people passing by clapped me on the shoulder in greeting. Nothing deep—just that small-town shorthand of *Hey, glad you're back,* without needing any words. Someone nodded at me like we'd known each other for years. I nodded back even though I didn't recognize them.

Kevin lifted his beer toward me.

"Speaking of being back...I heard a rumor Lou Calder might be your bench coach. Any truth to that?"

"There's no contract signed yet, but it's looking good."

Which was an understatement. Lou had basically given

me a verbal yes, and a promise from him carried more weight than ink. The guy never committed to anything lightly, and if he said he'd be there, he'd show up an hour early with his sleeves rolled and a clipboard full of ideas.

"Damn," Ryan said, impressed. "That's a hell of a pickup."

Tommy whistled.

"You're building a real staff."

"I'm trying," I said.

We kept talking—nothing serious, just noise to fill the space between thoughts. Unfortunately, mine weren't exactly staying at the table. I took a drink, eyes drifting across the room before I could pretend I wasn't looking for her again.

Quinn slid off her stool, still smiling. She touched Erin's shoulder in passing, said something to Tessa, then headed toward the back hallway that led to the restrooms. As far as I could tell, she still hadn't seen me.

I nodded along to something Tommy said about his youngest kid and basketball tryouts, but it was only half absorbed. I kept glancing toward the hallway. Nothing obvious, just little checks like I was waiting on a game score.

Quinn finally emerged a few minutes later, weaving through the crowd as she slipped her phone back into her bag, head tipped down just long enough to miss the guy approaching her.

He looked around my age, wearing a flannel shirt, and the kind of grin that meant he was at least three beers past polite. Hands tucked in his pockets like he practiced looking relaxed, he leaned a shoulder against the wall, blocking her path. Quinn stopped short and lifted her head.

She offered a friendly smile, and whatever he said made

her shake her head. He laughed at her response, though it was more disbelief than humor.

When he crossed his arms and widened his stance like he was claiming the space, it clicked. It's Todd Walker. He'd been a couple years ahead of me in school.

They went back and forth a few times, and Quinn looked more uncomfortable with each pass. Then he spoke again, clearly agitated, and I easily read his lips.

"Come on, just ONE song!"

My entire body went hot.

Of course. He wanted her to get onstage and sing with the band.

Quinn shook her head again, more firmly.

When she tried to pass, he blocked her path.

I pushed off my stool without even excusing myself.

"Where're you going?" Tommy asked.

But I was already moving and didn't answer.

I cut through the crowd and walked straight toward them.

"Hey," I said as I reached them.

Both of them turned.

Quinn's eyes widened, something like relief flickering there before she masked it.

Todd blinked at me, surprised.

"Benny Reed?" he said, grinning like we were about to high-five over old times. "Man, I didn't even see you—"

I didn't smile back.

"You okay?" I asked Quinn.

"Yeah." She nodded.

"I'm trying to convince her to sing a song with the band," Todd said. "I figured she'd jump at the chance. She used to beg people to let her sing anywhere in town. Now she's too big-time to belt one out at The Maiden?"

He chuckled like we were old buddies sharing a joke at Quinn's expense. Like I'd be impressed he remembered her history better than she did.

I didn't bother matching the grin.

"She said no," I said. "Seems like a clear enough answer."

I didn't raise my voice. I hoped I wouldn't have to.

Chapter Twenty-Six

Quinn

Benny's voice cut through the noise, even though he hadn't raised it.

I didn't like thinking of myself as a damsel in distress, and Benny definitely wasn't my shining knight in anything. But right now? Having him step in felt like a blessing. I'd spent most of my life on alert—trained to scan a crowd, read a room in seconds, and assume someone from security was watching my blind spots.

Since moving to Waypoint, I'd let that guard down. I never expected to need it at The Maiden, on a Friday night surrounded by people who remember me as the girl who used to sing in the gymnasium cafeteria.

"Relax, man. I'm just talking to her."

He'd introduced himself as Todd, with the confidence of someone who assumed I should know exactly who he was. I didn't.

"You're blocking her," Benny said, calm but immovable.

Todd shrugged, still trying to look cocky, but the confidence didn't land the way it had thirty seconds ago.

"I just asked if she'd sing a song with the band." He scoffed, then turned his glossy eyes to me.

I kept my voice even. "Today isn't a no because I'm 'too big-time.' It's just a no."

For a heartbeat, we just stared at each other.

Then he huffed a humorless laugh and shook his head.

"Whatever." He pushed off the wall, muttered something, and disappeared into the crowd.

Once he left, I realized I'd angled closer to Benny. I took a small step back, reclaiming my own space.

"You okay?" Benny asked.

His expression wasn't pitying or overbearing—just steady. Present. Something warm unfurled in my chest.

"Yeah," I said. "I'm fine. Just...annoyed."

"Annoyed," Benny echoed, a wry twist at his mouth. "That's fair."

"Thanks for coming over," I said. "I don't think I was in any real danger, but I'm glad you shut it down."

"I had a feeling you weren't enjoying the conversation," he said.

"Not even a little."

He nodded, but the moment didn't immediately dissolve. It lingered, warm and a little too aware, until I finally shifted my weight.

"I should get back," I said. "Before the girls send out a search party."

"Come on," he said, tipping his head toward the tables. "I'll walk you back."

As we approached the table, Sylvie looked up mid-laugh. Her smile froze, shifted, and turned curious.

"Oh. Hi, Benny."

Margot followed her gaze, eyebrows lifting like she was suddenly very interested in my life choices.

"Hi..." she echoed, drawing the word out just enough to count as commentary.

Tessa leaned slightly forward, her focus narrowing in on Benny and me. Erin stayed quiet, her interest obvious without a single word.

He gave them an easy nod. "Hey."

I slid back into my seat. The restless energy inside me hadn't calmed yet.

Benny leaned closer.

"Whenever you're ready to leave, let me know. I'll walk you to your car."

Before I could answer, Tessa asked, "Why does she need an escort?"

I lifted one shoulder in a half-shrug. "Some guy wanted me to sing with the band. I said no, but he didn't like that answer. Benny cut him short."

"Maybe we should tell the manager," Sylvie said.

"I think we're good," I said. "No reason to drag the manager into it."

They all looked ready to argue with me, but they didn't.

"I'll be right over there," Benny said, nodding toward a high-top across the room. "Whenever you're ready."

Before he could step away, Tessa nodded at him. "Thanks for stepping in."

"Anytime."

He headed off, weaving through the crowd with that steady, confident walk. I watched long enough to see him reach the table, then forced myself to refocus on mine.

Erin leaned in a little. "You okay?"

"I'm fine," I said, and I meant it. "Annoyed, but fine."

They all watched me for a second, just to be sure. When no one found cracks in my answer, the tension eased.

"Okay, since we've established that you're okay." Tessa

tipped her chin toward where Benny had gone. "I'm pivoting."

"Pivoting?" I asked.

"To Benny Reed acting like your personal security detail," she clarified.

Sylvie let out a low whistle. "*Very* personal security."

Margot propped her elbow on the table. "Does he come with benefits? Or is this like an unpaid internship situation?"

Erin's mouth curled the slightest bit. "If it's unpaid, I feel like he volunteered pretty fast."

All four of them stared at me. No longer worried, just waiting.

I raised both hands. "It wasn't a thing. Some guy pushed for a song, I said no, Benny stepped in. That's the entire story."

Sylvie glanced around the table like she was taking attendance. "Please tell me I'm not the only one who saw sparks?"

"You're definitely not," Tessa said. "And I watch sparks fly between those two every day at the stadium."

"You do not," I said.

Tessa shrugged. I focused very hard on my drink, because apparently denial pairs well with beer. No one pushed it further, thank God, and conversation moved on to safer topics. I laughed when I was supposed to, sipped my drink, even sang along when the band finally came back from break and launched into "The Anthem" by Good Charlotte.

Eventually, the crowd turned younger, like the universe reminding us it was past our bedtime. The girls declared themselves officially old and ready to go home.

Benny was still at the high-top across the room, talking

with three guys I didn't recognize. When I walked over, all of them glanced up, and Benny shifted just enough to bring me into the circle.

"This is Quinn," he said simply. Then he tipped his chin toward each of them. "Kevin. Tommy. Ryan."

We traded basic greetings and polite nods. Exactly the level of small talk I wanted at that moment.

"We're heading out," I said.

"I'll catch you later," Benny said as he tossed some money on the table and stood. No explanations, no lingering. He grabbed his jacket and fell into step beside me.

Outside, the night air was crisp enough to wake up whatever part of my brain had tried to deny sparks, tension, and everything my friends swore they saw.

Benny kept his pace aligned with mine.

"I'm pretty sure Todd's harmless," he said as we reached my car. "But regardless...I'm glad your dad's staying with you."

It would've been so easy to let that assumption sit. What's one tiny lie of omission between friends? But guilt rushed in before logic could catch up, and the truth slipped out anyway.

"He's in Philly for the weekend visiting my Uncle Mike."

"Then I'll follow you home."

"You don't have to," I said. "If it makes you feel better, I'll text you when I get inside."

"It would make me feel better to follow you," he said. "And watch you walk into the house."

I paused, weighing the argument I wasn't actually going to make, then let out a slow breath. "Okay."

The drive home was uneventful. No traffic, no surprises...just the hum of my tires and "Sugar, We're Goin

Down" blaring like someone mistook my brain for a teenage party.

But my thoughts weren't nearly as calm. I kept replaying the night— Benny stepping in without hesitation and the way my friends acted like they knew something I didn't. Or didn't want to admit.

And now he was following me home.

At a red light, I glanced into the rearview. His headlights stayed right behind me, steady as a heartbeat.

The girls were right—there were sparks, and they weren't exactly subtle anymore. And somewhere between the bar and my house, I'd stopped pretending otherwise.

He trailed me all the way to my driveway. I parked, stared at my front door, and made the decision that was absolutely, definitely, totally about being polite. Friendly. Grateful. I snorted out loud at my own lie.

Benny got out of his Jeep and followed as I unlocked the door.

"Do you want to come in?" I asked. "For a thank you drink."

One corner of his mouth lifted. "Sure."

Inside, I kicked off my boots by the door and hung my purse on the hook.

"What would you like to drink? I have water, sparkling water, tea, juice, beer, wine..."

"Water's good."

"Water it is." I poured two glasses and handed him one. Then I remembered the chocolate chip cookies I'd baked earlier and opened the jar and tilted it toward him, "I also have cookies."

He reached inside, grabbed one, and took a bite.

"Did you bake these?"

I did.

"They're delicious."

That stupid warm feeling inside me answered before I could.

"Thanks." I pulled a small plate out of the cupboard and set some cookies on it. "Come on," I said, nodding toward the living room.

The soft glow of the lamp cast everything in a cozy, slightly-too-intimate mood I hadn't planned on. He took the far end of the couch, and I sat at the opposite side.

We talked a little—about the Maiden crowd and how much we liked the band. It was easier to talk about familiar faces and nostalgic songs than to acknowledge whatever had been building between us for weeks.

I leaned back against the cushion and let out a slow breath. "It's...interesting being back home," I said. "People keep reminding me how I used to beg for singing gigs. I guess it's their way of keeping me humble."

He let out a quiet chuckle, and leaned forward to snag another cookie.

"Small towns have long memories for sure."

"Even after everything that happened in my entire career, I still remember hustling for gigs like it was yesterday," I said. "And it's not like I'm scared or don't like singing anymore, it's just easier to say no to everything. If I agree to sing at one charity event, or one festival, or one National Anthem, I end up having to explain why I'm not doing the others. My management team turns down requests for me every week—some of them tiny, some of them huge, some of them really meaningful or important. So I just don't sing at all." I let out a small laugh. "Although not singing one song with the band on a Friday night at The Maiden seems silly when I think about it."

"It's not silly, it's a boundary," he said. "It's *your* boundary...and boundaries are like the outfield wall. They mark the edge of what's acceptable, don't shift based on someone's mood or circumstances, and everyone has to respect them whether they agree with the placement or not."

I stared at him, stunned that something that sounds so simple could be so difficult. Then I chuckled.

"Where were you twenty years ago when my boundaries were like those moveable screens they use in batting practice?"

"Twenty years ago?" His mouth tugged into something crooked and unfairly charming. "I was probably busy trying to convince some girl to move her boundaries for me," he said, not proud, just matter-of-fact. "But I promise, I don't do that anymore."

I didn't know what to say to that—his blunt honesty, with no excuses attached.

Something inside me pulled tight, warmed, and twisted all at once. The silence between us got a little heavy, so I filled it with a small, almost embarrassed laugh.

"You make it sound simple."

"It *is* simple," he said, eyes steady on mine. "It's just not easy."

That word landed somewhere deep. Simple. Not easy. That had been my whole life, hadn't it? Singing should have been joy and sound and connection, but instead it became contracts and favors and expectations. Somewhere along the way, the thing I loved turned into something complicated.

I didn't respond right away, and he didn't rush to fill the silence.

"How did you get so wise?" I finally asked.

He shrugged. "Life. Baseball. Paying attention."

I shifted to tuck my legs beneath me. Nothing profound

came to mind, so I leaned forward and took another cookie, buying myself a moment. I brought it to my lips and took a bite, and that's when I realized Benny was watching me. Intently.

My heart kicked hard against my ribs.

The look on his face—focused, hungry, like he was starving and I was the only thing in the room—made heat flood through me.

"Want another one?" I gestured toward the plate.

"Maybe we can just share that one."

I blinked. "Oh. Yeah, sure."

He slowly shifted closer. The space between us shrank until I could feel the warmth of him, feel the moment stretching tight and inevitable. I still had the cookie in my hand, ridiculous proof I hadn't been prepared for any of this.

I lifted it halfway between us in some lame attempt at humor or a distraction or—honestly, I had no idea what I was doing. Benny looked at it for a beat, then his gaze lifted to my eyes before dipping to my mouth.

He closed the distance slowly, one hand sliding along the side of my jaw, his thumb resting in that sensitive spot just below my ear. His touch wasn't hesitant. It was intentional. Like he'd imagined exactly how this would go, and now he was simply following through.

His mouth found mine—warm, steady, tasting like melted chocolate and brown sugar. The kiss wasn't rushed, but it wasn't polite. It had heat underneath it, waiting, pressing, promising. I leaned in without thinking, wanting more of that slow, unguarded certainty.

The half-eaten cookie slipped from my fingers and hit the floor, forgotten. All I could focus on was the way he'd kissed me, like he'd already been here in his mind and was relieved he finally got to catch up to it in real life.

My lips parted and his tongue swept against mine, slow and thorough, like he was memorizing the taste of me. His other hand found my waist, fingers spreading wide, anchoring me to him. I made a sound low in my throat—need and surrender wrapped into one—and felt him smile against my mouth before kissing me deeper.

The kiss went on and on, minutes dissolving into nothing but sensation and heat. Somewhere in the haze of it, I'd found myself against the arm of the couch with Benny resting between my thighs, his weight a perfect pressure I didn't want to lose.

He ended the kiss but didn't move away, just rested his forehead against mine while we both tried to catch our breath. When he finally looked at me, desire was warring with restraint.

"We're getting to the point of no return here," he said quietly.

"Yeah," I said, my voice hoarse.

He searched my face, like he was looking for doubt, hesitation, or any reason to stop. I held his gaze, trying to let him see how much I wanted him even though my heart was hammering so hard I was sure he could feel it.

"You sure?" he asked.

"I'm sure."

He stood in one fluid motion, and I felt the loss of his weight immediately. A grin tugged at his mouth, slow and sexy.

"Where's your bedroom?"

"Upstairs."

He held out his hand and pulled me up from the couch,

but before I could get my balance, he bent and tossed me over his shoulder like I weighed nothing.

I let out a screech, my hands grabbing at his back.

"Benny!"

"Just making sure you don't change your mind on the way up," he said, and I could hear the smile in his voice as he headed for the stairs.

My heart was still racing, but now it had nothing to do with nerves and everything to do with the easy strength in the way he carried me, the certainty in his stride.

The world tilted and swayed with each step he took, but I felt steadier than I had in years.

This was happening. We were doing this. And for once, I decided not to overthink what came next.

Chapter Twenty-Seven

Benny

Quinn laughed against my back as I took the stairs two at a time, the sound bright and breathless.

"Benny," she squeaked, half-scolding, half-delighted. "You're ridiculous."

"Accurate," I said. "But you're still not asking me to put you down."

She made a noise that definitely wasn't a complaint, her hand fisting lightly in the back of my shirt. I could feel the small shifts of her body with every step, the trusting weight of her over my shoulder doing things to my heart and my self-control at the same time.

At the top of the stairs, I slowed, orienting myself in the dim hallway light.

"First door on the left," she said before I had to ask.

With a twist of the knob, I opened the door and stepped into her bedroom. Soft lamplight spilled across the space. It was simple, cozy, and more *her* than any backstage green room or hotel suite I'd seen in pictures. Books on the nightstand. A sweatshirt tossed over a chair. The faint, clean scent that was unmistakably Quinn.

I bent and set her down. She wobbled a little, hands grabbing my shoulders for balance, and laughed. The low, throaty sound had my heart racing.

"You'd think I could stand on my own by now," she murmured, but she didn't let go, and suddenly we were close enough that I could see all the different shades of blue in her eyes. Close enough that when she tilted her face up, her mouth was barely an inch away from mine. I kissed her, and whatever restraint I'd been clinging to dissolved the second her lips moved against mine.

Heat rolled through me like a slow wave, rising with every small sound she made—quiet, involuntary noises that told the truth before either of us said a word.

I moved my hands against her waist, her sweater soft under my palms. I'd spent too long pretending I didn't notice the way she filled out those T-shirts she wore at the stadium, the way her hips moved when she walked down the hall. There wasn't a lot of pretending happening now.

Quinn tugged at my shirt and I pulled back just long enough to pull it over my head. Her fingers traced down my chest, slow and curious, landing at the waistband of my jeans. If they got any more comfortable there, I wouldn't stand a chance. I caught both of her hands and slid them behind her back, pulling her in so she pressed against me. And I kissed her the way I've wanted to for weeks—firm and deep, with no patience left for anything halfway.

She didn't just keep up, she pushed right into it without hesitation. We locked in, like all the tension between us hadn't been building to break us apart, but to line us up for this exact rhythm.

I skimmed my hands up her sides, taking her sweater

with them and broke the kiss long enough to drag it over her head. For a second, I forgot how to breathe.

Black lace pushed her breasts together like it knew exactly what it was showing off.

"Fuck, Quinn..." It slipped out, quiet but rough, more prayer than curse.

Her cheeks flushed deeper, and that hit me harder than the lace itself. She wasn't posing or putting on a show. She was just there, soft and confident and completely knock-me-flat gorgeous.

I let my palms slide back to her waist, my thumbs brushing the warm skin just above the band of her jeans. She leaned into the touch, her chest brushing mine, and that small movement alone shot heat down my spine.

"You're killing me," I murmured.

Her eyes locked on mine, the corners of her mouth curling up. "What am I doing?"

"Making me want you so bad."

My thumb eased under the lace, slow enough that I felt the goosebumps rise to meet me.

"Making me want to put my mouth on every inch of you."

She swayed forward, gripping my shoulders.

"Making it nearly impossible to go slow when I'm trying not to rush this."

Her eyes darkened. "I don't want slow."

Then her mouth was on mine, hard enough that I felt the choice in it.

I kissed her back, met that want head-on, and let it pull me under. Heat hit with every sweep of her tongue against mine. Her hands slid up my neck and tightened in my hair, just enough to wreck my breathing.

Without breaking the kiss, I walked her backward

toward the bed. Her legs hit the edge of the mattress, and she arched into me with this soft gasp that hit me low and hard.

I pulled back and took in her flushed cheeks, swollen lips, and wild hair. She looked like every version of temptation I'd ever tried to ignore, but there was something else too —something real that made my heart pound.

"You're beautiful," I said, because not saying it felt impossible.

She didn't deflect with a joke like I half-expected. She just held my gaze, and something settled between us. Trust, maybe. Or just the simple fact that we were both choosing this with our eyes open.

I wasn't nervous because I didn't know what I was doing. I was nervous because I wanted this to matter.

"Lie back," I told her.

She eased onto the bed, and I followed her down just far enough to trace my mouth along her throat, across her chest, and down the line of her stomach. Her muscles tightened under every inch I passed.

When I reached the button of her jeans, I popped it open and eased the zipper down. Then I straightened, hooked my fingers into the waistband, and dragged the denim over her hips. She lifted for me without hesitation, and I pulled them the rest of the way off, letting my hands trail down her legs as I did.

"Damn..." The word came out rougher than I meant, but the matching lace hit me like a fastball to the chest.

I let my thumb trace the edge where it dipped low at her hip.

"You look even better than I pictured."

"You've pictured me?"

A slow grin pulled at my mouth.

"I'm taking the fifth on that one."

Her eyes narrowed, like she wasn't sure whether to call me out on that or pull me closer. I rested a knee on the mattress and hovered over her, nibbling along her collarbone and down the curve of her breast. Her breath stuttered, so I kept going, dragging my tongue over her nipple through the lace.

She gasped, and squeezed my shoulders.

I did it again, slower, letting the fabric drag against my tongue this time. The sound she made hit me low and fast, so I sealed my mouth over her and sucked, hard enough that her back arched into me.

Yeah. She liked that.

I pushed her bra up, and her breast filled my hand like it was meant to be there. Then my mouth was on her—hot, bare, better. I dragged my tongue slow from the bottom up, then sucked hard enough to pull a broken sound from her throat that I felt all the way down my spine.

Her fingers slid into my hair and held me there, like she needed the pressure as much as I did. So I gave it to her— steady, greedy pulls of my mouth, tongue flicking, sealing, sucking until she couldn't bite back the sounds anymore.

When I finally lifted my head, she was flushed, breathing rough, her eyes heavy and glassy. I kissed down the center of her chest, slow and unhurried. My mouth brushed the waistband of her panties as my hands slipped up the inside of her thighs, parting them for me.

I nuzzled against the lace, letting it brush my mouth before I bit down—not hard, just enough to make her feel me through the fabric. She choked on a sound, thighs tightening around my head.

Dragging my tongue over the damp lace, I tasted how warm and sweet she already was.

"Benny..." she groaned, and it wasn't a word anymore, it was need.

I dragged my tongue up the center, slow enough to feel every catch along the way. Her hips jumped, so I steadied her thigh and did it again—slower, deeper, until she trembled against my mouth.

"Please," she breathed.

Just one word. Barely there. But I heard it like an order.

I slid the lace aside and put my mouth directly on her. I licked into her and sucked slow, greedy, like I'd been starving for the taste of her.

She let go of my hair and gripped the sheets instead.

The sound she made wasn't even a word—just a rough, broken gasp that caught in her throat and fell apart on the way out. I pulled back just enough to look up at her over the length of her body.

"Don't bite it back," I said. "I want to hear you."

Without waiting for a reply, I put my mouth on her again, working my tongue in slow circles before sealing my lips around her and sucking hard.

A moan tore out of her, raw and unguarded.

Yeah, that's what I wanted to hear.

I shifted off the mattress, hooked my fingers under the scrap of lace, and dragged it down her legs before dropping to my knees. She gasped when I gripped her thighs and pulled her to the edge of the bed, legs falling over my shoulders, nothing left between my mouth and what I wanted. I didn't give her time to recover—just found the rhythm that made her cry out again.

Her hips bucked hard, and I pinned her in place, keeping steady pressure with my mouth until her whole body tightened, then shook. She came with a sharp cry that broke into something ragged and desperate. I kept licking her through the pulse of it, not rushing, not easing up until her thighs stopped trembling and she melted into the mattress.

I kissed the inside of her knee, letting my mouth linger there for a beat, then stood. She lay sprawled across the mattress—hair wild, chest heaving, eyes dazed like she'd forgotten how to speak.

Perfect.

Her heavy-lidded gaze tracked me as I stripped out my jeans and boxers. When I climbed back onto the bed, she reached for me without hesitation. Her fingers skimmed my stomach, then lower. Slow, teasing, purposeful.

"Quinn..." I rasped, because that one touch almost shut my brain off.

She didn't stop. Her palm slid along my length with a careful, curious pressure, like she was learning me through touch alone. I groaned low in my throat and shut my eyes, because if I watched her do it, I wasn't going to last long enough to be inside her.

I wrapped my fingers around her wrist.

"I'm at the end of my rope here," I said. "If you keep that up, it's going to be over before it starts."

Her mouth curved, looking inordinately pleased.

"Good to know."

Yeah, too good.

I kissed her once—slow, deep, and meant to make her forget her own name—then moved between her thighs, bracing a hand on the mattress beside her hip. The heat of her, open and ready, hit me all at once. I dragged my other hand up her thigh, almost exactly where I wanted to be when the realization hit me like cold water.

"Wait." My voice came out rough. "We need—"

"Top nightstand drawer," she said, breathless but sure.

Reaching over, I slid open the drawer and grabbed a foil packet. I tore it open and rolled the condom on with hands that weren't half as steady as I wanted them to be. When I looked back at her, my breath caught.

"Quinn," I said, but nothing else came out.

She reached for my jaw, her thumb brushing the corner of my mouth.

"Come here," she whispered.

I settled between her thighs and pushed in slow, letting every inch of her warmth take me. Slow enough that I felt her shiver all the way through it. She gasped, fingers clutching at the sheets, then at my shoulders, like she couldn't decide what to hold onto.

"Christ, Quinn..."

She arched against me, hips meeting mine, taking more —wanting it as badly as I wanted it. Like this wasn't casual. Like it had been building for weeks, and we finally stopped pretending we didn't feel it.

I set a rhythm. Not rushed or gentle...something right in the middle that felt like us. She met every thrust like she already knew the pace, like we'd done this a thousand times in another life and finally caught up to it in this one.

Her nails dragged down my back and I had to bite back a groan that probably would've scared the neighbors.

"Benny," she groaned. "Harder."

She said it, I did it. Simple, but not easy—because staying in control around her was work.

Her mouth opened on a sound that punched the air right out of me.

I planted a hand next to her head and let the other slide between us, finding her clit. She gasped again when my thumb pressed into her, when I worked her through every thrust.

Her breath broke, her thighs trembled, and she tightened under me.

"That's it," I whispered, lowering my forehead to hers. "Let me have it. Come on."

She wrapped her thighs around my waist, fingers gripping my shoulders like she was holding on for dear life. And then she broke—every muscle tightening around me, her heart pounding against my chest while I kissed her through it. The sound she made was raw, unfiltered, and absolutely perfect.

Her body kept pulsing around me, and I kissed her— harder and more frantic, like I needed her breath to finish the job. I drove into her once, twice, and then I was gone. Heat rushed through me, pleasure hitting sharp and low, and I had to bury my face in her neck just to get my bearings.

For a few seconds, neither of us moved. Nothing existed except the sound of us trying to breathe again.

Then she let out a little laugh against my shoulder, and something in my chest cracked wide open.

I kissed her forehead, and she slid her fingers through my hair, slow and easy, like she was still figuring me out.

"You okay?" I murmured, voice low.

She drew in a shaky breath and nodded. "You?"

A grin tugged at my mouth before I could stop it. "Never been better."

I stayed there a minute longer, letting our hearts slow down against each other. Then I slipped out of her carefully, tied off the condom, tossed it in her trash, and crawled right back into her arms like that was the only place I belonged.

She didn't say a word, just curled into my chest like she already knew I wasn't leaving.

And I wasn't.

Not tonight.

And hell if I knew how I was supposed to walk away after this.

Chapter Twenty-Eight

Quinn

I woke up feeling warm.

Not the heavy, overheated kind you get from a tangled blanket, but a steady, solid heat at my back, an arm slung around my waist, and a slow, even breath against the back of my neck.

Right. Benny.

Last night wasn't a dream. Or if it was, my dreams have upgraded significantly.

A smile tugged at my mouth before I even opened my eyes. My body ached in that good, used way, and the soreness between my thighs was a very specific kind of reminder.

My stomach chose that exact moment to growl loud enough to wake the dead. Because of course it did.

Behind me, Benny huffed out a sleepy laugh. "Was that you or a small bear?"

"That was a very dignified hunger protest," I mumbled, my voice scratchy.

"Dignified, huh?"

I glanced at the time projected on the ceiling. "And in its defense, I usually eat breakfast two hours ago."

He shifted closer, tightening his arm around me. "Dignified *and* on a schedule."

"Exactly," I said. "But I should probably make us some breakfast."

"Or I could. Just point me to the ingredients."

I twisted just enough to see his face. His hair was a sexy mess, eyes soft and half-lidded.

"You cook?"

"I've mastered breakfast," he said. "Anything after noon is a toss-up."

I grinned. "And he cooks, too."

"Don't oversell it," he said. "We're talking the basics, not a tasting menu."

"How are your pancakes?"

He kissed the tip of my nose.

"Fluffy and delicious." My stomach growled again, louder this time. "Message received. Let's get you fed."

We untangled ourselves and got out of bed. I shrugged into my robe, watching him as he stretched. God, he looked good in the morning light—all lean muscle and easy confidence.

"You take my bathroom, and I'll use the one down the hall." I grabbed my sweats and moved toward the door, then turned back. "Towels are in the cabinet, and there are spare toothbrushes in the top drawer. Meet you downstairs."

I slipped into the bathroom down the hall, caught my reflection in the mirror, and winced. My hair was a full-on cautionary tale—tangles, kinks, the whole post-sex greatest hits. But it was my neck and chest that stopped me. Pink patches bloomed along my collarbone and just under my jaw where his beard had scraped. There were more around my mouth and chin. It wasn't dramatic, but it was definitely noticeable.

I touched the tender patch of skin and shook my head.

"Well, that's going to be fun to cover."

Erin's voice popped into my head immediately. *So... beards. They're sexy until the morning after.*

After brushing my teeth, I ran a brush through my hair and twisted it into a messy bun. Then I pulled on my favorite sweatshirt—the oversized gray one with Stevie Nicks's face on it, *Don't be a lady, be a legend* splashed across the front—and the worn-in joggers.

I headed downstairs and found Benny standing by the kitchen window, hands in his pockets, looking out at the backyard. He'd pulled his jeans and T-shirt back on from the night before, but he'd skipped the shoes and socks. I'd never found feet particularly sexy before, but barefoot Benny in my kitchen was doing things to me.

He turned when he heard me come in and smiled.

"I spotted the flour and sugar," he said, gesturing to the canisters on the counter, "and found a whisk and spatula in that holder. But that's about as far as I got."

I moved to the fridge and pulled out eggs, bacon, and milk, setting them on the counter.

"Griddle and pans are in the bottom cabinet by the stove," I said, nodding toward it. "Mixing bowls are in the one above. What else do you need?"

"Butter, baking powder, and vanilla if you've got it," he said, already heading for the cabinet.

"Butter's right there," I said, pointing to the small ceramic crock on the counter.

He picked it up, examining it. "Is this a butter bell?"

"It is."

"I thought these were an urban legend."

"They're very real," I said, reaching into the cabinet for the baking powder and vanilla. "And perfect for when you make your own butter."

He looked up at me. "You make your own butter?"

"Sometimes."

He just looked at me for a beat, then smiled. "Yeah. That tracks."

I moved to the coffee maker while he got to work. He cracked eggs one-handed into the mixing bowl—smooth and efficient, like he'd done it a thousand times. There was something almost hypnotic about watching him work, the easy way he moved through my kitchen like he belonged there.

Morning-afters were usually awkward. That weird dance of trying to figure out if you were supposed to leave or stay, whether small talk was required or if silence was safer. This didn't feel like that.

I scooped grounds into the filter, watching him.

He glanced over, catching me staring. "What?"

"Nothing," I said. "You just look...comfortable."

"Good."

He turned back to the stove and started laying out strips of bacon in a pan.

There was something ridiculously attractive about how focused he was. No fumbling or macho showmanship. Just easy competence.

His T-shirt pulled tight across his back when he reached for a plate. I caught myself staring and dragged my gaze up to his neck instead.

It did not help.

"I can feel you thinking over there," he said.

"Thinking is generous," I said. "Mostly I'm ogling."

He laughed, and that little slice of domestic normalcy hit me right in the chest.

The coffee finished brewing and I poured us each a mug—mine with a Dolly Parton quote, "Find out who you are and do it on purpose," his with a faded Bergmann Brewery logo my mom had given me years ago.

"How do you take your coffee?" I asked, reaching for the milk he'd set out earlier.

"Black," he said, still focused on the stove. "You?"

"Cream, no sugar."

I set his mug on the counter beside him and stirred a splash of milk into mine. When I lifted it for a sip, the steam brushed the tender skin along my jaw. A zing of pain shot up and I sucked in a breath through my teeth.

Benny caught it instantly. "You okay?"

I touched the spot under my chin, trying not to smile. "Your beard should come with a warning label."

His mouth curved, slow and unapologetic. "Is that a complaint?"

"Only that I won't be able to hide this," I said, gesturing vaguely at my jaw and neck. "Tessa's going to take one look and know exactly what it's from."

He didn't even blink. "Is that a problem?"

"Not necessarily," I said, lifting the mug again, more carefully this time.

Benny turned back to the stove and continued cooking, like nothing about the moment had thrown him off. A few minutes later, he split the pancakes and bacon onto two plates and brought them to the island.

We sat on the stools, plates steaming in front of us.

I drowned my pancakes in syrup, took a bite, and groaned.

"These are amazing."

"Told you," he said. "Fluffy and delicious."

We ate in comfortable silence for a few minutes. The kind that would have felt awkward with the wrong person but didn't with him. Then he set his fork down and leaned back, eyes fixed on me like he was shifting into game-planning mode.

"Okay," he said. "Twenty questions."

My eyebrows shot up. "Twenty?"

"Fine, we'll see how far we get before you tap out." He lifted his mug. "Question one...what perfume do you wear?"

Of all the places I thought he might start, that wasn't even on the list. I blinked.

"My perfume?"

"Yeah." His gaze didn't waver. "Your scent has been haunting me. I've never smelled anything like it."

That did things to my insides I was not prepared for.

"It's a custom blend," I said, a little shy despite myself. "There's a perfumer in Portland named Elise Roman who does small-batch, mostly organic blends. I met her backstage at one of my shows and she smelled incredible, so I asked what she was wearing. Turns out she made it and offered to create something for me." I took a sip of coffee. "Then she made add-on vials for different seasons—like jasmine and orange blossom for summer, amber and cardamom for winter. I used to switch them up, but lately I've just been wearing the base on its own." I paused. "Sorry, that was probably more detail than you wanted."

"Don't apologize," he said, the corner of his mouth curving up. "Every time I think you're just a regular woman, you drop something like 'my custom fragrance from my artisan perfumer in Portland' and remind me you're absurdly famous."

"It sounds worse when you say it out loud," I muttered, even as I laughed.

"It doesn't sound bad." His tone softened. "Just...big. And I forget about it sometimes." He held my gaze. "You just feel like Quinn to me."

Warmth bloomed in my chest. "I am just Quinn."

He held my gaze for a beat, then nodded.

"Okay," I said. "My turn.."

He gestured with his fork. "Hit me."

"Why did you take the job with the Lagerheads?"

He wiped his hands on his napkin.

"Couple reasons. I like the idea of building something from the ground up." He paused. "But honestly? Grace and Charlie are here. I've always tried to be part of their lives, but doing it from across the country was hard. This way I get to see them regularly, even during the season."

He stated that like it was a practical career decision.

But the way he said *Grace and Charlie* told a different story.

Instead of pressing deeper, I said, "Your turn."

We traded questions until our second cup of coffee went cold. We didn't quite make it to twenty, but we learned some interesting things about each other.

I learned his favorite ice cream is vanilla—which he insists is "not boring, just underrated." He eats the crust first on a slice of pizza, sets three alarms then wakes up before all of them, and thinks his biggest flaw is that he's terrible at asking for help.

In return, I told him I eat the broken French fries in a basket first, organize my books by mood instead of author or genre, and that my favorite ice cream is mint chip because it tastes like childhood.

"We actually have something in common you might not know about."

"What's that?"

"We're both named after our moms' maiden names," I said.

"That is a fun fact." He narrowed his eyes. "How'd you even know that?"

I stood and started gathering our plates before he could read too much in my face.

"That's a story for another day."

Instead of pressing, he said, "I'll hold you to that."

He helped me carry the plates to the sink. I rinsed and he loaded the dishwasher like he'd done it a hundred times instead of never. When we were done, he didn't act like he was in a hurry to leave.

"You have plans today?" he asked.

"Not really."

He nodded, slow.

"Mind if I hang out for a bit?"

"I'd like that."

He checked his phone and groaned.

"Can I borrow a charger?"

"Yeah, sure." I headed into the living room and looked around, but didn't see one. "I must have left it in my office."

I started down the hallway and he followed.

In the office, I flipped on the overhead light and crossed to my desk. A few notebooks were stacked off-center on top of each other, and the charger cable was peeking out from under them. I tugged it free.

"Here it is."

He didn't answer.

When I turned back around, he was studying the

framed photos hanging on the wall above the piano. His shoulders were relaxed, hands in his pockets. He wasn't searching for anything, just looking.

There were pictures of my parents at a festival, Erin and me backstage through a decade of hair disasters, and one of me beside Mr. Bergmann from a few years ago, both of us laughing like the photographer had caught a joke we weren't finished telling.

Benny nodded toward it.

"Looks like you two were pretty tight."

"We were," I said, simple as that. I came over and stood beside him, not touching the frame, just close enough to see it the way he did. "He was one of my biggest supporters. If it wasn't for him, I don't know if I'd have a career. He knew a guy who knew a guy who liked the way I sang. That's how it all started."

Benny glanced at the photo again, slower this time, like it meant more now.

"I'm sure he helped, but I think you would have made it either way," he said quietly.

I didn't know what to say to that, so I just handed him the charger. He took it, but his eyes stayed on the wall a beat longer, like he was filing something away.

When he finally turned, his attention shifted to the built-in bookshelves on the opposite wall. I'd had them custom made when I bought the farmhouse—floor-to-ceiling walnut, and deep enough to hold the oversized music books I pretended to use.

Some shelves were packed tight with notebooks in different colors and sizes, others held framed drawings from kids, various photos, and a bright orange award shaped like a slime droplet from a kid's choice award I won years ago.

A couple of industry plaques were tucked there too, half-hidden between a stack of magazines and a crooked clay mug a fan handed me at a county fair. Nothing was arranged by importance. It was all just...there. Stuff that mattered, regardless of who said it should.

Benny wasn't looking at any of the awards, not even the slime one. His gaze skipped right over them and landed on the notebooks.

"Are all those full?"

"Most," I said. "The ones on the bottom shelf are still waiting their turn."

His gaze moved from the notebooks to me.

"What's in them?"

"Ideas," I said. "Lyrics, scraps of melodies, lines I haven't figured out how to use yet. Stuff that might matter later or might never matter at all." I shrugged. "Some of it's just for me."

He studied the shelves a moment longer.

"Is that all of them, or do you have more somewhere?"

"That's a good chunk of them." I nodded toward the wall. "There are older ones at my mom's house."

He took that in, eyes tracing the rows again.

"That's a lot of notebooks."

I looked at the shelves, then back at him.

"Some people write their life in journals. I write mine in lyrics."

Benny didn't say anything. He just nodded, like that told him everything he needed to know.

His attention shifted again, this time to a framed photo tucked between a stack of journals and a small glass Billboard award that looked more like décor than a trophy. Erin and I were squeezed into the shot, cheeks pink, hair messy, a piano buried under sheet music. She was laughing at something that apparently required a full-body reaction. I was next to her, clutching a notebook like I expected someone to steal it.

"Was that taken at Waypoint High?"

I nodded.

"In the music room. December of our junior year," I said. "Erin and I were killing time before winter break." I hesitated, then added, "I left for Christmas and never came back to school after that."

He didn't say anything. Just took a second, looking at the picture like he was lining up the girl in it with the woman standing next to him.

"How did I not notice you back then?"

It wasn't a line meant to flatter. It sounded like he was genuinely annoyed with his younger self for missing something obvious.

"You were the guy who had it all together," I said. "I was the girl hiding in the music room, trying to figure things out."

He huffed out a breath—part disbelief, part something else.

"You think I had it together?"

"Didn't you?" I asked.

He shook his head, one short, honest motion.

"I was just trying not to screw up. If I struck out, my dad acted like I'd ruined the month. Confidence was...whatever I needed people to believe so they didn't look too close."

I glanced at the photo again. Teenage me looked afraid someone might notice what mattered to her. Teenage him acted like nothing did.

"Funny how we miss whole people," I said. "Even when they're right there."

This time, he didn't look at the photo.

He looked at me.

"I'm not missing you now."

Chapter Twenty-Nine

Benny

I'd sat through hundreds of meetings in my career. Thousands, probably. Budget reviews, roster discussions, strategy sessions that stretched past midnight. I knew how to focus, how to keep my head in the game even when exhaustion was clawing at my edges.

But I'd never had to sit across a conference table from a woman whose bed I'd only left twelve hours ago.

Quinn sat two chairs down from me, flipping open a notebook like she was about to solve world peace with a ballpoint pen. Across from her, Tessa typed on her laptop, her fingers moving with the rapid-fire efficiency of someone turning a meeting into an action plan.

"Alright," Tessa said, glancing between us. "GM candidates. We need to narrow, not expand."

"We've talked to six," I said, keeping it simple. "Three were impressive on paper, but none of them fit."

Tessa nodded sharply. "I agree. We don't just want someone to check a box, we're looking for a person who's on board with what we're looking to build."

We spent the next few minutes trading names. Former

front office guys, recommendations from colleagues, a couple executives testing the market. Maybe one or two worth a deeper conversation, but no one who made us both sit up and say, "that's the one."

Quinn didn't jump in with opinions, just listened, scribbling notes like she was absorbing it all. She wasn't pretending to know baseball operations, which I respected. She asked smart questions when she needed clarity. That mattered more than being an expert.

I watched her tuck a loose strand of hair behind her ear, and my mind flashed to Sunday morning when she'd done the same thing while watching me cook breakfast. Quinn glanced up and caught me looking. Her mouth curved into a small smile.

Tessa's typing stopped.

"Where are we with coaching hires?"

Time to focus on baseball, not Quinn's eyes.

"Lou Calder's signing his contract this week, so bench coach is covered. That leaves two positions—first base and assistant hitting coach. My main focus is first base. Marin's solid enough to handle hitting on her own if she has to."

"So we're getting there." Tessa looked at Quinn. "How's the renovation budget?"

"We're still on track," she said. "Under on clubhouse finishes and signage, over on the scoreboards thanks to price hikes, but the savings from equipment and some of the interior materials make up the difference. We're not touching the contingency yet."

Tessa shook her head and smirked.

"I still can't believe you track a multi-million-dollar renovation in a notebook."

Quinn gave me a quick glance. "It's what I do." She pointed to the printout next to Tessa's laptop. "Though I'm sure you sleep better knowing my finance team plugs everything into actual software and double-checks my work."

"I do," Tessa said with a chuckle, then quickly added, "Not that I doubt you."

"Of course not." Quinn tapped her pen against her notebook. "When are you available to do the walk-through with the contractors next week?"

"Whenever. I'm pretty open."

I blinked. Last week her calendar was a disaster of double bookings.

Quinn's eyebrows went up. Clearly she was thinking the same thing.

"Since when?" she asked.

"Since your mom saved my life," Tessa said, leaning back in her chair. "Jo jumped back in like she didn't miss a beat. If she hadn't stepped in at the brewery, I'd still be buried."

Quinn's expression softened, quick but real. "She likes being back."

"She frees me up to actually focus on this team instead of running two businesses at once. I don't know what we'd do without her." Tessa chuckled. "I hope she knows I'm not letting her retire again."

Quinn's mom was helping from behind the scenes, just like Quinn was. No fanfare. No spotlight. Just doing work that mattered.

I glanced at Quinn again. She was already studying her notes like none of this was personal, even though it obviously was.

Tessa clicked a few more keys, then paused.

"We talked about coaching staff, GM candidates, budget, renovation timeline. Anything else we need to discuss?"

"One thing. When the clubhouse is done, I want controlled access. Key-card only. No casual tours or sponsors wandering around looking for photo ops."

"People really do that?" Quinn asked.

"Rumor has it, Tessa's dad had to chase a brewery guest out of a batting cage once," I said.

Tessa winced. "He said he thought it was part of the tour."

"That doesn't explain why he was standing at home plate with a bat and the pitching machine on."

They both chuckled at that.

"Okay, you got it," Tessa said. "Limited access until spring training officially kicks off. I'll let the marketing department know."

Quinn scribbled something in her notebook. I tried not to stare at the way her handwriting tilted a little to the right, like it was leaning into a thought.

"Is that it?"

"I'm good," I said.

"I'm all set," Quinn said.

"Perfect." Tessa snapped her laptop closed. "Then we're officially efficient today, which means I get to feel smug about it for the rest of the week."

I checked the time on my phone.

"I've gotta run. Grace and Charlie have a half day," I said. "If you need anything, shoot me a text. Otherwise, I'll see you tomorrow.

I stood, slinging my bag over my shoulder.

"Yep," Tessa said.

"See you," Quinn said.

Our eyes met, and the corner of her mouth lifted slightly before the door clicked shut between us. I shook my head with a soft laugh as I made my way to the elevator.

The doors opened immediately, like the universe was helping me escape before I did something stupid like go back in there.

I'd gone my whole career shutting everything out except the game. That single-mindedness had always served me. Kept things simple.

But today, focusing had been damn near impossible. Between flashes of Quinn's Sunday morning smile and trying not to stare at the beard burn her makeup hadn't quite hidden—just like she'd warned—keeping my head in the game had taken more effort than it should have.

I could navigate roster builds and bullpen structure in my sleep. *This* I was going to have to figure out.

I walked out of the building to the parking lot and climbed into my Jeep, but instead of starting the engine, I pulled out my phone and typed before I could overthink it.

I'll call you later.

Simple. Nothing over the top. But it was a promise, and I meant it.

I hit send, set the phone in its mount, and pulled out of the lot with the stupidest smile tugging at my mouth.

I'm definitely in uncharted territory.

Chapter Thirty

Quinn

My phone buzzed, and I smiled before I could stop myself.

Heat flared in my chest, sharp and ridiculous. It was four words and a period, not a sonnet, but my brain still did a little cartwheel.

I stared at the screen, rereading four words like they required analysis.

"Okay. Spill."

I jumped. "What?"

Tessa leaned her elbows on the table, eyes narrowed like she was interrogating a suspect.

"You're literally glowing. Like you just came back from a yoga retreat that specializes in orgasms."

"I—what—no—" I sputtered, because apparently full sentences were no longer available to me.

"That's a yes," she declared.

I pressed a palm to my cheek, partly because it was hot,

partly because I needed something to ground myself in real-ity. She smirked like she'd just solved a crime.

"And don't even think about denying it. Because that beard burn has Benny Reed written all over it."

Of course she noticed. I'd done my best to cover it up, but makeup can only do so much.

For a second, my brain presented the wrong slideshow... Benny in my kitchen barefoot, whisk in hand. Benny leaning over me in bed, eyes dark, teeth dragging along my throat. Benny's beard doing...well. Exactly what it had done.

Tessa leaned back in her chair and grinned. "Oh, this is gonna be good."

I huffed out a breath and set my phone facedown on the table. "You're making a lot of assumptions."

"Please," she snorted. "I've been watching the two of you circle each other for weeks. I assumed it would happen. I just didn't know when."

The old impulse rose automatically—deflect, joke, mini-mize. Make it seem like nothing. But I wasn't seventeen anymore, hiding from cameras and gossip columns. This wasn't a scandal. We were adults who'd had sex...*amazing sex*...and I wasn't going to pretend that was something to be embarrassed about.

I let out a slow breath. "Saturday night."

Tessa's smile went full wattage. "There it is."

"You're enjoying this way too much."

"I need details. He walked you to your car at The Maiden and then what happened?" She sat back in her chair like she was settling in for a story.

"Yes, Benny walked me to my car and said he was 'pretty sure Todd's harmless,' which is usually how horror movies start, but then he mentioned being glad my dad was staying with me. It would've been so easy to just let him think that."

"But you didn't." Tessa snorted. "Of course you didn't. You're incapable of lying, even when it's convenient."

"Correct," I said, deadpan. "So I told him my dad was actually in Philly visiting my uncle. And before I could offer to text him when I got home, he said, 'Then I'll follow you.'"

Tessa's eyes widened but she stayed quiet.

"I told him he didn't have to, and even offered to text when he got home if it would make him feel better." My stomach flipped at the thought of his next words. "He looked me dead in the eye and said it would make him feel better to *follow me home and watch me walk inside.*"

"That's some serious romance novel energy right there," Tessa said.

"I know," I muttered. "Which is why I said okay instead of arguing like a stubborn gremlin."

She leaned forward. "So he followed you."

"All the way. His headlights were glued to my bumper the entire drive. I kept checking the rearview at every red light. It should've been overkill, but instead it was kind of perfect."

"That's...weirdly romantic."

"By the time I parked, I'd already stopped pretending I didn't want him there. So I invited him in for a drink." I paused. "A *thank you* drink."

Tessa leveled a look at me that said she could see straight through that and into the exact moment my clothes ended up on the floor.

"Sure," she said. "A polite beverage."

"Exactly," I nodded. "Extremely polite."

"Okay, so...do you two have plans to see each other

again outside this conference room? Or was this a one-night thank you beverage plus bonus activities?"

I held up my phone.

"Does that answer your question?"

Tessa's eyebrows shot up, then her mouth curved into a smug grin.

"A phone call? That's practically an engagement." She made a sound I could only describe as a squeal. "Oh my God, you and Benny are actually happening."

I held up a hand.

"Don't shout it from the rooftops. I haven't even told Erin yet."

"Your secret's safe with me." She grinned. "Though between that beard burn and the way you're glowing, Erin's going to figure it out the minute she looks at you anyway."

"I'm stopping by her house after work, so I'll tell her then."

Tessa nodded, then studied me for a beat. "How are you feeling about it?"

I picked up my pen, tapping it against the notebook. "Honestly? Really good, which is new." I glanced up at her. "It feels easy with him. Comfortable. Like I can just be myself without performing or managing an image or worrying about what he wants from me."

"That's a good thing."

"Yeah, but being with me gets complicated. The attention, the scrutiny. Men usually have a hard time with that part. They say they're fine with it until they're not."

"But you're retired now," Tessa pointed out gently. "It's not like you're on tour or doing press junkets."

"I don't think that will matter."

"Well, what does matter is that Benny doesn't seem like the kind of guy who scares easily."

"I'm not worried about him," I said quietly. "I'm worried about everything that comes with me." I paused, then shook my head. "And I'm already getting ahead of myself. It was one night."

"Sure. But sometimes one night with the right person tells you more than six months with the wrong one."

Chapter Thirty-One

Benny

Quinn shifted in her seat as I parked in front of Erin's house. It was the kind of quiet cul-de-sac where every house looked cared for but lived in—basketballs by garages, leaf piles along the curb, mismatched chairs on front porches. A neighborhood built for family pictures and ice cream trucks.

"You ready for an interrogation?" she asked.

"Absolutely."

"Thanks for coming tonight." She glanced at me, something like nerves and amusement tangled together. "But honestly, if you hadn't, Erin probably would've hunted you down and dragged you here herself."

"I'm here because I want to be," I said, then added, "Although Erin trying to drag me might've been entertaining."

"She has alarming upper-body strength. Don't underestimate her."

"Not a chance." I cut the engine. "Especially since I'm hoping she'll tell me all your embarrassing stories."

"Erin would never. She's got my back." She chuckled.

"Besides, there are enough of my embarrassing stories online. They're just a Google search away."

"I'm glad she has your back." I met her eyes. "And I don't want to research you. I want to get to know you."

She looked surprised at first, then her mouth curved into a smile that hit like a damn fastball to the chest. She leaned in, kissed me once, then pulled back with a look that said *yeah, I want this too.*

"You," she murmured against my mouth, "just might be perfect."

"Keep thinking that."

We lingered for one more breath, then Quinn looked toward the house.

"We should go in before Erin sends a search party."

She reached for the door handle, but I touched her wrist lightly. "Sit tight."

One corner of her mouth lifted, amused but not arguing. I slipped out of the Jeep and circled around to open her door. She waited, pretending she hadn't been ready to bolt out on her own a second ago.

"So chivalrous."

"Only on special occasions and Wednesdays."

When she stepped out, I caught her hand and tugged her in for a quick kiss, just enough to make her laugh against my mouth. Then I let go and shut the door.

"Don't forget the apple crumble," she said.

As if I could. It's been making the Jeep smell like cinnamon all the way here. Not that I was complaining. I opened the back door and picked it up carefully, making sure not to tilt it.

I followed her to the front door, where she knocked twice, then pushed it open without waiting.

The house was warm and lived in, with the kind of kid-filled energy you could feel the second you stepped inside. Shoes were kicked off by the door in a pile only a family could decipher, and the smell of garlic and roasted chicken wrapped around me in welcome.

Voices drifted from deeper inside, threaded with the soft clink of pots and cabinet doors opening and closing. We rounded the corner into the kitchen, and I caught sight of the fridge sporting a color-coded calendar hung crookedly— Rosie's dance classes in pink, Liam's basketball tryouts in blue, school picture day circled three times like someone wasn't taking any chances.

Erin was checking something in the wall oven, while Scott hovered over the stove, stirring with the kind of concentration usually reserved for bomb defusal. Whatever was in that pot had his full attention.

"It smells amazing in here," Quinn said.

Erin's head snapped up and her whole face lit.

"I'm glad you finally came inside. I thought I was going to have to send Liam out with plates."

She closed the oven, crossed the kitchen in three quick steps, and pulled Quinn into a hug that was all warmth and familiarity. She whispered something that made Quinn chuckle. She pulled back with a look that was half *Erin, behave* and half *I knew this was coming.*

Quinn stepped back, one hand still resting briefly on Erin's arm.

"Benny, this is my best friend in the world, Erin Driscoll, now Merrick. And I think you and Scott know each other from high school."

"It's nice to officially meet you, Benny," Erin said.

Scott glanced over his shoulder from the stove, not missing a beat as he kept the wooden spoon moving in steady circles. "Hey, man. It's good to see you again," he said. "I'd come shake your hand, but if I stop stirring this gravy it'll turn into wallpaper paste, and Erin will never let me hear the end of it."

I grinned. "Good to see you again, Scott." I looked between them. "Thanks for having me. Quinn's right...it smells amazing."

Erin's gaze dropped to the dish in my hands, and her eyes widened.

"Please tell me that's apple crumble."

Quinn laughed. "It is. I made it this afternoon."

Erin pointed at the island like she was directing traffic.

"Set it right there before I steal it out of your hands and dig into it."

I placed it on the island, and before I could even step back, Erin lifted the foil.

Warm cinnamon drifted up, and she inhaled dramatically, then sighed like someone witnessing a small miracle.

Before anyone could say more, footsteps sounded in the hallway.

"Aunt Nini!"

Rosie burst into the room first, all ponytail and bright eyes. She wrapped her arms around Quinn's middle with a practiced familiarity.

"You're finally here," Rosie said, muffled against her sweater. "We were listening for the door."

Liam arrived a second later. "Hey, Aunt Nini," he said, hugging her other side

Quinn smiled and squeezed them both.

Erin looked at me and grinned. "One of Quinn's superpowers is getting my kids away from their screens just by showing up."

"Yeah," I said, watching Rosie still clinging to her. "I see that."

She released them and stepped back. "This is my friend Benny. Benny, this is Liam and Rosie."

"It's nice to meet you two," I said.

"Hi," Liam said, offering a quick wave.

Rosie tilted her head, studying him with open curiosity. "Are you Aunt Nini's boyfriend?"

Quinn froze. I bit back a smile.

Before I could answer, Scott said, "Rosie, don't interrogate our guest before dinner."

I met Rosie's eye and gave her a slight nod. Her whole face lit up.

"What can I help with?" Quinn asked, looking between Erin and Scott.

"Yeah, just tell us what you need," I added.

Scott lifted the gravy pot off the stove with a triumphant grin and turned off the heat. "Gravy's done. Which means it's time to eat."

Erin pointed at Quinn. "Grab a bottle of wine from the rack?" Then she looked at me. "Benny, do you drink wine or would you prefer a beer?"

"A beer would be great."

She opened the refrigerator and peeked inside

"I have Bergmann Lager, Harvest Amber, and one Trail Mix Shandy left."

"I'll take an Amber."

"And I'll take the Trail Mix," Scott said.

Erin handed me the two bottles. Quinn returned from the pantry with an open bottle of wine.

"We'll bring everything in," Erin said. "You two go sit."

Quinn led the way to the dining room, where the table was already set. She moved to one end of the table and poured wine into a glass, then shifted to the seat beside it and filled that one.

I stood there, a beer in each hand, not sure where to go.

Rosie appeared in the doorway. "I usually sit there." She pointed at the chair beside Quinn, then gave me a small smile. "But you can sit next to Aunt Nini tonight."

"Are you sure?" I asked.

She nodded, then pulled out the chair directly across from Quinn and settled in.

"That's so sweet, Rosie," Quinn said, as she pointed to the end of the table. "Scott sits there."

I set his beer down there, then took the seat beside Quinn.

"Yes, thank you, Rosie."

Liam took the seat next to Rosie just as Scott and Erin came in carrying platters of chicken, roasted potatoes, and green beans. They set everything down center table and took their seats.

"This looks amazing," I said.

"Wait till you taste it," Quinn said, reaching for the potatoes. "Erin's roast chicken is the best."

"She's not wrong," Scott said, already carving into the bird.

We passed our plates down one by one, and Scott added slices of chicken to each. Then we passed the sides around...the potatoes started one way, green beans the other.

I took the bowl of potatoes from Quinn and went to hand her the green beans.

She shook her head. "No thanks."

"You don't like green beans?" I asked as I set the bowl down.

"Aunt Nini's allergic to vegetables," Rosie announced.

I raised a brow and looked at Quinn.

"All vegetables?"

Her cheeks went pink as she focused intently on pouring gravy over her plate as she nodded.

I glanced at Erin, then Scott. They were both grinning.

"Allergic," I said slowly.

"It's a real condition," Quinn said, still not looking up from her plate.

"Uh-huh."

Rosie nodded seriously. "They make her sick."

"That's terrible," I said, trying to keep my face neutral.

Quinn's eyes flicked up to mine for half a second. The corner of her mouth twitched.

Scott snorted into his beer. Erin wasn't even trying to hide her smile.

"It's very tragic," Erin said. "She's suffered her whole life."

"Since childhood," Quinn confirmed, reaching for her wine.

I spooned potatoes onto my plate. "Good thing there's plenty of chicken."

Dinner settled into an easy rhythm after that. Rosie kept up a steady stream of chatter about her newest dance routine and how she and her friends were arguing over whether their recital costumes should have sequins or feathers.

Liam was mostly quiet, but kept stealing glances at me, obviously working up to something.

Anytime Rosie paused long enough to take a bite, the rest of us drifted into the kind of conversation that felt easy and familiar—Quinn giving Erin a hard time about already testing holiday cookie recipes, Scott retelling the chaos of chaperoning Liam's planetarium field trip, Erin admitting she was thrilled travel ball was finally over because she wanted her weekends—and her voice—back. They pulled me into all of it without hesitation, looping me into their ongoing pizza-place feud like I'd earned a vote just by showing up. And the longer we talked, the more I noticed Liam homing in on every baseball detail that slipped into the conversation, like each one nudged him closer to the thing he was working up the nerve to ask.

At the next break in conversation, he set his fork down and rested his elbows on the table, eyes darting to mine like he'd decided this was his moment.

"Benny, my dad says I'm too young to throw a curveball," he said, trying to sound casual. "But a bunch of my friends do. He told me if I don't believe him, I should ask you why I shouldn't."

Erin lifted her brows like *good luck,* and Quinn hid a smile behind her wine glass.

"Your dad's right," I said. "Curveballs aren't a great idea at your age because your elbow's still growing, and that twisting motion puts stress on the parts that aren't ready for it yet. You won't feel it now, but it can cause problems down the road."

Liam frowned, obviously not happy with my answer.

"But that doesn't mean you're stuck," I added. "Have your dad teach you a circle change. It moves enough to keep a hitter off balance, which is basically the whole point of mixing pitches." I smiled. "And I know your dad can throw that pitch because he used to strike me out with it all the time."

He looked at Scott, who smiled and nodded, then turned back to me, eyes sharp with interest.

"And in the meantime?" I added. "Work on your location. The best pitch is a fastball to a specific spot. If you can put it exactly where you want it, you'll beat most hitters without needing a curveball."

"So...fastball, circle change, and hit my spots."

"Exactly," I said. "You do that, and you'll be ahead of every kid trying to impress people with a curveball they're not ready for."

Liam seemed satisfied with that and went back to eating.

Dinner eased back into an easy rhythm, everyone finishing the last bites of their meal.

Once we all cleared our plates, Erin announced dessert like it was a national holiday.

"I hope everyone saved room for the apple crumble."

And of course they did—Quinn's crumble disappeared fast, the kind of fast that said everybody meant it when they asked her to make it again next week.

When it was time to leave, Rosie hugged me without warning, and Liam said goodbye with a lot more enthusiasm than he'd said hello. Erin told me to come back anytime, and I believed she meant it.

Outside, Quinn exhaled. "That went weirdly smooth."

"I had fun," I said, and I took her hand as we walked toward the Jeep.

"Me too."

I opened her door and watched her climb into the Jeep, and the truth settled in before I could talk myself out of it.

I didn't just want to know Quinn. I wanted to fit into her world. Her people. Her life.

And tonight, I could actually see what a relationship with her might look like.

And it didn't feel out of reach. It just felt right.

Chapter Thirty-Two

Quinn

The Ridge Road trail was mostly empty this time of year, the trees bare and the air carrying that cold November bite that promised winter wasn't far behind. Leaves crunched under our boots in uneven bursts as we walked, close enough that our arms brushed now and then.

"It's freezing, but annoyingly pretty," I said.

He smiled at that, the unguarded kind he didn't hand out often, and gave a small nod like he agreed.

We kept walking, our steps falling into the same easy rhythm, the woods settling into a soft hush around us.

After a while, he cleared his throat. "Thanksgiving's next week."

I glanced over. "Yeah. It snuck up fast."

"Cat's hosting lunch," he said. "She asked if I wanted to invite you."

My heart skipped, then started pounding.

"Oh," I said. "And did you...did you tell her? About us?"

"About *us*?" he repeated.

"Us as in—I mean…" I gestured vaguely between us as I trailed off, hoping it would finish for me.

He stopped walking just long enough to look directly at me, eyes warm and annoyingly amused.

I groaned and shoved at his arm. "You're such a jerk," I said with a chuckle.

"Why? I just asked a question." We started walking again. "You're doing great answering, by the way. Very clear."

I nudged him harder this time, and he slipped an arm around my shoulders like it was the easiest thing in the world, pulling me into his side.

"I told her I'd ask what your plans were," he said into my hair.

Then he pressed a quick kiss to the top of my head before letting his arm fall away so we could navigate a narrow stretch of trail.

"I'm having dinner at my mom's," I said. "But I could do lunch." I glanced at him. "And maybe you could come to dinner at my mom's, too?"

"Sounds like a perfect day."

We walked a little farther and a pair of hikers approached from the opposite direction. With their thick coats and knitted hats, they looked like the kind of people who did this every Saturday regardless of the temperature.

"Afternoon," the man said with a friendly nod.

"Afternoon," Benny replied, and I echoed him with a smile.

The woman gave a little wave. "Watch for ice up by the bend," she warned. "It sneaks up on you."

"Thanks," I said. "We'll keep an eye out."

They continued on, their footsteps fading into the trees behind us.

"Since we were talking Thanksgiving," I said. "What's your favorite side dish?"

"Mashed potatoes," he said immediately. "Whipped with real butter and cream. No lumps. Preferably with gravy that doesn't turn into wallpaper paste."

I snorted. "So Scott was fighting a real battle in that kitchen."

"He was," Benny said with mock solemnity. "And he won. That gravy was delicious."

"What about yours?" he asked.

"Stuffing," I said. "It has to have the crispy edges, though."

We kept going, our footsteps crunching through what leaves were left on the trail—until we rounded the bend the hikers mentioned.

Benny spotted it first. "Careful," he said, reaching out instinctively.

Before I could ask what, my boot hit a slick patch of ice hidden under a thin layer of leaves. My foot skidded, and I lurched forward with a very ungraceful, "Oh—nope—nope —nope—"

His hand closed around my elbow, anchoring me before I could face-plant.

"Thanks." I adjusted my coat. "Good to know you still have those catcher reflexes."

He chuckled, not letting go until he was sure I had my footing.

"You okay?"

"Yep." I blew out a breath. "Only my pride was hurt."

He brushed a bit of leaf debris off my sleeve before letting his hand fall away. "Your pride's tough. It'll survive."

"Barely," I muttered with a smile.

We kept walking, the trail flattening out as the trees

thinned toward the far end. The sky was that washed-out November blue that always made me think of early dismissals and breath turning white in the air.

"Okay," I said. "Important question."

"More important than mashed potatoes?"

"Much," I said. "What's your favorite music?"

He lifted a brow. "If I don't say you, are you going to be offended?"

I snorted. "I'd be shocked if you did."

"Well," he said, sliding his hands into his jacket pockets as we walked, "I've heard your songs played in more stadiums than I can count. Pregame playlists, batting cage mixes, walk-up songs...a lot of my teammates listened to you. So it wouldn't be that shocking."

I blinked, caught off guard. "Seriously?"

"Seriously." He shrugged. "But to answer your question, my favorite music is the stuff I grew up with...nineties and alt rock. But I like classic rock too, and some pop."

Then he cut his eyes toward me, a subtle, knowing look that said and *yes, yours* without making it weird.

A flush crept up my neck before I could stop it.

"What about you?" he asked.

"I love most music," I said.

"Most?" he echoed, amused.

"I'd rather listen to nails on a chalkboard than death metal. And I'm not a fan of old-school honky-tonk country. But everything else works for me."

He nodded, like he was storing that away for later. "So who were your inspirations?"

"Stevie Nicks, Joni Mitchell, Carole King, Bob Dylan, Carly Simon, James Taylor, Cat Stevens, Jackson Browne, Paul McCartney, Alanis Morissette." I chuckled. "I could go on and on..."

"That's a hell of a list," Benny said, voice softening. "Makes sense, though."

"Why's that?"

He shrugged, eyes on the path ahead. "Your songs feel like all of them, with your own pop twist."

It landed in every soft, squishy part of me I usually tried to guard.

I blew out a slow breath. "Well...I'll take that. Thank you."

We rounded the last curve of the trail, the trees thinning until the gravel path opened onto the small lot where Benny had parked. His Jeep sat alone beneath a line of bare maples, the afternoon sun already dipping low and turning everything that hazy November gold.

"End of the road," he said, brushing his glove against mine as we stepped out of the woods.

"That was a good walk," I said, tugging my hat down over my ears. "Minus the part where I almost died on invisible ice."

"You lived," he said. "And I didn't even have to carry you back."

He walked to the passenger side and pulled the door open, holding it with one hand and bracing the other on the frame like he was making sure it wouldn't so much as wobble.

"After you," he said.

I climbed in, the seat warm from the sun, and before I could reach for the handle, he gently closed the door behind me. By the time he rounded the hood and settled into the driver's seat, I'd just managed to stop smiling at the dashboard like a complete idiot.

"Did you want to head home?"

"I was going to."

He eased the Jeep out onto the narrow road, fingers loose on the wheel. "I was thinking we could go back to my place. Order pizza. Maybe watch a movie."

Heat unfurled through me, delicious and impossible to hide. "Pizza and a movie sounds perfect."

"Good," he said. "I was hoping you'd say yes."

He turned left toward his place and reached over, lacing his fingers through mine.

Benny's house sat at the far end of the street, tucked behind a line of tall pines that made it feel private without being remote. He pulled into the driveway, tapped the opener, and the door lifted with a soft whir.

He eased the Jeep inside and killed the engine. I looked around the space while the door closed behind us. A row of shelves held organized bins and boxes, all labeled in Benny's blocky handwriting. A few free weights sat stacked in the corner, and his bike hung on the wall like it was waiting for spring.

Then he glanced over with a smile.

"Come on," he said. "Let's go in."

Before I could reach for my seatbelt, he was already out of the driver's side and coming around the front of the Jeep. He opened my door like he always did and waited for me to hop down.

"Thank you," I said, my breath catching a little at the gentleness of it.

"Always," he murmured.

He placed his hand on the small of my back, leading me to the door.

Reaching around me, he pushed it open, then straightened so I could go in first.

I stepped into the mudroom that doubled as a laundry room. A washer and dryer sat along one wall, and across from them was a long bench with cubbies beneath it and hooks above. Functional. Efficient. Lived in without being cluttered. Very Benny.

We hung up our coats and peeled off hats and gloves. I stepped out of my boots, and Benny placed his beside mine. It made the whole space feel shared, somehow. Or maybe that was just me reading into things.

We stepped through the doorway into the kitchen, and Benny immediately crossed to the counter and dropped his keys and wallet into a small black tray nestled beside the coffee maker. It felt oddly domestic—like watching someone ease into the rhythm of their own home.

The warm overhead lighting glowed against espresso cabinets and pale gray subway tile. The granite counters were a deep stormy gray with silver flecks that caught the light, and the stainless-steel appliances looked sleek without trying too hard. It had clean lines and was masculine without being cold.

"This is really nice," I said, brushing my fingers lightly along the edge of the counter.

"Thanks," he said. "I got lucky. I liked everything about it, so it was pretty much move-in ready. The only thing I had to do was shove my crap in the closets."

"It's perfect, and really suits you."

"I thought so," he said. "As soon as I saw it, I made an offer before someone else could. Figured it was time to stop renting if I was really going to be here long-term." He pushed off the counter. "Want the tour?"

I smiled. "Obviously."

Maybe focusing on the tour would keep me from spiraling over the word *long-term* he'd just dropped like it was no big deal.

He led me through the open layout—living room with a

big sectional, a wall of built-ins with his TV, and a few framed photos on the shelves. Grace and Charlie with ice-cream-smeared faces. Another of the three of them at the ballpark, the kids bundled in sweatshirts and beaming, Benny in the middle looking proud and exactly like the man I'd come to know. The whole space felt lived-in and steady in a way that made perfect sense for him.

The photos pulled at something warm in my chest, and when I looked up, he was watching me with a shy smile. He tipped his head toward the hallway and I followed, my socks sliding softly over the hardwood as we walked.

"There are three bedrooms, and I use this one as an office." Benny said as we passed the first door on the right. He nudged it open with his foot.

I peeked inside.

A desk with dual monitors and an ergonomic chair sat right in the middle. On the corner sat a well-worn glove with a baseball tucked in the pocket. A couple of unpacked boxes on the floor held framed photos and old awards he clearly hadn't gotten around to hanging.

"Still settling in?" I asked.

"Just figuring out what matters enough to put on the walls," he said with a small shrug.

He gestured to the next door to the other bedroom.

"Those two rooms share a Jack-and-Jill." He walked across the hall, opened the door, and stepped aside. "And this is my room."

I walked into a space that was Benny down to the bone. Clean lines, navy-and-gray bedding, a solid wood bed frame that looked handmade. A dresser and a wall-mounted TV faced the bed, lamps balanced neatly on each nightstand. There was no clutter, no chaos—nothing overly decorative, just quiet order.

"So," I said lightly, leaning a hip against the doorframe, "this is where the magic happens."

One corner of his mouth tugged up. "If by magic you mean sleeping and SportsCenter, then yeah."

A laugh escaped before I could stop it, warm and a little breathless. "Right. Obviously."

But even as I joked, my gaze snagged on the big, neatly made bed, the only thing in the room my brain wanted to zoom in on.

Because *yes*, sex with Benny was...Amazing. Addictive. The kind of mind-melting, toe-curling, body-singing sex that made a girl consider writing a thank-you note to the universe.

And it was fun—which was a glitter-bomb-to-the-face combination. Sparkly, distracting, impossible to ignore.

Sure, we were still in that early stage where everything felt like chemistry and luck and *oh-my-God-again-please*. But I had this tiny, traitorous suspicion—the kind I refused to look at too closely—that with Benny, even twenty years from now, it'd still be the good kind of dangerous.

"And the basement's finished, but we don't have to go down there," he said, pulling my attention back to him. "It's currently home to absolutely nothing."

"That's a bold design choice."

He huffed a laugh.

"I haven't figured out what to do with it yet. Home gym? Entertainment room? Batcave?"

"Batcave," I said immediately. "No contest."

"Obviously."

A beat of silence stretched as we stood there, his body angled just slightly toward mine, like gravity was doing most of the work.

His eyes dropped to my mouth for half a second. Maybe less. But I felt the shift all the way down my spine.

"You hungry?" he asked, voice lower.

"For pizza?" I asked.

His look made it very clear pizza was not the first thing on his mind. Which was good because it wasn't on mine either. So I didn't answer with words. I rose onto my toes and kissed him—slow at first, then deeper until he answered with that low sound I'd started to crave.

He slid his hands to my hips, pulling me flush against him.

"Quinn," he murmured against my mouth.

Whatever plans we'd had evaporated instantly, replaced by one very clear, very delicious priority...the bed behind him.

Chapter Thirty-Three

Benny

When Cat opened the door, she looked like she was bracing for impact—shoulders tight, eyes wide, a polite-but-strained smile already forming.

Then she saw me and the tension melted like someone had cut strings.

"Oh thank God," she exhaled, grabbing my sleeve. "I thought Mom and Dad were here early."

"Happy Thanksgiving to you too," I said.

She huffed out a laugh, brushing her hair off her forehead.

"Sorry. I'm just behind. Charlie decided to 'wash his hands like a real chef,' which somehow turned into soap on the walls, all over the floor, and—don't ask me how—behind the toilet."

"You should have called me. I would have come and cleaned it."

"Sure, you say that now."

"Smartass."

Inside, the house was surprisingly calm. Soft holiday

music hummed in the background, the smell of turkey filled the air, and sunlight warmed the dining room table already set with Cat's good dishes.

Charlie was on the living room floor, sorting Legos by color like it was a sacred ritual. He looked up long enough to wave. "Hi, Uncle Benny."

"Hey, bud."

Grace burst into the hallway with perfect dramatic timing, wearing a gold sequin hat that glittered like a disco ball.

"Uncle Benny!" she gasped, looking behind me like I might have Quinn tucked in my back pocket. "Where is she?"

"Hi, Grace. It's nice to see you too," I said.

"Hi." She blinked. "Where's Quinn?"

"She's helping her mom meal prep for later. But she'll be here for dinner."

Grace released a breath like she'd been holding it since dawn. "Okay. I'm going to watch for her out the window."

"I'm here an hour early, so it's probably going to be a while."

"That's okay!" she called over her shoulder, already halfway to the living room.

I looked at Cat and she shrugged.

"She'll last about five minutes." Cat sighed and washed her hands. "She's been like that since breakfast. Which, for the record, was *early*."

"She's excited," I said.

"She's obsessed," Cat corrected, but she was smiling.

I leaned against the counter, crossing my arms. "What do you need? Put me to work."

Cat hesitated only a second before her whole posture

relaxed. "If you could put together the veggie tray and make the dip, that would save me so much time."

"Easy enough," I said.

"Veggies and sour cream are in the fridge," she said, then pointed to the cupboard over the oven. "Platter's in there, and the dip mix is in the spice drawer." She paused. "And please make it look nice. Mom will judge."

I collected everything I needed.

"She judges everything," I said. "But I'll still make it look nice."

"Thank you."

After washing my hands, I got to work.

"So," Cat said, pulling something from the oven. "Things are going well?"

"With the dip?" I deadpanned.

She rolled her eyes. "With Quinn."

I shrugged and focused on stacking celery on the platter.

"Yeah. They are."

"Good 'they are' or pretend-you're-casual-but-you're-actually-smitten 'they are'?"

"Cat."

"You never bring women around, Benny. So if you're bringing someone to Thanksgiving, I get to ask questions."

I stopped what I was doing and looked at her. "Really good."

Cat leaned against the counter, her expression softening.

"Good. I like her." She nudged me lightly with her elbow. "And you seem different since you're with her," she added.

I went back to crafting my masterpiece. "Different how?"

"Relaxed," she said. "Happy, maybe. I don't know. Just...lighter."

I didn't have an answer because she wasn't wrong.

Before she could poke at it more, Grace screamed from the living room:

"I SEE A CAR!" She rushed into the kitchen. "IT'S HER!"

I wiped my hands on a towel and headed for the front door, but Grace had raced in front of me and was already there, pulling it open.

Quinn stood on the porch, cheeks pink from the cold, holding a tin in both hands. The second she spotted Grace, her whole face lit up.

"Grace," she said, delighted, "that hat is *everything*. You look incredible."

Grace froze for half a beat—like her brain short-circuited—then let out a tiny gasp. "It's like the one from The Last Verse Tour."

Quinn grinned. "It's perfect. You wear it way better than I ever did."

Grace nearly levitated.

Only then did Quinn shift her gaze to me.

"Hi," she said quietly.

"Hey."

I nudged Grace gently to the side and stepped back. "Come on inside."

Quinn moved past Grace, just far enough into the foyer so I could swing the door shut behind her. Without thinking, I leaned in and brushed a quick kiss against her mouth.

Grace spun and bolted down the hallway, her sequined hat bouncing with every step.

Her stage whisper carried easily back to us as Quinn and I followed her toward the kitchen.

"Mom! Uncle Benny kissed Quinn!"

Cat made a choking sound as she turned to look at us.

Quinn seemed more amused than anything. "She's not wrong," she said.

"Hi Quinn," Cat managed, clearly trying not to laugh. "I'm so glad you could join us."

"Thanks so much for having me." She held the tin out. "I brought Welsh cookies."

Cat's face lit up immediately. "I *love* Welsh cookies." She pointed to the counter beside the serving dishes. "You can set them right there."

She set the tin down where Cat pointed just as Grace was at her side again.

"Quinn, can I show you something in my room?"

"Absolutely. Lead the way."

Grace beamed at her like she'd been handed the keys to the universe and grabbed her hand, tugging her down the hallway.

Cat watched them go with a smile. "She's going to show her the collage poster she made."

"What poster?"

"The one of all things Quinn." She chuckled. "If Quinn gets within two feet of that thing, she'll have glitter all over her." She pointed her spatula at me. "And I'm sure some will end up on you."

I tried to hide the grin that pulled at my mouth, but failed miserably. "If I'm lucky."

Cat went still, spatula suspended mid-air, and just looked at me.

"Well, damn," she finally said.

"What?"

"That's the biggest smile I've seen from you in a long time."

I opened my mouth to respond—something deflecting or sarcastic—but before I could get a word out, the doorbell rang.

Straightening, I said, "There goes the smile."

"Behave," she warned, tossing the towel at me.

I caught it before it hit my face. "I'll try my best."

She leveled a look at me. "Try harder than that."

"I'll get it!" Charlie shouted from the living room. His footsteps thudded across the hardwood before the front door creaked open.

"Grandmom! Grandpop!" Charlie said, muffled by what was probably a hug.

Dad's reply followed. "Happy Thanksgiving, buddy."

A moment later, they appeared in the kitchen.

Mom paused just inside the doorway, slipping her gloves off, her eyes sweeping over the counters, the half-assembled side dishes, the serving platters lined up and ready.

"Happy Thanksgiving," she said to the room at large.

Dad inhaled deeply. "Smells good in here."

"Thank you," Cat said brightly, crossing over to hug them.

Mom returned it with a polite pat to the shoulder.

Dad nodded at me. "Benny."

"Dad," I said.

I walked over and gave my mom an obligatory kiss on the cheek.

Cat glanced past all of us into the living room. "Charlie, are your Legos picked up?"

"Not yet."

"We're having hors d'oeuvres in there," she said, pointing toward the living room. "Go clean them up, please."

Charlie groaned theatrically but hopped up and ran off to do it.

Mom watched him dash out of the room, then folded her hands neatly.

"So Cat," she said. "Are you sure you don't want to join us at the club tonight? They always make such a lovely dinner, and I'm sure there will be plenty of eligible men there."

Cat's expression didn't change, but she let out a soft breath that was basically an eye roll disguised as politeness.

"Thanks, Mom, but no," she said. "The kids and I are staying in. We're going to watch a movie and have a fun family night."

Mom pressed her lips together, clearly unhappy with her answer, but wisely choosing not to push further.

A beat later, laughter drifted down the stairs—Grace's bright squeal layered with Quinn's quieter laugh.

All four of us turned toward the sound.

Grace rounded the corner first, still glowing like she'd swallowed a star. She went straight to my mom and dad.

"Grandmom! Grandpop!" she said, giving each of them a hug and a kiss.

Mom hugged her tightly. "Happy Thanksgiving, darling."

Dad tapped the brim of her hat. "Looking sparkly today."

There was definitely a shimmer of glitter on her cheek. And as Quinn stepped into the room, I noticed some on the back of her hand and in her hair.

Mom's eyes flicked between the two of us, then down at Grace. "Who's your friend, sweetheart?"

Before Grace could answer, I stepped forward.

"Mom, Dad—this is Quinn Logan," I said. "Quinn, these are my parents, John and Vera Reed."

Quinn offered a polite smile. "It's so nice to meet you both. Happy Thanksgiving."

Dad shook her hand. "Welcome."

Mom followed, her expression composed but undeniably surprised. "We're glad you could join us."

There was a flicker — something taking shape behind both of their eyes — and every part of me knew exactly what that was.

Cat clapped her hands once. "Okay, into the living room, everyone. I'll bring hors d'oeuvres."

"What do you need help with?" Quinn asked.

"Nope, I've got it," Cat said, pointing the spatula at her. "You're a guest. Go socialize."

Quinn laughed and let Grace tug her toward the living room, where Charlie had finished picking up the Legos and was now sitting cross-legged, waiting for her like she was the main event.

I followed, taking a seat beside Quinn on the couch while Mom and Dad settled into the chairs across from us.

Dad crossed an ankle over his knee. "So," he said, with one of those chuckles he did when he was trying too hard to sound casual, "I guess what I've been seeing online is true, then."

Quinn's expression didn't change, but I felt the shift— the way she went rigid, the quick breath she tried to hide.

She glanced at me, like she was waiting to see whether I'd stiffen or shut down.

I didn't do either.

"We've been spending time together," I said simply, letting it sit there.

Dad nodded, pleased with himself. "A few of the sports sites mentioned it."

Of course they had.

He still followed a bunch of MLB channels, and anything remotely connected to baseball—including who former players were seen with—ended up in his feed.

Mom's gaze lingered on Quinn, assessing, probably more surprised I'd brought someone to dinner than anything else.

Cat swept into the room then, balancing a tray of appetizers like she'd been waiting for the exact second the conversation needed rescuing. "Help yourselves, everyone."

Quinn handled my family beautifully, smiling without flinching. Charlie proudly showed her his latest Lego creation, Grace talked about everything from her birthday to her hat to her favorite Quinn song, and Dad stayed weirdly friendly, which was its own kind of red flag.

When my dad was impressed, it was almost always because of money, fame, or status. Quinn hit the trifecta.

We settled into a rhythm of small talk, laughter, the kids bouncing between us.

Grace tiptoed over to Cat, whispering something fast and breathless against her ear.

Cat smiled. "If you want to, honey."

She spun around and crossed the room in a few determined steps, stopping right in front of Quinn.

"Quinn?" she said, hands clasped behind her back like she was physically holding in her excitement. "My family birthday party is next week, and I was wondering if you'd want to come."

"I'd love to," she said.

Grace squealed and threw herself at Quinn, who

hugged her back without hesitation. A little more glitter jumped to Quinn's sweater.

"We're going to The Copper House," Grace announced. "Mom let me pick my dress. It's blue and twirly."

Quinn's face softened. "I love a twirly dress."

The rest of the afternoon rolled by easily. Dinner was simple—good food, predictable small talk, the kids talking nonstop, and my parents pretending not to check their watches every ten minutes.

After dessert—pie, brownies, ice cream, and Welsh cookies—Cat grabbed another cookie, took a bite, and let out an appreciative hum.

"These cookies are *insane*," Cat said. "I've tried making Welsh cookies twice and both attempts tasted like disappointment. Do you have a recipe you'd be willing to share? Because whatever I'm doing is not this."

"I don't really have one," Quinn said with a shrug. "I use an old coffee mug to measure everything, which isn't an exact science." She smiled. "But I'll be making more for Christmas. If you want to come over, maybe we can actually measure things and turn it into a real recipe."

Cat brightened. "I'd love that."

"Can I come too?" Grace asked, bouncing in her chair.

"Of course," Quinn said.

Something warm tugged in my chest at the sight of Quinn fitting in here, sharing pieces of her life so easily, like she'd always belonged.

Eventually Dad cleared his throat. "We'd better head home. We have to get ready for the club."

Black tie. Of course.

We all stood and Mom pressed a kiss to Cat's cheek,

gave Charlie and Grace hugs, and then offered Quinn a small, polite smile. "It was lovely to meet you."

"Same here," Quinn said warmly.

They left in a swirl of coats and perfume.

Once the door shut behind my parents, the whole house seemed to exhale. Cat gathered a few plates, I grabbed the serving dishes, and Quinn stacked the dessert plates before carrying them to the sink.

"I should head to my mom's," Quinn said, drying her hands. "I'll go say goodbye to Grace and Charlie first."

She slipped into the living room. Grace let out a dramatic, drawn-out "noooo," while Charlie offered a quiet goodbye. After assuring Grace she'd see her next week, Quinn came back putting on her coat.

"I'll help finish up here and be right behind you," I told her as I walked her to the door.

I leaned in and kissed her goodbye.

"I'll see you at my mom's," she whispered.

Quinn slipped out the front door with a soft *bye* and one last quick kiss. I watched her head down the walkway before closing the door.

Cat was at the sink, rinsing the last bowl. She didn't look over when she said, "She fits. You know that, right?"

I swallowed. "Yeah."

"And you're different with her."

I didn't answer. Mostly because she wasn't wrong, and I didn't know how to put words to the way my chest kept catching up to itself.

Cat finally turned, drying her hands. "Don't overthink it, Benny."

I wasn't. But what I felt hit me harder than I expected—that being with Quinn felt right in a way nothing else ever had.

Chapter Thirty-Four

Quinn

By the time I got back to my mom's, the house smelled like Thanksgiving—roasted turkey, cinnamon from the pies cooling on the counter, and the yeasty aroma of rolls she'd just pulled out of the oven.

It was the kind of smell that felt like a warm hug.

I slipped off my boots and went straight into the kitchen, where Mom had already pulled out half the cookware she owned. Steam clouded the windows, smooth jazz drifted from the little speaker by the microwave, and the heat from the oven wrapped around me like a blanket.

"There you are," Mom said without turning around. She was stirring something in her favorite copper pan—the one she claimed cooked vegetables better than "any modern nonsense." "Where's Benny?"

"He's helping his sister clean up," I said. "He'll be here soon."

She squinted then pointed to my cheek.

"Is that glitter?"

"Benny's niece Grace showed me a poster she made. A very sparkly one."

"Looks cute," she said, fighting a smile.

I rolled my eyes, but it tugged a grin out of me anyway. "What do you need me to do?"

We'd done most of the major prep this morning. Now we were mostly in waiting mode, assembling what we could while everything finished cooking.

"You can work on the charcuterie board."

I grabbed the wide wooden board from the cabinet above the coffee maker. I'd made a charcuterie board on a whim one year, and it ended up becoming a permanent Thanksgiving staple alongside Mom's classics.

After setting everything on the counter, I fell into the familiar rhythm of arranging it without needing to think too hard. Mom moved around me automatically, checking the timer, stirring whatever was in the copper pan, sliding a casserole dish onto a trivet to cool.

A cheer went up, followed by my dad's "Finally!" and my brother's "Took them long enough." Mom and I shared a look that lasted only a second but held years of identical holidays.

"Men," she muttered fondly. "Remind me why we feed them?"

"Tradition," I said.

"Terrible reason."

But she was smiling. Growing up, holidays always looked like this—Mom and me in the kitchen, Dad and Miles yelling at whatever game was on. We'd fallen into those old-school holiday roles without ever really discussing them, the kind that would probably make a think-piece somewhere roll its eyes.

But I never minded it.

Especially not during the years I lived with Dad in L.A. while Mom and Miles were still here in Waypoint. Back then, these kitchen moments were rare and precious. Just the two of us moving in the same space, the same rhythm, like we'd never been apart at all.

I placed a folded slice of salami on the board, then glanced at her. "How are things at the brewery?"

She let out a soft breath, the kind that said she was choosing her words.

"Busier than I expected," she admitted, shifting a dish a little farther from the stovetop heat. "The girls have been doing their best, but Walter ran that place without much outside input. They've been trying to untangle years of his system."

"I know they appreciate having you there."

"Mostly because I know how he organized things. After Walter passed, so much changed so fast, and nobody could find anything."

"So basically, you're the keeper of all the brewery secrets." I said as I tucked a cluster of grapes into place.

She snorted. "If only they were interesting secrets like a hidden recipe vault or a scandalous brewer feud."

"But it's good? Being back?" I asked.

"It is. At first I wasn't sure I had the stamina for it anymore. Getting sick knocked me around more than I expected."

My chest tightened.

"I know."

"But easing back into a routine? Being around people again? Feeling useful?" She gave a small, honest nod. "It's helping. More than I would have guessed."

"I can tell," I said. "You seem lighter."

She laughed softly. "You spend years dreaming about

retirement, then find out you still need purpose. You can only plant so many gardens and go to so many lunches before you start going a little stir-crazy."

"Never thought I'd hear you say that."

"Me neither." She peeked at the turkey through the oven window, her voice dipping just a little. "Things moved so fast for so long, and then when I got sick, it all just stopped. It was a lot to get used to." She gave a small shrug. "It's nice to have a reason to get up and go out again. And Tessa said my schedule can be flexible, so it really is the best of both worlds."

"And if it ever feels like too much, you can always take a break."

Before either of us could say more, a firm knock sounded at the front door. My stomach flipped, which is ridiculous because I just saw Benny less than a half hour ago.

"I'll get it," I said, wiping my hands on a towel before heading down the hall.

I opened the door to Benny—coat unzipped, hair ruffled from the cold, a soft smile pulling at the corner of his mouth. A single fleck of glitter clung to his sleeve like Grace had tagged him before he left.

"Hey," he said quietly.

"Come in." I stepped back and let him inside. "Perfect timing."

From the living room came a loud groan, followed by my dad's "You've gotta be kidding me," and then Miles's "That was holding!" layered right over top.

Benny's brows lifted. "Officiating trauma. I know it well."

"That's just my dad and brother," I said, laughing. "Football brings out their...passion."

He smirked. "I get it."

We walked into the living room, where Dad was planted in the recliner and Miles was leaning forward on the couch like his willpower alone was going to affect the score.

"Benny, this is my dad Mark and my brother Miles," I said, feeling that flutter of nerves again but warmer this time, "Dad, Miles, this is Benny."

Dad stood and shook his hand. "Good to meet you."

"You too, sir," Benny said, firm handshake, good eye contact—my dad's three love languages.

Miles hopped up next, grinning. I thought he was going to say some embarrassing brother thing, but he just said, "Nice to meet you."

The commercial break ended, and before they could try to entice Benny to stay with them, I touched his arm.

"Come meet my mom," I said, leading him toward the kitchen.

The second we stepped through the doorway, Mom was setting the turkey on the counter.

"You must be Benny," she said warmly as she slipped off her oven mitts.

"Yes, ma'am." He stepped forward. "It's nice to meet you, Mrs. Logan."

"Call me Jo," she said, pulling him into a hug.

"Okay. Jo," he said once she let him go, a little startled but smiling.

Mom squeezed his arm once before stepping back. "I'm glad you could join us." She looked at me "Quinn, honey, why don't you bring the charcuterie board and the appetizers into the dining room?"

"Got it," I said, grabbing the board.

Benny stepped aside to let me pass and snagged a grape in one smooth, sneaky motion.

"Thief," I muttered under my breath. He just grinned.

"What can I help with?" he asked.

"Since you asked..." Mom handed him a plate of stuffed mushrooms and another of cranberry brie bites.

He took both without hesitation. "Lead the way."

I headed to the dining room, the board balanced in my hands. Benny followed close behind, his footsteps quiet on the hardwood, careful in that way people are when they're in someone else's home for the first time.

The dining room was already set, the mismatched chairs Mom refused to replace pulled up around the table because "they have personality."

After setting the charcuterie board down, I gestured for Benny to do the same. Once he did, he paused, taking in the room—the family photos lining the wall, the too-full china cabinet Mom refused to declutter, and the faded runner stretched down the center of the table, softened from years of use.

I struck a match and lit the taper candles, their glow catching on the glasses and silverware.

Mom's voice floated in from the living room—warm, commanding, and amused.

"Alright boys, it's time."

Footsteps shuffled, the TV clicked off, and a moment later Dad and Miles filed into the dining room like soldiers answering a summons. Mom swept in right behind them, apron gone, hair fluffed, a bottle of wine in her hand.

She gave the table a once-over. "Perfect," she said, satisfied. "Everyone grab some appetizers and sit."

As everyone shifted toward their seats, Benny hesitated for only a second, before settling beside me.

My family slipped into the easy hum of its usual holiday soundtrack as everyone reached for appetizers. And Benny joined right in. He filled half his plate with veggies and dip, then piled on a bit of everything else. His plate tipped slightly as he added a stuffed mushroom, and a carrot slipped off and landed near my hand.

I picked it up and held it out to him. "You dropped something."

A slow smirk spread across his face. "Wow, look at you touching a vegetable. I'm glad to see close contact doesn't cause an allergic reaction."

"You're hilarious."

Mom finished pouring wine into her glass and shot me a look. "Are you still telling people that?"

"It's not a lie if you believe it's true," I said.

"Seriously?" She rolled her eyes.

Miles chuckled. "I can't believe you just quoted George Costanza to prove your point."

"Seinfeld is a classic," I said with a shrug.

Benny finally plucked the carrot from my hand—his thumb brushing mine for just a second, but it was enough to spark something warm and ridiculous blooming in my chest.

"Well," he said, popping it into his mouth, "at least you're making progress."

"Careful," I warned, bumping my elbow into his. "Keep teasing me and I'll make you eat all the green beans."

He leaned in just a little, voice low and only for me. "Joke's on you. I actually like vegetables."

His whisper lingered at my ear way longer than necessary—through appetizers and right into dinner—like my brain had decided to replay it on a loop.

Dad reached for the rolls and glanced at Benny. "So, I hear the Lagerheads are shaping up."

"Yeah. Better than I expected, honestly. There's a lot to get in place before the season starts, but we're making progress."

Miles perked up. "The team looks good?"

"The team looks great," Benny said, pride threading through his voice. "We're getting the roster where it needs to be, and the coaching staff is coming together too." He paused, then added, "It's mostly Tessa, Quinn, and me doing the heavy lifting behind the scenes, but we're getting it done. We make a good team."

When he said those last three words, he glanced at me. It was brief, but it landed like a touch.

"And Jo," Benny added, turning toward her, "you've really taken a load off Tessa. She's had more time to focus on the Lagerheads since you're helping her out at the brewery."

Mom blinked, surprised. "Oh. Well...I'm glad I could help."

Dad angled his fork toward Mom. "Things just run smoother when you're in the mix, Jo. The brewery, this family... you keep things steady."

Mom smiled and lifted her wine glass in a small toast before taking a sip.

Watching the two of them like this always threw people —everyone assumed my parents were still together. And honestly? Moments like this made it easy to see why.

But I remember the years when it wasn't this easy, when everything between them felt tight and tired. They're better now. Calmer. Softer with each other because they don't have to be anything else.

The rest of dinner was filled with easy conversation, overlapping stories, and laughter that bubbled up without warning. And Benny slipped into the pattern like he'd been part of it for years. He didn't try to take over or impress anyone, he just eased into the space with this steady calm, like he already understood the rhythm here.

Mom slid the basket of rolls toward him. "Take another. I made extra this year."

Benny grinned. "These are unbelievable. Quinn's been holding out on me."

"I have not," I protested.

"You kind of have," he murmured, nudging my knee again.

Dad pointed his fork at him. "You keep talking like that and Jo's going to send you home with a dozen of them."

Benny didn't miss a beat. "And I'd be fine with that."

As the plates emptied and the conversation softened into that comfortable after-dinner lull, Benny turned his head just slightly toward me, his voice low enough for only me to hear.

"Thanks for inviting me," he said. "I—" He paused, like he was searching for the right word. "I like it here."

A simple sentence, but it still managed to knock the air out of me in the softest way. I let the warmth of it settle next to everything else the day had stirred.

"You're welcome," I said. "Anytime."

And for the first time in a long time, surrounded by family and with Benny's knee brushing mine under the table, *anytime* didn't feel like a throwaway promise.

It felt like the start of something real.

Chapter Thirty-Five

Benny

The Christmas tree was heavy and awkward, but I managed to keep a grip on it as I made my way toward Cat's front door. Grace and Charlie marched ahead of me like they were leading a parade.

"Alright, you two, inside," Cat called from the doorway, stepping back to hold it open. "And give your uncle room unless you want to get smacked in the face with a rogue branch."

Grace darted through with a dramatic duck, giggling. Charlie followed, doing an exaggerated sideways shuffle like the tree was some wild animal I was wrestling into submission.

"Do you need any help?"

I shook my head, adjusting my hold to keep the trunk from going rogue on me.

"I've got it," I said, even though the bottom branches kept catching on the doorframe. "Mostly."

"Just don't drop it on my children or my furniture."

"No promises," I muttered, shifting my grip to keep the trunk from sliding. "This thing's got a mind of its own."

She snorted. "Good. It'll fit right in."

I shuffled forward until the tree finally cleared the doorway.

"Victory," I muttered.

"Not yet," Cat said, nodding toward the corner of the living room. "Base goes there. And try not to impale anything on the way."

Charlie bounced across the room like he was narrating a live disaster broadcast.

"Will he make it? Will he crash into the lamp?"

Grace chuckled.

"Will Mom kill him if he does?"

"I heard that," Cat said. "And nobody's dying today, thank you."

I lowered the tree into the stand with only minimal chaos, leaned down to tighten the screws, and stepped back. "Behold. The Fraser fir."

Grace clapped like I'd just performed a magic trick. "You got it in the stand!"

Charlie nodded. "It smells like Christmas."

Cat put a hand on her hip, assessing it like a general inspecting troops.

"Not bad," she said. "It's upright and nothing broke. I'll take it." She turned toward the kids. "Take your coats and boots off and we'll make hot cocoa."

Grace and Charlie immediately scattered, shedding their coats off on their way out of the family room.

"Hang them up in the mudroom," she called after them. "Don't just throw them on the floor. I mean it."

She pivoted toward me, sweeping a stray needle off her sweater.

"Thanks for helping out. Your reward is leftover pie and

hot cocoa," she said. "The real kind, not the mix. We're feeling festive."

"Fancy," I said.

She shrugged. "It keeps them busy. And happy. And out of the way while you"—she pointed at the bound branches still netted tight—"cut that thing open."

"On it."

She started toward the kitchen, then paused in the doorway, arching an eyebrow at me.

"Be careful you don't take a branch to the face."

"No promises," I said again, and she snorted before disappearing into the kitchen, to herd the kids.

I pulled a knife out of my pocket and got to work.

"Alright, buddy," I muttered to the tree like it was a skittish horse. "Let's not take my eye out."

A few careful cuts later, the branches shook free instead of exploding out, and the tree settled into something that actually looked intentional. There were needles everywhere, but no one was bleeding, and nothing was broken, or tipped over, which I counted as a win.

I wiped my hands on my jeans and nodded.

"Good enough."

With that, I headed toward the kitchen, following the sound of kids arguing cheerfully about whose turn it was to stir the cocoa.

Cat stood at the stove, with a kid on each side of her, stirring the pot while they watched with eager eyes.

"Tree's up," I said.

"Can we decorate now?" Charlie asked.

"It needs to settle first," Cat said. "So we're going to have hot cocoa and dessert while we wait."

Grace took the whisk and immediately went at it like

she was trying to create a vortex. Somehow all the liquid managed to stay in the pot.

"How was Thanksgiving at Quinn's mom's?"

"It was good."

"Just good?"

"Yeah. Good."

I couldn't help the small smile that tugged at my mouth.

Cat took the whisk from Grace and told her and Charlie to grab their mugs.

"You like her."

"I'm not sure what you want me to say to that." I chuckled. "Obviously I like her."

She softened, the teasing fading. "You're good together. That's all I'm saying."

Before I could comment, Grace set her mug on the island with a little thunk and climbed onto her stool. Charlie scrambled up beside her, already reaching for the marshmallow bag like he had a claim on it.

"Hold on," Cat said, sliding the pot off the burner. "Don't touch them until I pour."

Both kids froze like she'd hit them with a spell.

Cat filled each mug carefully, then handed them over one at a time. "Okay. You get six mini-marshmallows each. *Six*," she repeated, narrowing her eyes at them like she expected negotiations. But there were none. She filled another mug and handed it to me. "You can have six too."

"I'm good," I said with a chuckle.

"Quinn's still coming to my birthday dinner, right?" Grace asked.

"Grace," Cat warned gently, "you already asked Quinn that twice."

"And she said yes twice," I added. "Pretty sure she meant it."

Grace beamed and took an enormous gulp of cocoa, immediately hissing through her teeth when it was too hot. Charlie chuckled, because that's what brothers do.

Cat grabbed two pie containers from the fridge and set them on the counter.

"We have apple and pumpkin," she said.

I leaned my elbows on the island. "Pumpkin for me."

"Same!" Grace declared immediately.

Charlie considered the options like he was signing a binding contract. "Apple. With extra whipped cream."

Cat shot him a look. "So, the normal amount."

I snorted as she plated the slices and slid them to the kids. Grace didn't even wait—she dug her fork straight in, marshmallows still half-melted on her upper lip. Charlie followed, humming happily like apple pie was a spiritual experience.

For a few minutes the kitchen went quiet except for forks scraping crust and little contented sounds.

When everyone finished, Cat wiped her hands on a towel and nodded toward the living room. "Alright, troops, let's go see if the tree is ready." She looked at me. "Would you go grab the ornaments and lights from the garage?"

Grace got off her stool so fast, she slipped when her socks hit the floor. But she caught herself and kept going. Charlie followed, both of them barreling into the living room like the tree might wander off if they took too long.

I headed out while they went into the living room. A few minutes later, I returned with the plastic storage tubs. As soon as I set them down, the kids got on the floor and popped the lids off with more enthusiasm than coordination. Charlie pulled out a spool of lights—thank God they were neatly wound—and Grace dove in after him, dragging out another one.

"Can I do the lights?" Charlie asked.

"Uncle Benny's going to do the lights," Cat said, nodding in my direction. "He's tall enough to reach the top without us dragging out a ladder."

Grace stopped mid-reach into the bin and looked up at me, sizing me up. "You're really tall."

"It's one of my better qualities," I said, taking the spool from Charlie.

"I'm going to put on some music," Cat said.

Grace perked up. "Can we do Mariah?"

"No," Cat and I said at the same time.

Grace groaned. "You guys never let me have fun."

Cat rolled her eyes but was smiling as she scrolled through her phone. A moment later, Johnny Mathis' rich, honeyed voice filled the house with "It's Beginning to Look a Lot Like Christmas."

I got to work, circling the tree and weaving the lights through the branches as I went along. The three of them directed the placement from the floor, each with their own opinion on how loopy or tight the strands should be. I mostly ignored them and kept going.

When I finally stepped back, Cat folded her arms and pretended to judge. "Looks good. Uneven in a charming way."

"It's called organic placement," I said.

"It's called good enough," she corrected. "Go ahead, Grace."

Grace plugged them in, and the tree lit up—warm, soft, and perfect.

"Time for ornaments!" Charlie shouted, reaching for the bin.

The next ten minutes were chaos in the best way.

Charlie hung every ornament at his eye level, creating a

dense cluster on one side. Grace favored the top, handing things to me to reach the branches she couldn't. Cat circulated behind them, quietly shifting ornaments to balance things without the kids noticing.

The tree was a total mish-mash of ornaments—kid-made crafts with too much glitter, wonky clay shapes, and lopsided paper snowflakes—plus the occasional fancy glass ball that had probably been purchased before Grace and Charlie came along.

Nothing like my mom's curated, themed trees—always color-coordinated, magazine-perfect, and untouched by kids' fingerprints or crooked construction-paper crafts.

I found myself wondering what Quinn's trees looked like growing up—probably more like Cat's than my mom's. Full of mismatched memories.

"Looks good," I said.

"Looks chaotic," she corrected. "But in a good way."

"In the best way."

"Did you decorate your tree yet?" Grace asked me.

"I don't usually get a tree."

Grace gasped like I'd confessed to a crime. "You don't get a tree?"

I shrugged. "I usually come home for Christmas, so it didn't seem worth it."

Charlie stared at me like I'd announced I didn't believe in oxygen. "You *have* to have a tree."

"Do I?"

"Yes!" all three of them said at once.

It's honestly not something I've ever considered.

I held up my hands. "Alright, I'll think about it."

That seemed to satisfy them.

Cat dropped onto the couch with a tired sigh, and I joined her. The kids took over the floor, laying out the

Christmas village under the tree. Grace was insistent the skating rink needed to be in the center. Charlie disagreed.

"You seeing Quinn tonight?"

I shook my head. "No. She's going out with the Bergmann sisters. I might grab a drink with the guys."

"But you're seeing her tomorrow?"

"Yeah." I scratched my jaw. "Not sure what we're doing yet."

Cat gave me a long look. "Well...if you *did* get a tree, I'm pretty sure she'd have fun decorating it with you."

I paused. "You think so?"

"Duh."

I didn't bother arguing. Mostly because I wasn't entirely sure she was wrong.

Grace popped up from the floor when she noticed me standing, brushing glitter from her hands.

"Uncle Benny, did you see? We put the skating rink right in the middle."

Charlie, still crouched beside the Christmas village, let out a dramatic groan. "Because *she* said it *has* to go there."

"It *belongs* there," Grace insisted, like this was a matter of national importance.

I stretched out my back. "Alright, I'm gonna get out of your way while you settle that debate. I can see this is above my pay grade.

Cat pushed herself off the couch and walked me toward the door. "Thanks for helping out today," she said, pulling her cardigan tighter around her.

"Anytime," I told her, and I meant it. "Plus, I got pie and hot cocoa out of the deal. Hard to beat."

She smiled and opened the door. "Drive safe."

"I will."

I stepped out into the cold, the scent of pine still

clinging to my hands. My breath puffed white in the air as I crossed the short walkway, boots crunching over the thin layer of frost on the concrete. As I climbed into the Jeep, the seat was freezing, and the steering wheel colder, but the warmth from their house still sat somewhere in my chest as I shut the door.

I started the engine and eased down the driveway.

Halfway home, it hit me—I kind of wanted a tree. My own tree. In my own house.

So instead of heading home, I turned toward the store. Ornaments and lights first, and then back to the tree lot.

Because apparently this year, I was doing Christmas for real.

And if things went the way I hoped, I wouldn't be decorating it alone.

Chapter Thirty-Six

Quinn

Benny kept one hand on the wheel and the other on my knee the entire drive from the restaurant to his house—steady, warm, and casual in that way that absolutely did *not* feel casual at all. Every bump in the road sent a little spark up my thigh, and by the time he pulled into the garage, my brain was embarrassingly tuned to that touch.

He shifted into park, killed the engine, but didn't move his hand. Instead, he looked at me—soft, a little nervous, but also like he was trying not to smile.

"I've got something to show you."

A dozen thoughts flashed through my head, none of them rated PG.

I raised a brow. "You're going to have to narrow that down, because my imagination is running wild with 'I've got something to show you.'"

That earned me the full Benny grin—slow, a little crooked, the kind that made my stomach feel too warm.

"Not that," he said, giving my knee a squeeze that did *not* help settle my thoughts. "But...maybe later."

After raising my temperature at least a gazillion degrees, he removed his hand and got out of the Jeep. I watched him come around to my side to open the door, like he always did.

I put my hand in his, stepped out, and followed him into the house. Once inside the living room, he stopped, just for a second, like he was suddenly unsure.

"So. This is what I wanted to show you."

He stepped aside and revealed a whole, full-sized, completely undecorated Christmas tree.

"You got a tree?" I whispered.

He shoved his hands into his pockets like he suddenly had no idea what to do with them.

"Yeah, I thought maybe..." His eyes flicked toward mine. "You might want to help me decorate it."

And that simple nervous confession felt more intimate than anything else he could've shown me.

"Oh, Benny," I said, stepping closer. "I'd love to."

His shoulders actually dropped, like I'd just told him he passed a test he didn't realize he was taking. The surprise of it tugged at something deep in my chest. Did he really think I'd say no?

"Okay. Great."

He grabbed two shopping bags off the floor and set them on the coffee table. "Full disclosure...I panic-shopped."

I peeked inside and found lights still in plastic, ornament boxes taped shut, and at least three color schemes fighting for dominance.

"Benny," I said, trying not to laugh, "you bought every possible option."

He grimaced. "I didn't know what the rules were."

"Haven't you ever decorated a tree before?" I asked, half-teasing.

He rubbed the back of his neck. "Not in my own house."

That answer was simple, honest, and so very him. I squeezed his arm gently, then turned back to the boxes.

"Alright," I said, turning back to the boxes. I dug through the bags and picked up two sets of lights, one white, one multicolored. "Which do you like better?"

He didn't even look at the boxes. His eyes went straight to me.

"Which do *you* like?"

I huffed out a little laugh. "Benny, it's your tree, not mine."

"Yeah," he said, voice low and simple in a way that hit deeper than it should have. "But I'm hoping you spend a lot of time here looking at it with me."

"Have you always been this sweet?" I asked with a flirty smile.

Instead of answering right away, he crossed the room in three easy steps, slid his hands around my waist, and pulled me against him.

"Definitely not," he said quietly, eyes locked on mine. "Guess you bring it out in me."

And then he kissed me—slow at first, then deeper, his tongue sliding against mine in a way that scrambled every coherent thought I had. By the time he pulled back, my brain had to reboot.

I cleared my throat. "Okay. Um. I prefer white lights. And I don't like them blinking."

His mouth kicked up in that crooked almost-grin that always did me in. "White it is."

"See? You're a natural," I said.

"Pretty sure I'm just following your lead." He handed me the box, then took the spool of lights for himself. "I'll handle the lights," he said, as if there was ever a universe where he wouldn't be the one doing the reaching and looping.

I stepped back to give him room, watching as he reached up easily and started weaving the strands through the branches—careful, methodical, tongue pressed to the inside of his cheek in concentration. There was something grounding about this big, steady man doing something so ordinary because he wanted to share it with me. It tugged at a place no one has reached in a long time. If ever.

When the lights were done, he gave me a hopeful look. "Good?"

"Perfect," I said. And it was.

Ornaments came next—simple ones, nothing fancy. We moved around the tree, our hands brushing as we reached for the same branches.

At one point he moved past me to hang a wooden star, his chest grazing my shoulder. I felt it everywhere.

I could tell he noticed by the way he froze for half a second, then stayed close.

"Tree is looking good," he murmured.

"Yeah, it is."

I reached past him to adjust a pinecone ornament, trailing my fingers against his stomach, and he sucked in a sharp breath. I froze, keeping them in place. Slowly, he covered my hand with his.

"Quinn." His voice dropped lower. "Keep touching me like that and we're not finishing this tree."

"Maybe I don't care about the tree right now."

His eyes dropped to my mouth, then back up.

"Good. Neither do I."

Benny skimmed his hands along my waist and, with the gentlest pressure, guided me backward. One step. Then another. Until my back met the wall beside the tree and there was nowhere to go except closer.

Bracing one hand beside my head, he claimed the space between us in a way that lit up every nerve I had. I curled my fingers into the front of his sweater to steady myself.

"You okay?" he asked, his forehead resting against mine for a beat.

"Yes," I breathed against his mouth.

He dipped his head and kissed me, like he'd been holding himself back and finally decided not to anymore. Then his hands were on my ass—big and warm and certain.

I tugged him closer, dragging my fingers into his hair, and he let out a breath that shuddered right through both of us. He kissed me again, slower this time, as he shifted his hands lower and effortlessly lifted me.

"I got you," he said as he dragged his mouth across my jaw, to my neck. "Bedroom?" he asked, his voice a rough whisper against my skin.

I nodded, because using words felt like advanced calculus at this point.

"Say it," he murmured.

"Bedroom," I whispered.

He slid his hands under my thighs and pulled me away from the wall. My legs tightened around his waist automatically, and he carried me down the hall with that steady, unshakable confidence that always stole my breath.

The second he set me on the bed, he was right there with me, his mouth on mine like he'd been exercising restraint and was done with it.

His hands slid under my sweater, those calloused palms dragging over bare skin—stomach, ribs, the underside of my bra. He pushed the sweater higher and I lifted my arms, letting him strip it off. He tossed it aside and lowered his mouth to my collarbone, kissing a slow, torturous path across my chest that made my whole body tighten. His hands found my back, unclasping my bra with an ease that should've been illegal. He pushed the straps down my arms, slow and sure, and the second my breasts were bare, his gaze dropped—hungry, awed, almost reverent.

"Quinn..." His voice scraped low, like he'd been punched in the lungs. His thumb brushed the side of my breast, gentle but possessive. "You wreck me."

"Good," I whispered.

Before he could pull himself together, I slid my hands to his shoulders and pushed—just enough to roll him over. He let me, falling onto the mattress with a low chuckle that did things to me.

"Oh," he murmured, eyes darkening as I straddled his hips. "We're doing this."

"Mm-hmm." I slipped my bra completely off, and tossed it behind me. "I have plans."

I leaned forward long enough to grab the hem of his sweater. "This needs to go."

"Yeah," he said, sitting up as I peeled it off him.

The second it was gone, his arms wrapped around my waist, pulling me flush against him. My breasts brushed his warm chest, and the jolt of it punched a tiny gasp right out of me. Before I could recover, his mouth found mine—deep, hungry, unhurried—and I kissed him back, letting myself sink into it for a moment.

Then I pulled back, pressing my palms against his chest to push him back down onto the mattress.

"Don't distract me," I said.

His rough laugh vibrated under my palms. "Wouldn't dream of it."

Scooting back along his thighs, I popped the button of

his jeans, slow and purposeful. The zipper followed, a low metal rasp in the quiet room that made his jaw clench. I tugged the denim open far enough to free his straining cock.

I glanced up at him through my lashes as I wrapped my hand around it and slowly stroked.

"You doing okay?"

He dragged a hand over his face like he was trying to hold onto his sanity.

"I'm fantastic," he rasped.

"Good," I murmured, giving him one slow stroke from base to tip. "And you're about to be even better."

His breath hitched, and that alone made heat curl through my stomach.

I shifted off his hips and worked his jeans and boxer briefs down. He lifted his hips to help, jaw tight, , those steel-blue eyes gone dark and hungry, following every move I made like he was already half gone.

Resting my knee on the bed between his thighs, I wrapped my hand around him again and stroked once—slow, deliberate—just to watch the way his abs tightened in response. Then I leaned in and dragged my tongue from the base of him to the tip, tasting the heat of his skin, feeling the way his breath stuttered above me.

I did it again, slower this time, circling the tip with my tongue before closing my lips around him and taking him into my mouth. His groan hit me like a pulse, low and rough, vibrating straight through my body.

Hollowing my cheeks, I took him deeper, one hand braced on his thigh, the other stroking the part of him my mouth couldn't reach. I set a rhythm—lazy, unhurried, and meant to undo him piece by piece. Every time he exhaled, his stomach tightened, and every time my tongue swept along the underside of him, his hips twitched like he couldn't help it.

"Fuck..." His voice was a raw scrape of sound.

His hands slid into my hair—not guiding me, just holding on.

I bobbed my head, steady and controlled, letting my lips slide down the thick length of him before pulling back just enough to swirl my tongue again, loving every ragged breath pouring out of him.

His fingers tightened against my scalp, tugging just enough to get my attention.

"Baby...stop."

I let him slip from my mouth with a soft, wet pop and looked up at him. One hand was still tangled in my hair like he hadn't quite convinced himself to let go. His chest rose and fell in quick, uneven pulls. God, I loved that I did that to him.

When he reached for me, I went—crawling up his body, swinging a leg over his hips, and settling onto him like it was the only place I wanted to be. My hands braced on his chest as his slid up my thighs, gripping, guiding, worshipping. His eyes tracked every inch of me like he was memorizing it.

I rose up onto my knees, lining us up, and Benny's hands tightened as I sank down onto him in one slow, claiming glide.

His head slammed back against the pillow with a broken sound that made my whole body tighten around him.

I rolled my hips slowly, getting used to the stretch, the delicious fullness of him. His gaze locked on mine—dark, hungry, undone—and that alone sent a shiver through me.

"Tell me what you need," he rasped.

"You," I breathed, lifting and sinking again, finding the rhythm that made both of us gasp. "Just...you."

Every roll of my hips dragged a deeper sound from his chest, every downward slide made his jaw clench like he was fighting for air.

"Quinn..." His voice cracked. "You feel—you feel so damn good."

I rode him slow, then faster, chasing that sharp edge building low in my stomach. Benny met me thrust for thrust, eyes locked on mine like he couldn't look anywhere else if he tried.

"You gonna come for me?" he asked, voice rough, breath ragged.

"God, yes," I groaned and rolled my hips in a slow circle that made both of us gasp. His hands tightened on my thighs, and I kept moving, finding the rhythm that made his breath catch and mine come faster.

And then I hit *that* spot.

A bright, sharp bolt of pleasure shot up my spine, and my hips moved on instinct—faster, harder, chasing that perfect friction. Benny's hands slid up to my waist, fingers digging in like he needed the anchor while I rode him, deliberate at first, then losing the thread of control as heat unfurled low and fast inside me.

"Quinn..." he rasped, voice breaking apart. "Fuck—you feel—"

I kept grinding down, hitting that spot over and over until my vision blurred and my breath stuttered.

"Come on, baby...give it to me."

He slid his thumb between us and pressed against my clit. The sensation zinged straight to my nipples, making everything in me tighten and coil, heat winding low and fast.

"Benny—"

My voice cracked.

And then I shattered.

My climax tore through me in a blinding, consuming rush, every muscle tightening around him. Benny groaned—deep, raw, helpless—as my body clenched around his.

"Quinn—" he choked out, thrusting up into me once, twice, before he followed, his whole body tensing beneath mine as he came hard, buried deep inside me, breath ragged against my throat.

I collapsed onto his chest while aftershocks trembled through me. For a long moment, neither of us moved. We just breathed—messy, uneven, wrapped up in each other.

Finally, Benny lifted a hand to my cheek. "Hey," he murmured, still breathless, still wrecked in the most beautiful way. "You okay?"

"Better than okay," I whispered.

He kissed me once, then eased out of me and slipped off the bed, disappearing into the bathroom. I tugged the blankets down, slipped beneath them, and let my body melt into the pillows. My pulse was still thudding through my fingertips when he came back.

Without a word, Benny slid into bed behind me and pulled me back against his chest. His arm slipped around my waist, holding me like we'd been doing this for years.

He pressed a soft kiss to the back of my head.

Then another to my shoulder before he pulled me closer, like he couldn't get enough contact.

After a beat, his voice came low and rough against my skin.

"Quinn...this thing between us?" Another kiss to my shoulder. "It's getting serious."

My chest warmed in a way that had nothing to do with

sex. I reached down and threaded my fingers with his where they rested against my stomach.

"Yeah," I whispered. "Seems that way."

"I'm good with that. If you are."

"I'm more than good with it."

He exhaled and pressed one more kiss to the back of my head, lingering there.

"Okay," he murmured, settling against me fully. "Then we're doing this."

I smiled into the pillow, my whole body softening as his breathing evened out behind me.

Yeah. We were.

And for the first time in a long time, everything felt exactly, perfectly right.

Chapter Thirty-Seven

Benny

Quinn stepped outside just as I pulled up, the porch light catching the soft waves in her hair, a small gift bag dangling from one hand. And —*Christ*. The little black dress hugged every curve it touched and skimmed the rest, which was somehow worse. Or better. I'd lost track of which was which. Black patent Louboutins added four inches to her height and reduced my vocabulary to about three words.

I was out of the Jeep before she reached the bottom step.

"You're trying to kill me," I said.

She smiled like she knew exactly what she was doing. "It's a birthday dinner. I dressed up."

Understatement of the century.

I tugged her close and kissed her, lingering just long enough to feel her melt—that soft exhale against my mouth before she pulled back with a smile. It took me longer than it should've to step back and open the passenger door.

The drive to The Copper House didn't take long, but with Quinn's perfume drifting over the console and her thumb brushing absently over my knuckles, it felt like its own warm, private world.

A hostess led us to a round table tucked in the back corner—far enough from the crowd to keep my parents from defaulting to whisper-sharp commentary about people's outfits or table manners.

Grace spotted Quinn's shoes before we even made it to the table. "Quinn! Your shoes are so pretty!" She wrapped her arms around Quinn's waist, then immediately stepped back to show off her own twirly blue dress, spinning twice for good measure. "I can't wait until I can wear heels like that."

"Beautiful," Quinn said, gesturing to the spinning skirt, and Grace beamed.

After a round of hugs and hellos, we settled in.

Charlie, dressed in khakis and a blue button-down that coincidentally matched Grace's dress, gave Quinn a shy wave. Thankfully, he grew out of the sticky-hands-and-run-around-the-restaurant phase years ago.

The server came by for drink orders. Quinn ordered a glass of wine, and I went with a beer. Grace and Charlie ordered Shirley Temples with extra cherries. We also had her put in some appetizers for the table.

Once she left, conversation drifted easily. My mom asked Quinn polite questions about her family. My dad launched into a story about his recent golf trip to Hilton Head, complete with stroke-by-stroke commentary on "the best round he'd played all year," which made Charlie's eyes glaze over until Quinn leaned close and whispered something that made him chuckle.

The appetizers arrived—fried mozzarella sticks, spinach artichoke dip, and calamari. Grace and Charlie dove for the mozzarella while the adults passed the other plates around.

"You mentioned making Welsh cookies together," Cat said to Quinn. "Is that offer still open?"

"Absolutely," Quinn said.

"I get to help, right?" Grace asked.

Cat glanced at Quinn. "Fair warning—she'll want to take over the entire operation."

"I'm very good at measuring and cracking eggs," Grace said seriously.

Quinn laughed. "Then you're hired. When works for you, Cat?"

"Sunday?"

"Perfect."

Conversation circled the table in comfortable loops as we waited for dinner, with everyone talking over each other just enough to feel lively but not chaotic. Quinn fell into the rhythm like she'd been part of it for years. She listened when people spoke. She asked the right questions. She laughed at the dry comments my dad thought no on ever caught. Even my mom—who rarely warmed to anyone quickly—seemed to soften in her direction.

Grace kept sliding little glances at Quinn—not the starstruck looks from Thanksgiving, but something quieter. She was watching her the way kids watch people they're starting to trust, curious and comfortable, like Quinn was becoming real to her in a way that had nothing to do with music.

The entrées arrived—steaks for most of us, pasta for Cat, mac and cheese for Charlie, and an impressive lobster for Grace. She attacked it like it might escape, and Quinn leaned over once to show her the trick with the claw. Grace beamed like she'd just learned a cheat code.

Every so often, Quinn glanced at me. Just a small smile,

private and warm, but enough to knock me sideways each time.

The server cleared our plates and reappeared with a chocolate layer cake covered in sprinkles and one glowing candle on top. Grace gasped, hands clasping under her chin like she hadn't known this was coming, even though we did this every year.

Half the wait staff joined us in singing "Happy Birthday"—enthusiastic and only slightly off-key. Grace leaned forward and blew out the candles in a single, dramatic puff.

The server cut slices and handed them out, starting with the birthday girl. Grace immediately scooped the frosting off the top with her fork and made a sound like she'd just tasted the best thing ever created. But she only managed a few more bites before her eyes drifted to the small pile of gifts beside Cat's chair.

"Alright, birthday girl, you can open your presents," Cat said, smiling. "Let's start with this one."

She handed over the package from my parents.

Grace peeled back the tissue paper and lifted a small jewelry box.

"Oh!" She flipped it open, and her eyes went wide.

Nestled inside was a delicate silver necklace with her birthstone cut in a teardrop shape.

My mom reached over and lifted the delicate chain from the box, the small blue stone catching the light.

"It's your birthstone," she said. "Blue topaz."

"Thank you."

Grace pushed back from the table and wrapped them both in a hug—my dad first, then my mom, who softened in a way she rarely did.

"Turn around. I'll put it on for you," my mom said.

Grace nodded and turned around, lifting her hair. My

mom fastened the clasp with careful fingers, adjusting the pendant so it sat just right. When Grace turned back around, she touched the stone lightly, like she was making sure it was real.

"It's perfect," Quinn said, leaning in to admire it.

Grace beamed, and for a second she looked less like a kid at a birthday party and more like someone who'd just been given something she'd keep forever.

When she settled back into her seat, Cat handed her my gift.

Grace tugged out a small box wrapped in navy paper. She opened it slowly, like she already suspected something big was inside.

The moment she saw the card on top—*The Radio City Christmas Spectacular*—her whole face lit up.

"Wait—" Her head snapped toward me. "We're going to New York?"

"Yep," I said, grinning.

"There's more," Cat said with a smile. "Tell her the rest."

"We're staying overnight," I said. "We'll catch the show, see the tree, explore the city—the works."

Grace's mouth dropped open. "Overnight? Just us?"

"Just us."

Grace was out of her chair and around the table before I could blink, throwing her arms around my neck hard enough that I had to brace myself against the table.

"Thank you, thank you, thank you," she said into my shoulder, and I caught Quinn's eye over Grace's head. She was smiling—soft and warm and something else I couldn't quite name.

Once Grace released me and dropped back into her

seat, Cat slid the last gift bag across the table. "This one's from Quinn."

Grace reached for the white tissue paper, pulled out the first item, and blinked at it.

"It's...my hat."

"No, sweetheart," Quinn said gently. "It's mine. It's been with me a long time. Now it's yours."

She clutched the hat to her chest, her voice going quiet. "Wait—this is *your* hat? Like, the one you wore on tour?"

"That's the one," she said. "I wore it to close every show on The Last Verse Tour." Quinn touched the brim lightly, like she was saying goodbye.

Grace's chin wobbled, and she pressed her lips together hard as she stared at the hat.

Cat's eyes flicked to me, one brow lifted like, *Did you know about this?*

I lifted a shoulder—nope, I was just as surprised as she was.

Grace turned to Quinn and wrapped her arms around her—gentler than the hug she'd given me, more careful, like Quinn was something precious. "Thank you," she whispered, her voice thick.

Quinn's hand came up to rest on Grace's back. "You're welcome." When Grace finally pulled back and wiped at her eyes, Quinn nodded toward the gift bag with a small smile. "There's one more thing in there."

She reached into the bag again and pulled out a leather-bound notebook—light pink, with tiny silver stars and her name stamped on the front—and a fat pack of colored gel pens.

Grace looked around the table, clutching the notebook to her chest. "Thank you. I love all my presents."

"Best birthday yet?" Cat asked, smiling.

Grace nodded, adjusting the hat on her head. "Best birthday ever."

Eventually, dessert plates were cleared, the check was paid, and the familiar post-birthday-dinner lull settled over the table. My parents bundled up, Cat wrangled Charlie into his coat, and Grace—now wearing the hat at a slightly crooked angle—hugged Quinn one more time, still clutching the notebook and pens.

We walked out into the cold December night, breath misting in the air. Grace was chattering about New York— what we should see first, whether wed have time for the M&M store, if I knew the Rockettes did that famous kick line—and Cat was doing her best to corral the excitement into something resembling a reasonable bedtime.

My parents said their goodbyes, my mom pulling Quinn into a brief, slightly stiff hug after kissing me on the cheek. Grace hugged Quinn twice more before Cat finally managed to steer her toward their car.

"We'll see you Sunday," Cat said to Quinn.

"I'm looking forward to it."

"We'll do something fun while the ladies bake," I told Charlie.

"Awesome!" he said, then climbed into the SUV.

Then it was just the two of us, walking back to the Jeep under the glow of streetlights.

Quinn was quiet as I pulled out of the parking lot, her hand finding mine on the console like it always did.

"That was really generous," I said after a minute. "Giving Grace your hat."

"She's a good kid. I wanted her to have something special."

I squeezed her hand.

"And that notebook's going to be her most prized posses-sion, right after the hat."

"I love that you're taking her to the Radio City show," she said.

"Yeah. I do experiences instead of gifts for their birth-days. They don't need more stuff, and when I didn't live here, it was one way to make sure we actually spent time together. Grace has wanted to go for a couple years. Cat thinks she's finally old enough to really take it in."

"That's really thoughtful," Quinn said. "Those are the things they'll remember."

"It used to be a lot cheaper," I said, grinning. "We'd take a trip to the zoo or the movies. Now Grace wants Broadway shows, and I'm sure soon enough Charlie will be asking for something that costs real money too."

Quinn laughed, the sound warm in the quiet cab of the Jeep. "Sounds like you're in trouble as they get older."

"Worth it, though."

She turned to look at me, her expression soft in the dashboard light. "You're really good with them. With your whole family, actually. Tonight was..." She trailed off, like she was trying to find the right word.

"A lot?" I offered.

"It was perfect," she said.

I brought her hand to my lips, kissed her knuckles, and kept driving. The city lights blurred past, the radio playing something low and easy, and for the first time in a long time, everything felt exactly right.

Chapter Thirty-Eight

Quinn

The knock came as I was checking the butter. Perfect. I wiped my hands on a dish towel and opened the door.

Cat, Grace, Charlie, and Benny were on my front porch bundled against the cold, breath puffing into the December air.

Grace stood front and center, wearing the sequin hat I gave her like it was a crown. The sparkles caught the porch light, and honestly, the hat had never looked better.

"Mom said I can wear it here," she declared without preamble, "but not out anywhere else because I might lose it. But if I lose it here, it's okay because you'll find it."

"That makes sense. Now come on in before you all freeze."

I stepped aside so they could spill into the warmth of the house, shaking off the cold as they came inside.

Benny leaned in and pressed a kiss to my cheek as he passed—quick, casual, but the kind of connection that meant something. "Hey," he murmured.

"Hi," I said softly.

Grace took off her coat and looked around like she was absorbing every detail, her sequin hat bobbing as she craned her neck to take in the entryway, the living room, and the big framed photo over the mantle.

"Your house is so cozy," Cat said.

"Thank you," I said. "I renovated most of the downstairs and my bedroom when I first moved back. I actually stayed with my mom during all of it so I didn't have to live through the construction mess."

Cat winced in sympathy. "Smart. I lived through a kitchen reno once. Worst decision of my life."

"Exactly," I said.

Charlie had already wandered a little farther in, peeking at the books on my shelf and the framed photo of me and my parents from a holiday long before the world knew my name.

Grace, meanwhile, was doing a slow, delighted spin in the living room. "It smells pretty," she declared. "Like cookies and warm."

"Warm is an excellent design aesthetic," I said. "Come on—I'll give you a quick tour before we ruin the kitchen."

I led them through the living and dining rooms, then the bathroom I'd had gutted and rebuilt last spring. Cat paused in the doorway of the laundry room.

"Okay, I'm jealous," she said. "This is nicer than my actual bedroom."

"That's because I wasn't living here during the demo," I said. "Otherwise I would've abandoned the whole project halfway through."

We continued down the hall.

"And this," I said, "is my—"

Grace darted forward, then stopped dead and gasped so loudly I swear the air rippled.

"IS THAT *LADY MILLICENT VON HARMONSHIRE?*"

Benny came skidding around the corner like he thought someone had broken a limb. "What happened? What's wrong?"

"She just saw Millie," Cat said.

"Who's Millie?"

Grace turned to him, still reverent but with a look that suggested he'd just asked who Cinderella was. "Lady Millicent Von Harmonshire. Quinn's first guitar." She crossed my office like she was walking into a sacred temple, eyes huge as they locked on Millie, gleaming on her stand in the corner. "I can't believe she's just sitting here in your house."

"Where else would she be?" I asked, smiling.

"I thought she'd be in a museum," she breathed. "Or some kind of locked case. Or—Mom, what's it called when fancy things are behind glass at the mall?"

"A display," Cat said, fighting a smile.

"Yes, *a display.*"

Behind me, Benny whispered, "What did she call the guitar?"

"Lady Millicent von Harmonshire."

He blinked like I'd just given him the coordinates to Atlantis. "Of course."

Grace pressed both hands to her sequin hat to keep it from falling forward. "She's perfect," she said reverently.

The look on her face was better than any award on the wall.

"Would you like to hold her?"

Grace's eyes went even wider. "Really?"

"Of course." I gestured to the chair. "Have a seat."

Grace sat down carefully like sudden movements might make the offer disappear. I lifted Millie from her stand and settled her gently into Grace's lap, adjusting the angle so the weight rested comfortably.

"There," I said. "Just like that."

Grace's hands hovered for a second, like she was afraid to actually touch. Then she placed one palm flat against the body, fingers spread wide, and exhaled slowly. She strummed once, very softly. She looked up at me with something close to wonder.

"Thank you," she said, voice thick.

From the doorway, I caught Benny watching, his expression soft. Cat had her phone out, snapping a picture before Grace noticed.

"Alright," Benny said gently, eyes flicking to me first. "I think Charlie and I should hit the road if we're gonna make the movie."

His voice broke the spell in the lightest way possible—not harsh, just enough to bring us all back into motion.

Cat slipped her phone into her pocket. "We should probably start baking anyway."

I took Millie from Grace, cradling the familiar weight as I crossed the room to place her back on her stand.

We filed out of the office together, the magic of the moment easing into the normal sounds of the house. In the living room, Charlie was curled into the corner of my couch, completely absorbed in a bright blue Nintendo Switch Lite. The screen cast soft flashes of color across his face as his thumbs tapped steadily.

"Let's go buddy." Benny ruffled Charlie's hair lightly. "If we leave now, we'll make the previews."

Charlie paused the game and slipped the Switch into its zippered case before hopping off the couch.

After giving him a hug, Cat said, "Have fun, and be good for Uncle Benny, okay?"

"I will," Charlie said, already buzzing with excitement.

Benny held the door open for him, then leaned in and pressed a quick kiss to my lips. "See you in a couple hours," he murmured.

"I'll be here," I said.

Then he and Charlie headed out, the door clicking shut behind them, leaving the house suddenly quieter—still warm, but now humming with anticipation.

I smiled "Okay. Now we bake."

Cat laughed. "We're ready to follow your commands."

The island was already lined with bowls, measuring cups, and ingredients. Grace looked at the setup like it was Disney World.

"Do we want to use aprons, or live dangerously?"

Grace held out her arms instantly. "Apron!"

Cat chuckled. "Apron for me too. I've seen what she can do with a bowl of flour."

"Aprons it is," I said, heading to the pantry and pulling three off their hooks—one green with candy canes, another solid red, and my own well-worn navy one that had battle scars from years of baking projects. I handed the festive one to Grace and the red to Cat. "Fair warning," I said. "I'm a messy baker."

Cat tied Grace's apron strings, then her own. "Messy how?"

"Messy as in I'll probably need to wipe down every surface in here by the time we're done." I grinned. "But the results are usually worth the cleanup."

Grace beamed like that was a promise straight from the universe. "Let's start!"

She climbed onto the step stool like she owned the place, her apron slightly crooked but her confidence perfectly straight.

When I reached for the flour container, I automatically grabbed the old chipped coffee mug I always used.

Cat blinked. "Is that your measuring cup?"

"Technically," I said. "It's my grandmother's. This is how she measured everything. So it's what I use for all her recipes."

Grace giggled like I'd told the greatest secret in the universe as she filled the mug with flour.

I transferred each mugful into a real measuring cup, and Cat wrote down the amounts like she was deciphering a code. "One mug equals...okay, wow, that's a smidge over a cup and a half."

We did the same for the sugar before I handed Grace the eggs.

She cracked them into a small bowl—firm tap, clean break, no shells. Over Grace's shoulder, Cat gave me a look that was half pride, half amusement.

"Looks like you've done this before," I said.

"Mom taught me," Grace said with a shrug. "I'm really good at the egg part."

The stand mixer brought the dough together for the first batch of traditional currant cookies. Grace stirred in the currants herself, folding them through the dough with neat, deliberate strokes.

"This is what you're looking for," I told her, pressing a fingertip into the dough. "Soft, not sticky."

They both nodded solemnly, absorbing every detail.

Then we made the second batch—same process,

different mix-in. Grace dumped the mini chocolate chips in with zero hesitation and twice the enthusiasm.

"Okay," I said, wrapping the dough in plastic wrap. "Both batches go in the fridge for a little rest."

"For how long?" Grace asked, hopping off the stool to open the refrigerator door.

"Fifteen to thirty minutes," I said. "Just enough time to make them easier to roll out."

Cat glanced around the kitchen. "Which is also enough time to clean this disaster zone."

"I like to call it 'creative ambiance,'" I said, flicking a little flour off the counter.

Grace leaned toward me, lowering her voice to a stage whisper. "Can I go look at Millie again?"

Cat opened her mouth—probably to say no—but I beat her to it.

"Of course," I said. "Just don't touch her or anything in there, okay?"

Grace nodded solemnly, like she'd just been given the nuclear codes, and scampered down the hall, her sequin hat bobbing with every step.

Cat watched her disappear, shaking her head with a soft, affectionate exhale. "She adores you," she said quietly. "Thank you for being so good with her and Charlie."

"They're easy to be good with," I said, gathering up the used measuring cups and placing them in the dishwasher. "And Benny's great with them. They light up around him."

"He is. I don't know what I'd do without him." She paused, her voice still soft, still just a sister speaking truth. "They're lucky to have him."

I hesitated, not wanting to overstep but curious, and maybe a little protective of the two kids I've quickly fallen in love with. "Can I ask you something? And tell me to mind my business if it's too personal."

"Of course," Cat said as she wiped down the counter.

"Where's their dad?"

Cat didn't tense or turn defensive, she just huffed a small breath that sounded almost like a laugh. "It's not too personal. And honestly? It's not a dramatic story. Just a very Manhattan one."

I waited, giving her room.

"After Charles and I got married, we moved to the city and were supposedly living the dream," she said, wiping another streak of flour off the counter. "He hit the ground running as what people now lovingly call a 'finance bro.' Long hours, big personality, suits that cost more than my car in college. And I got a job at a really good firm. We were both climbing."

"That sounds like a whirlwind," I said softly.

"It was...a lot," she agreed. "We were making great money, had this gorgeous apartment in Battery Park City with floor-to-ceiling windows and a view that made you forget rent was practically the GDP of a small country." She smiled at the memory, then softened. "It worked for a while. The city. The grind. Us."

She leaned her hip against the counter.

"But when we had the kids, everything changed. Or things about him that were manageable before suddenly weren't. He loved the *idea* of a family. But the reality?" She shrugged gently. "He wasn't built for the everyday parts. Started staying out later and later. Then not coming home at all." She paused. "I knew he was cheating, so I asked him to move out."

A quiet ache threaded through her tone, but it wasn't bitterness, just resolution.

"The divorce took forever—lawyers, paperwork, all of it. I stayed in the city for about a year after everything was final, thinking maybe he'd show up for the kids once the dust settled." She shook her head slightly. "But he didn't. So I moved us back to Waypoint. We're close to my parents, the cost of living is lower, and now they have Benny."

"That must have been so hard. Starting over like that."

"It was," Cat admitted. "But it was the right call. And now—" She gestured vaguely to the window, toward Waypoint in general. "Now we're where we're supposed to be."

"I get that," I said softly. "Coming home felt like that for me too."

Cat's smile softened, shifting into something more thoughtful. "You know...Benny's always been good to me. And the kids. I've seen that warm, easy side of him my whole life, but no one else really has."

"No?" I asked softly.

She shook her head and continued.

"He's always tried to be whatever people needed him to be," she went on. "The easygoing star athlete. The guy who's got it all handled. But with you?" She shook her head gently, almost fondly. "He doesn't look like he's performing anymore. He just looks happy."

Something eased and tightened at the same time, a soft pull in my chest. I hadn't known I was being let into a part of him he rarely shared.

"I thought that was just what he was like once you got past the surface," I said. "I didn't realize I was seeing something different."

"Well, you are." Cat's expression softened. "And for what it's worth? I'm really happy he found you."

Before I had to decide how to respond—to deflect, or to

admit what that stirred in me—the timer beeped, cutting through the moment.

Cat pushed off the counter, giving me a small, knowing smile that didn't demand anything more. "Dough's ready," she said. "Let's get these cookies rolled out before Grace comes back and starts swinging the rolling pin like Thor's hammer."

Chapter Thirty-Nine

Benny

The Maiden always looked different in December —same scarred tables, neon beer signs, and outdated jukebox—but the string lights and haphazard Christmas decorations gave everything a softer edge. And after two hours of pickup basketball with the guys at the old rec center, sitting here with a cold drink and sore shoulders felt damn near perfect.

Tommy sat across from me wearing a shit-eating grin. "So we're just not gonna talk about you getting your shot swatted into the bleachers?"

I took a long pull from my beer. "Ryan fouled me. He practically climbed my back."

Ryan lifted his hands, indignant. "I barely brushed you. You just lost your touch, old man."

Kevin snorted. "Please. You all lost your touch. That was the slowest pickup game I've ever played in."

"Speak for yourself," Tommy said. "I'm still in peak condition."

"You rolled your ankle walking into the gym," Ryan deadpanned.

Tommy flipped him off without missing a beat.

It felt good. Normal. Like I wasn't a visitor anymore—just one of the guys again.

The server dropped off another pitcher and took our food orders. Kevin topped off our glasses while Tommy reenacted—poorly—the moment Ryan tried to do a behind-the-back pass and sent the ball directly into the wall.

Ryan groaned. "Why are we friends with you again?"

"My charm," Tommy said. "And also because Benny used to bail your ass out of every stupid situation in high school, so now we're all bonded for life."

"'Bailed out' might be the wrong term. If anything, I barely managed to slow him down."

Tommy snorted. "Remember the Fourth of July bonfire incident?"

"Nope," I said immediately. "We're not revisiting that."

Which, of course, guaranteed that we were absolutely revisiting that.

Kevin leaned in, grinning. "He pulled you back before you somersaulted straight into the bonfire."

Ryan groaned. "I tripped."

"You were running *toward* the fire," Tommy said.

"I was running past it!"

"You were heading straight for it," I said. "Like it was a finish line."

They rolled right into a handful of other stories—things I hadn't thought about in years but came back like they'd happened yesterday.

It was easy.

Comfortable.

Like slipping into an old jersey—worn, familiar, and still fitting in all the ways that mattered.

The food arrived and we all shut up long enough to

destroy the burgers and half the fries. Then the conversation settled into low-key stuff—basketball, work, and other normal shit. Until Ryan's phone buzzed on the table for the tenth time in as many minutes.

Tommy nodded toward it. "Dude. Seriously. Who keeps texting you?"

Ryan ignored it. Or tried to. The phone buzzed again.

Kevin raised a brow. "What is that, Tinder blowing up? Secret girlfriend?"

Ryan shot him a look. "My wife would kill me for that joke alone." The phone buzzed again, and he flipped it face down. "It's not—just drop it."

Which obviously guaranteed none of us were dropping it.

"Come on," Tommy pressed. "If you're getting catfished, we deserve to know."

Ryan groaned, scrubbing a hand over his face. "I have a Google alert on Benny, okay?"

The whole booth went silent.

I blinked. "On *me?*"

He shrugged, embarrassed. "I set it up forever ago. Back when you first got drafted. It was the easiest way to keep track of what was going on with you. And now I don't know how to turn it off."

Something stupid and warm moved in my chest, but I kept my voice light. "That's...borderline creepy."

"Yeah, well," Ryan muttered, "the internet won't shut up about you today."

I straightened. "About what?"

Tommy already had his phone out. "Oh damn."

My stomach dropped as I pulled out mine.

Multiple photos, all of Quinn and me. The holiday market last weekend. Leaving The Copper House after

Grace's birthday dinner. Me holding the door for her at that coffee place on Main Street. Apparently people had been paying attention without us noticing.

Beneath them, dozens of comments speculating about everything from how long we'd been together to whether I'd convinced her to come out of retirement. Someone had started a thread analyzing our body language. Another claimed this explained why I'd turned down offers from other teams.

"He's totally in love with her."

"New power couple incoming."

"Omg look how he looks at her."

"If he breaks her heart, we riot."

Ryan winced. "Quinn's fans are...intense."

I stared at the comments. At strangers dissecting us like we were entertainment.

A familiar prickle crawled up the back of my neck—the same one I always got before a bad inning, when too many eyes were on me. Except this wasn't about baseball, and it sure as hell wasn't just about me.

But she wasn't just a pop star to me. She was Quinn. The woman who baked cookies with my niece and used color-coded notebooks in meetings and fit into my life like she'd always belonged there.

"You freaking out?" Kevin asked.

"No." I shook my head as the realization settled in, calm and sure.

"Man is zen," Tommy said. "If the internet was yelling about me, I'd change my name and move to Montana."

"It's just noise," I said. "People can talk. They can post. Quinn and I know what we are. We don't have to live small just because somebody takes a picture."

Ryan blinked. "That's...unexpectedly healthy of you."

I shrugged. "She deserves a life that isn't hidden. And I'm not interested in pretending I'm not crazy about her because someone might post about it."

"Never thought I'd see the day you went full romantic on us." Tommy raised his beer. "It looks good on you."

"Shut up."

But I didn't deny it.

Couldn't deny it.

Not when every damn part of my life felt better when she was in it.

Kevin angled his head, studying me. "So if this blows up bigger—like article big, sports outlets big—you're good?"

"More than good," I said. "I'm proud she's with me. Whoever has a problem with that can go pound sand."

Laughter erupted around the table.

"To Benny Reed, local celebrity boyfriend," Ryan said with a grin.

I groaned but clinked my glass against theirs anyway.

Because honestly? If that was the headline, I'm okay with it.

Chapter Forty

Quinn

By the time I topped off our wineglasses, the fire was blazing high enough to make the living room glow, the soft crackle mixing with the Christmas carols drifting from my speakers. The room smelled like cinnamon and vanilla courtesy of the candle Erin had given me for Friendsmas.

Erin and I were curled up on opposite ends of the couch, legs tangled in the middle under the same plush throw blanket. Somewhere during the second glass of wine, she had commandeered the throw pillow with the embroidered gingerbread men and declared it the emotional support pillow of Friendsmas.

It was perfect.

"Okay," Erin said, lifting her glass. "Friendsmas toast. To another year of not letting geography, obligations, or questionable boyfriends stop us from doing this. Although having you home for good and with someone who's actually drama-free may make this the best one yet."

I clinked my glass against hers. "Amen."

Friendsmas had started our junior year of high school—

one last sleepover before I flew to L.A. right after New Year's. We'd sworn we'd keep the tradition alive every December twenty-third no matter what. And we had. Some years it was over Zoom. A couple times she'd flown to wherever I was so we could make it happen.

"So," Erin said, curling her legs under her. "Tell me again what Benny said about the internet stuff. The part where you pretended to be chill but were actually spiraling internally."

I groaned and buried my face in my wineglass. "I wasn't spiraling."

Her eyebrows did the disbelieving arch—the one she'd perfected around age twelve. "Quinn. You spiraled so hard you texted me ten screenshots and a voice note I still can't translate."

"That was not spiraling," I said. "That was information sharing."

She snorted. "You sounded like a dial-up modem."

I shoved her foot with mine, but I couldn't stop the smile tugging at my mouth.

"He said he's fine with it. The photos. The posts. The comments dissecting our body language like we're a season finale." I pulled the blanket tighter around myself. "He said he doesn't want us to live small because someone might take a picture."

"Okay, so if he's fine with it, what's wrong?"

"He *said* that, but I also know it's...a lot. " I said. "I've done this before, and as you know, it doesn't always end well." My voice dipped. "The internet turns ugly fast."

"So you think he'll bail?" Erin asked gently.

I hesitated just long enough that we both heard the truth.

"It's not that I think he will," I said. "It's that I'm scared he could. Or that the pressure will change him. Or us."

Erin leaned forward. "Hey. Look at me."

I did.

"Don't judge him by the men who didn't deserve you," she said. "And don't punish him for a past he wasn't part of."

My throat tightened.

"I'm not trying to," I whispered.

"I know," she said. "But you're protecting yourself so hard you're missing the part where he's actually showing up."

I swallowed. "You think so?"

"I know so." Erin took a long drink of wine. "He's all in, Quinn. I saw him last week when he picked you up from my house. The man looked like he would've handed over a kidney if you asked him."

A laugh escaped me, half-choked and soft. "I don't want his kidney. I just want him."

"Then you're in luck, because he wants you right back."

For a moment, it was quiet—just the fire snapping and a soft instrumental version of "Have Yourself a Merry Little Christmas" drifting through the room. It wrapped around us like the kind of peace that only happens once a year, when everything feels a little gentler.

Erin stretched, grabbed her empty glass, then checked her phone. "Okay, Scott texted that he'll be here in five minutes."

"You sure you don't want to stay longer?" I asked, already knowing the answer.

"I would if we hadn't already polished off two bottles of wine." She stood, and I followed her into the kitchen. "I promised Liam I'd help him finish his gingerbread house in the morning. You know he'll be up at the crack of dawn for that. Besides, Benny will be here soon."

"Fair enough."

She pulled me into a tight hug. "Tonight was perfect."

"I know." My voice softened. "I love this tradition."

"Me too," she said. "Can we have it here again next year? It's so cozy, plus there aren't any kids."

"Deal."

She pulled her coat from the hook, buttoned it, and gave me a look—one I knew by heart. "Don't overthink it," she said. "Don't overthink him."

"I'll try."

"No," she said, then launched into a truly awful Yoda impression. "'Do or do not. There is no try.'" I couldn't help but laugh. She tapped my forehead. "Let yourself be happy."

"Okay."

Headlights washed across the front window.

"My chariot awaits." She hugged me once more, then headed out into the cold. "Text me tomorrow," she called as she climbed into the passenger seat. "I want to know what Benny got you."

"I will," I said, closing the door behind her.

I'd barely turned the lock when another set of headlights swept across my driveway.

Benny.

I lingered by the door, heart doing that soft, traitorous lift as his Jeep rolled to a stop. A moment later, I was opening the door again just as he was stepping onto the porch.

"Hi," he said, voice low in that way it got when it was just the two of us.

"Hi," I said.

He stepped inside, pulled the door shut behind him, and kissed me—quick and warm, like he'd been thinking about it the whole drive over. He had gift bags in one hand, the tissue paper crinkling softly as he set them on the entryway bench before shrugging out of his coat.

When he straightened, his gaze flicked to the two empty wine bottles standing side by side on the island like little soldiers.

A smirk tugged at his mouth.

"So...Friendsmas was productive," he said.

I nudged him with my hip on my way past. "It was festive. There's a difference."

"Mm-hmm." He grabbed the gift bags again and followed me toward the living room.

"Can I get you anything to drink?" I asked.

"No, I'm good for now," he said, setting the gift bags on the coffee table.

He lowered himself onto the couch, and I sat beside him, close enough that our shoulders brushed. His arm came up along the back of the couch, and I leaned in to settle against him.

"Tell me about Friendsmas," he said, his voice warm against my temple.

"It was good," I said. "It always is."

"You've been doing it since high school?" Benny asked, his thumb brushing lightly along my shoulder.

I nodded and filled him in on the tradition Erin and I started decades ago—how we kept it going whether we were in the same living room or on opposite coasts.

When I finished, I tipped my head back to look at him. "What about you? How was your day?"

He gave a small huff of a laugh. "Not nearly as fun as

yours. I cleaned out my gutters and finally installed the gutter guards I bought months ago."

I twisted a little so I could see him better. "Wait—you were outside on a ladder all afternoon? Were you freezing?"

He shrugged. "Nah. It wasn't that bad once I got moving."

"That sounds like a lie," I said, narrowing my eyes.

"Okay," he conceded, smiling. "It was cold. But not frostbite cold."

A slow smile tugged at my mouth. "Benny that's...sexy as hell."

His eyebrows lifted. "Cleaning gutters?"

"Competence is hot," I said. "And ladders help."

"Good to know."

I settled back against him, and his arm tightened, pulling me closer.

"Mmm, this is nice," I murmured.

His breath warmed my temple. "Yeah. It is."

We sat like that for a while—long enough that the fire settled into a low, steady burn. My eyes drifted shut without my permission, and I must've dozed off, because the sharp crack of a log collapsing made me jolt against him.

His hand slid up my arm, steadying. "Hey," he murmured. "You okay?"

"Yeah," I said, flushing a little. "I'm just really relaxed."

He laughed against my hair. "I can tell."

I tried to blink myself fully awake, but the warmth, the wine, and the fire all kept pulling me under.

"You can sleep on me, you know."

That warmth in my chest stretched wide. "I don't want to sleep."

A beat passed. "Then maybe we should open presents?"

He pressed a kiss against my forehead. "That should keep you awake."

I smiled and pushed myself upright, stretching as I stood. "Okay. Presents. Stay here—I'll grab yours from my office."

His eyes warmed. "I'm not going anywhere."

I gathered the stack and held them to my chest on my way back. When I reentered the living room, Benny was exactly how I left him, lounging on the couch, forearm draped across the backrest, watching me with that warm, focused attention that always made my breath hitch.

"That's a lot," he said, eyes flicking to the pile in my hands.

"Don't worry, it's not all extravagant," I said.

His smile went crooked. "I'll be the judge of that."

I set everything on the coffee table beside the bags he'd brought. "You first?"

He shook his head. "Nope. You're exhausted. You go first. Then you'll be awake long enough to laugh at my wrapping job."

He pushed one of the gift bags toward me. Tissue paper crinkled as I reached inside and lifted out a notebook.

My chest warmed. "You got me a notebook?"

"Turn it over," he said, his voice low and a little shy.

I flipped it in my hands, and my breath caught.

The cover was stamped with soft metallic musical notes, subtle enough to shimmer only when the light hit it. But at the center, clear and bold, were the words:

Some people write their life in journals,
I write mine in lyrics.
— Quinn Logan

I traced a thumb over the smooth cover. "I love it."

"There's more," he said, nodding at the bag.

Inside was a pack of gel pens—a special-edition set I didn't even know existed.

"Benny," I whispered. "These are gorgeous."

He shrugged like it wasn't a big deal, but the faint flush on his cheekbones told another story.

Another bag appeared in my lap, this one smaller. It held a blue velvet box.

My fingers trembled just a little as I lifted the lid.

Inside was a delicate white-gold chain with a pendant where a Q merged seamlessly with a musical note—minimal, elegant, unmistakably me.

"Oh," I whispered. It was all I could manage.

He cleared his throat, suddenly looking almost shy. "I, uh...wanted something that felt like you."

"I love it."

"Can I put it on you?" I nodded and turned, lifting my hair. His fingers were warm against my neck as he fastened the clasp. When I faced him again, his gaze dropped to the necklace, then back to my eyes. "Yeah," he murmured. "That's perfect."

I held the necklace out from my chest, looking down at it, smiling.

After a few seconds, Benny shifted beside me. "Last one," he said.

I took the bag from him then reached in and pulled out a white Lagerheads jersey, crisp and bright, the blue pinstripes running clean and straight down the front.

"Turn it over," Benny said.

I did.

REED

22

Air rushed out of me in a warm, shaky exhale. "Benny..."

"I know you can get your own, but I wanted you to have one from me." He rubbed the back of his neck, eyes dropping for a second before meeting mine again. "It would mean a lot if you wore it to a game," he added, softer now. "No one who mattered—not like you do—ever wore my jersey before."

Something deep and tender cracked open inside me.

"Of course I'll wear it," I whispered.

His smile was small but full and warm in a way that made my heart ache—like he hadn't just given me a piece of fabric, but a piece of himself.

I kissed him, slow and grateful, my fingers curling into the front of his shirt.

"Thank you," I murmured, pulling back just enough to meet his eyes. "Seriously."

He touched the necklace lightly at my throat. "I'm glad you like everything."

"Oh, I do." I nudged his knee with mine. "Now scoot over, baseball boy. It's your turn."

Chapter Forty-One

Benny

Quinn slid the largest of my gifts across the table toward me, cheeks still pink from our kiss. I pulled it closer and started unwrapping. When the last of the tissue paper fell away, I went still.

A quilt.

Not just any quilt. A whole damn lifetime stitched together in squares. Little League. Travel ball. High school tournaments. Jerseys I hadn't seen in years.

My chest did that stupid stretching thing it always did around her. Like my ribs didn't know how to handle how much I felt.

"I can't believe you got me a memory quilt," I said, my voice rough.

Quinn shook her head, almost shy. "I made it."

I stared at her. "You...made this?"

Quinn nodded, eyes shining.

The stitches were small and even. Careful. Precise. I ran a hand over my first travel-team jersey, faded but unmistakable. "Where did you even get all these shirts?" I looked up at her.

"From your mom."

"*My mom?*"

"With Cat's help," she said. "I felt weird just calling your mom out of nowhere asking for old shirts. So Cat reached out first and explained what I was making. Then we went over together and sorted through boxes of your stuff."

"She still had all this?"

"They were in neatly labeled boxes in the attic." Quinn's smile softened. "She knew exactly where everything was."

For a second, I just stared at the quilt because I couldn't speak. Finally, I cleared my throat.

"It's..." I forced out a breath. "I don't even have words."

"I'm glad you like it," she said softly.

I carefully set the quilt down, then leaned forward and kissed her slow and deep—the kind that said everything I couldn't.

"Thank you," I said against her mouth.

"You're welcome."

Her eyes were bright, a little glassy. She took a breath, then handed me a red foil envelope. "This one's different."

I opened it carefully and slid out the paper inside. It took a second to register what I was looking at.

"Daytona?" I asked.

"Yep," she said, grinning. "A NASCAR Racing Experience at Daytona. You get to drive a real stock car on the track. Plus I got them to throw in some fun extras, but you'll have to wait to see what those are." Her smile softened. "You inspired me with all those experiences you give Grace and

Charlie. I wanted to do the same for you. I figured we could go right after New Year's—make it a long weekend, relax a little before the craziness of the season officially starts."

My laugh wasn't even close to smooth — it was surprised and warm and hit somewhere deep in my chest.

"I've always wanted to do this," I said.

"Good."

"You're an amazing gift-giver," I said, leaning over to give her a quick kiss.

She smiled against my mouth. "You're not so bad your-self." Then she pulled back slightly. "But you're not done."

She handed me a flat, rectangular box.

After unwrapping it, I lifted the lid and found a framed piece of paper with Quinn's handwriting, the looping, slanted script I'd seen in meetings. But these weren't notes. They were lyrics for *Lost in the Chorus*. The whole song, handwritten with scratched-out lines and revisions in the margins.

"This..." I whispered. "Quinn. This is your first hit."

Her eyes held mine. "I wanted you to have it."

I stared at her, grateful but confused.

"Because it was about you," she finally said.

For a second, all I could do was sit there, trying to wrap my head around what she just said.

"The only other person who knows that is Erin," she said.

I didn't know how to reconcile the fact that her first hit song—the one that won her awards and launched her entire career—was about me.

Then something clicked.

"Does that mean..."

"Yes, Bennett Reed," she said, a little sheepish. "I had a huge crush on you back then."

"I had no idea."

"Obviously." She snort-laughed. "You didn't know I existed."

"For how long?" I asked.

"I quietly pined from middle school on, but my sophomore year—your junior year—it went off the charts."

"Why?"

She dragged her fingers through her hair, held it back for a second, then let it fall.

"I was at a keg party—my first and last one—and I got my period and bled through. But you noticed before I realized and came over and gave me your sweatshirt to tie around my waist so no one would see."

She picked up the last present and handed it to me. I reached in and pulled out a Waypoint High baseball sweatshirt.

The memory was hazy—some party, a girl who looked panicked, me handing over my sweatshirt without thinking twice. I'd never gotten it back.

I looked up at her. "I can't believe that was you."

"And I can't believe you didn't tell anyone."

I rubbed the back of my neck. "Yeah. I figured if Cat ever had something like that happen, I'd want someone to help her without telling the entire world. So I gave you my sweatshirt."

"I thought you would," she whispered. "I thought the whole school would know by Monday." She touched the sweatshirt like it was something precious. "I was going to give it back, but I was so embarrassed." She paused. "But that's when I realized you weren't just the hot, confident jock. You were a good guy. And that made my crush so much worse. So I poured all of it into a song," she added with a chuckle.

"I'm glad I got one thing right back then," I said, a small smile tugging at my mouth.

Taking her hand, I turned it gently in mine. Instead of lifting it to her knuckles, I brought her palm to my lips and pressed a slow kiss right in the center.

I'd been clueless about a lot. But at least in a moment that mattered, I hadn't blown it.

Chapter Forty-Two

Quinn

Half the world was already back in full grind mode, and I was only just dragging myself out of the holiday haze. To be fair, my haze lasted longer than usual. A long weekend in Daytona the week after New Year's had stretched it in the best way possible—sun on my skin, salt in the air, and evenings spent wandering along the shoreline.

But the highlight was watching Benny. He grinned nonstop—from the moment they strapped him into the stock car through the private track tour and garage walk-through I'd set up. Eyes bright the entire time, like a kid living his dream.

I'd never seen anyone look so good in a fire suit, and I hadn't expected the warm, melty feeling in my chest when he pulled off his helmet, hair a mess and eyes bright with adrenaline.

But real life was waiting back home. We got in late last night, and instead of going our separate ways, we ended up at his place. Neither of us said we weren't ready to be apart yet—we didn't have to. It hung in the air between us, soft and inevitable. So I stayed, and waking up wrapped in his sheets this morning felt less like a decision and more like the only thing that made sense.

Which is how we ended up arriving at the stadium together.

He leaned over and kissed me—soft, unhurried, the kind that settled low in my stomach and made it harder than it should've been to open the door.

"Ready?" he asked.

"Define ready," I muttered, earning that sweet laugh I'd started to crave.

But I followed him through the parking lot, the cold air snapping me fully awake. We headed toward the elevator, our footsteps echoing in the hallway, and as soon as we stepped inside, I glanced at Benny with a soft smile.

It felt like a lifetime since the first time I stood in this very elevator with him—awkward, curious, trying to figure him out. It was only a couple of months ago, but everything felt different now. Softer. Closer. Like the ground had shifted under us when I wasn't looking.

Funny how fast things could change.

When the doors opened, we stepped into the hallway and headed toward the conference room. Benny brushed his hand down my arm before letting go, a small gesture that felt as natural as breathing.

"I'm gonna run to my office real quick," he said. "Be right there."

"Okay."

I pushed into the conference room, and Tessa was already there—half hunched over her laptop, fingers flying across the keys. A coffee and a scatter of neon sticky notes surrounded her, half-filled with the kind of quick thoughts she jotted down just to keep her brain clear.

She didn't look up when I walked in, but the second I set my bag on the table, her head lifted.

"How was Daytona?"

"Sunny, relaxing, and hard to leave."

That was the truth, pared down to something I could comfortably share.

Tessa's smile widened like she knew more than I was saying but wasn't about to make it weird. "I'm glad you had fun."

Before I could respond, the rest of the team filtered in—Community Events, Marketing, Media Relations, all the usual suspects for event planning. Luke was carrying too many papers, Kelsey had her laptop, and everyone settled in with the practiced efficiency of people who'd done this a hundred times.

Benny slipped in last, easy and unhurried, taking the seat beside me.

Tessa stopped typing and glanced around the table. Then she pulled her laptop a little closer. "Alright, since we're all here, let's get started. Media Day happens first, so let's start there."

She tapped a key, and the agenda popped onto the big screen at the front of the room.

"After that, We'll start the day by taking the press through the renovated clubhouse, then out to the concourse so they can see the stadium upgrades." Tessa held up a hand and crossed her fingers dramatically enough for the whole table to see. "Assuming we don't get a foot of snow that morning."

That earned a chuckle. Everyone in this room had been burned by January weather before.

"We'll have a few of the coaches and some players who are already in town available for interviews, plus walkthroughs of the upgrades. We're keeping it structured, but not stiff."

From there, each department took turns running through all the moving parts that made an event like this look effortless on the outside.

"Anything else we need to talk about before we shift to Community Day?"

Ed Malone cleared his throat. "Just one thing."

He adjusted the papers in front of him, looking less relaxed than he had a moment ago.

"Some national outlets have confirmed, and local coverage will be heavy. Most of the coverage will be on the team and stadium upgrades, but..." His gaze flicked to Benny. "You might get a few questions about you and Quinn."

As the team's media relations manager, Ed's job was helping the players and staff be prepared for this kind of thing.

Beside me, Benny's energy shifted—a flick of tension under his calm surface.

He'd dealt with the press during his career, of course. But this was different. I'd had years of training on navigating that line, choosing my words carefully after getting burned early on. Not everyone gets that kind of preparation.

When Benny didn't respond, Ed continued.

"I'll put together a couple of media-friendly responses so you're prepared."

"I can have my team put together a few options too," I said. "They're used to dealing with this kind of attention."

Benny glanced at me and I caught the small tick in his jaw.

"Perfect," Ed said with a nod. "Loop them in and we'll coordinate on our end."

I scribbled a reminder in my notebook, even though it was too big to forget.

Tessa moved on to Community Day, but her words barely registered. My attention wasn't on the agenda anymore. I was thinking about Benny, the tension still coiled under his calm, and the sinking feeling that the little love bubble we'd been floating in might be starting to thin.

Chapter Forty-Three

Benny

I walked Quinn to the viewing suite, the small glassed-in space overlooking the press room below. She'd be able to see the whole circus without being seen.

Tessa was already inside, standing near the glass with her phone in hand, scrolling with quick, practiced swipes. She looked like she had ten tabs open in her brain.

"Morning," I said as we stepped in.

"Morning," Tessa replied. "Looks like a full house down there."

I stepped up to the glass and scanned the media room below. "I don't even recognize half of them."

"Ed did his job a little too well. Which isn't a bad thing," Tessa said lightly. "With the renovations and all the changes we've made, we want people to know it's a new era for the Lagerheads."

"Yeah, I get it," I said. "It's still my least favorite part of the job."

She slid her phone into her back pocket. "Well, too bad —you're good at it. Let's go give them something worth writing about."

"Go get 'em, Coach," Quinn said, giving my arm a quick squeeze.

"Yeah, yeah," I murmured, but the corner of my mouth tugged up into a smile anyway.

"Kick ass," she told Tessa.

Tessa winked. "Always."

She headed for the door, and I fell into step beside her in the hallway.

"Ed said he's starting with the stadium renovations since the media just got back from their tour."

"Yeah, that makes sense."

We rounded the corner toward the press room, the noise growing louder—chairs scraping, people settling in, mic checks echoing off the walls.

Tessa didn't slow. She pushed through the door, and I followed her into bright lights and the low buzz of pre-conference chatter.

We took our seats at the long table at the front of the room. The setup was the usual press-day configuration...a table for Tessa and me, and a podium set slightly to the side where Ed stood ready to run point—call on reporters, redirect questions, shut down anything that wandered off-topic. A wall of cameras and reporters faced us, already settling in.

Ed leaned into the mic.

"All right, everyone. Let's get started," he said. Once the room quieted, he continued. "Thank you for being here. Joining us today are Tessa Bergmann and the Lagerheads' new manager, Benny Reed. We'll start with questions on the stadium renovations."

A reporter in the middle row raised his hand first.

"Will the renovations be 100% complete by Opening Day?"

Tessa leaned into the mic, completely at ease.

"Yes. What you saw today is about ninety percent complete. We're on schedule — the interior work wraps in mid-February, and the rest will be finished shortly after. Everything will be ready well before Opening Day."

More hands went up, one after another. Questions about budgets, scoreboard and display capabilities, and the upcoming Community Day—all in Tessa's lane.

I sat back, half-ass listening and nodding when appropriate. Cameras clicked in uneven bursts. Someone typed too hard on a laptop.

Ed caught my eye, gave a small nod, and shifted the room.

"Let's take a few questions about the baseball side."

He pointed to a guy along the right wall.

"What are your priorities for spring training? Anything specific you want to focus on?"

I leaned into the mic.

"Fast starts. Clean defense. Situational hitting. Spring training is where you set your tone, so we'll be dialing in fundamentals right away."

My answer got a few nods. Someone murmured "good answer" under their breath.

Ed called on someone in the second row next.

"What style do you see this team playing under your leadership? More small ball? More aggressive on the basepaths?"

I shrugged.

"Depends on the roster. We've got some speed, some power, and we'll use all of it. I'm not locking us into one style when we have versatility. We'll play the game that puts us in the best position to win."

A few more questions came at me in quick succession—rotations, conditioning plans, bullpen usage, how early I planned to set the Opening Day lineup. Easy stuff. The kind of questions I could answer half-asleep.

This—talking baseball—was where I lived. Where I excelled.

And then a hand in the back shot up with a different kind of question.

"Rumor has it the Lagerheads are bringing in a female coach this season. Any truth to that?"

I sat a little straighter—not defensive, just clear.

"Yes," I said. "Marin Hollis will be joining us as our new hitting coach."

Murmurs rippled through the room. Cameras clicked. Hands shot up. And of course there was a follow-up.

"What was your motivation for hiring her?"

Motivation.

Like I'd been doing someone a favor.

Like it was a PR move.

Like she hadn't earned every damn bit of it.

Heat flickered low in my chest, but I kept my tone even, steady.

"The same motivation I'd have for hiring anyone," I said. "She's the best person for the job."

Another reporter jumped in before Ed could redirect.

"Do you expect any pushback from players or fans about bringing a woman into the coaching staff?"

I resisted the urge to sigh. They never stuck to baseball.

"No," I said, keeping my voice even. "Marin's résumé speaks for itself. She's sharp, connects with hitters, and knows the game as well as anybody I've worked with. That's what matters in a clubhouse."

Ed stepped in smoothly, calling on a reporter he'd clearly been saving for a safe baseball question.

"Mark? I think you had a question about pitching?"

The man in question stood. "What are you looking for out of the rotation heading into spring training?"

"Consistency. We've got a mix of veterans and younger arms, and spring training will tell us who's ready to take on what role. Nothing's set in stone yet, but we're in a good place."

A few more hands went up, but they stuck to normal stuff—bullpen usage, defensive metrics, lineup rhythm.

Straightforward. Expected.

And then a hand in the front row shot up.

Ed pointed to him. "Go ahead."

"Coach Reed," the reporter said, "photos surfaced recently of you with Quinn Logan in Daytona. Is she taking on a new role with the organization?"

"No," I said plainly. "Quinn's involvement is exactly the same. She's an investor and a supporter of the organization."

"So the two of you being seen together...is that personal or team-related?" the same reporter pressed.

Ed stepped in. "We'll stick to baseball questions. Next—"

But they talked over him before he could finish.

"Will she be traveling with the team this season?"

"Did she influence your decision to hire a female hitting coach?"

"You had other offers. Did Quinn sway you toward the Lagerheads?"

Their voices stacked on top of each other, sharp and impatient.

I exhaled and glanced at Ed.

He caught my eye and gave a short, steady nod.

Right.

The polished answers.

"Quinn and I both care about this organization," I said. "My focus is the team and preparing for the season."

It should've been enough, but it wasn't.

"So just to be clear," another reporter cut in, louder, "does she influence personnel decisions? Coaching choices? Your role with the organization?"

Something in me tightened.

I'd played nice.

I'd given the PR answers.

They weren't accepting them.

I lifted a hand—controlled and deliberate.

"Quinn Logan writes the checks," I said. "That's it."

Cameras clicked in a scattered burst of sound as I looked out over the room.

"Now," I said, voice clipped, "does anyone have a baseball question?"

Ed jumped in immediately, redirecting. "We'll take a couple more."

A few safe, predictable questions followed—bullpen roles, bench depth, young player prospects. The kind of things I could answer on autopilot, and honestly, that's pretty much what I did. Short, controlled responses. No elaboration. No personality. Just enough to get us to the end.

When no more hands raised, Ed wrapped things up. He thanked everyone, and the whole place shifted into cleanup mode.

Tessa barely had time to stand before someone from stadium operations approached, murmuring something about a contractor.

"I need to deal with this." She chuckled. "It's always something, right?"

She was gone before I could respond, already pivoting to whatever fire needed putting out.

I pushed back from the table and headed for the exit.

A couple reporters called my name on the way out, probably trying to get some off-the-record angle. I looked straight ahead and kept moving straight to the viewing suite.

The hallway was quieter now—just the low hum of vents and the distant clatter of people packing up gear. When I reached the suite, I expected to see Quinn still inside, but the room was empty.

She must've slipped out early. Sitting through a press conference wasn't exactly thrilling.

I pulled out my phone and texted her.

> Where'd you run off to?

After a beat, I shrugged and headed for my office. I pushed open my door, grabbed my keys and jacket from the back of the chair, and checked my phone again.

Nothing from Quinn.

She could've been catching up with Tessa. Or ducked into her own office. Or talking to one of the departments about something for Community Day. She had half a dozen reasons to be somewhere else.

Still...we came in together. It wasn't like her to just wander off without saying anything.

I shot her another text.

> You hiding from me?

Still nothing.

I headed down to the conference room to check there. It was empty and dark. Chairs were tucked in like no one had been there all morning.

Okay.

I rounded the corner toward her office, and stepped inside.

Empty.

No bag. No coat. No Quinn.

I pulled my phone out again, thumb hovering over her name. Calling felt like overkill, but the longer I stood there, the more out of place the silence felt.

I hit call.

It rang and rang, then went to voicemail.

I rubbed the back of my neck, confused. "Okay..."

We'd planned to grab lunch, and she hadn't mentioned changing plans.

I let out a breath and looked around the empty office.

Well...if she wasn't here and she wasn't answering, her house was the best place to check next.

The drive to Quinn's was quick. There was barely enough time for the heat to come up, or for me to decide whether I was overthinking all of this or not thinking enough.

Mostly, I just wanted to see her and make sure she was okay.

I pulled into her driveway and parked in front of the house. After killing the engine, I stepped out of the Jeep and headed up the steps to the porch.

"Quinn?" I knocked on the door in a steady, familiar rhythm. "It's me."

I knocked again, a little louder this time.

Still no answer.

I headed off the porch, pulling out my phone to call her as I went.

It rang once. Twice. Then to voicemail.

A small pinch formed low in my chest—not panic, just the feeling that something was off.

Before I even put the Jeep in reverse, my phone lit up with a text from Erin.

> Hey. Quinn's with me.

Relief hit first. Then confusion right behind it.

> Is she okay?

Three dots appeared, vanished, then appeared again.

> Physically, yes.

Physically? What the hell does that mean?

> Is she at your house? I can come get her.

Her reply was immediate.

> That's not a good idea tonight.

My stomach twisted.

> What's going on?

Another pause. Longer this time.

She'll talk to you tomorrow.

Tomorrow.
I stared at that single word until it blurred.

Okay. Let me know if she needs anything.

I got a thumb's up in response.
Not exactly reassuring.
And definitely not an answer.
But I didn't know what else to say, so I didn't say anything at all.

Chapter Forty-Four

Quinn

I got up, showered, and made coffee. I wasn't spiraling, rehearsing, or trying to talk myself into or out of anything. I knew what I needed to say, even if I didn't want to say it.

I picked up my phone and stared at Benny's name longer than I meant to.

Are you home?

His response came immediately.

Yeah.

I slipped into my coat, grabbed my keys, and headed out.

When I pulled up in front of his house, I stayed in the car for a moment, hands resting on the steering wheel.

Not afraid of the conversation, just sad that it was necessary.

The front door opened before I reached the porch.

Benny looked like he'd gotten about as much sleep as I had.

"Hey," he said.

"Hi."

He moved like he was going to kiss me.

I stepped past him into the house.

"Do you want—"

"No," I said gently before he could finish.

He nodded once and stepped back. I walked inside and settled at the kitchen island. He pulled a chair to the opposite side and sat.

"Are you okay?" he asked.

I nodded. "I wanted to talk."

"Okay."

"Yesterday, at the press conference," I said. "When they asked about us, you said 'Quinn Logan writes the checks. That's it.'"

He shifted. "They were implying—"

"I know what they were implying," I said. "And I know you were trying to shut it down. I get it."

"Then what's the problem?"

"The problem is that you left me out to make it easier."

His jaw worked. "I was trying to keep them from turning us into a story."

"Benny, we *are* a story. We're always going to be a story." I kept my voice steady. "I'm not just some regular person. You know that."

"I know."

"Then you should also know that the questions don't stop. The scrutiny just gets worse."

He didn't respond.

I took a breath and let it out slowly.

"I've been here before," I said. "With men who said they could handle it."

"That's not fair."

"I know," I said. "I'm telling you why yesterday scared me."

He held my gaze.

"But you told me we should live our lives," I continued. "That we shouldn't hide. And I believed you. I thought you were different."

"I am different."

"Are you?" I asked. "Because yesterday, when someone asked about us—when it got even slightly uncomfortable—you took me out of the conversation."

His hands flattened on the counter. "Quinn, I didn't mean it like that."

"Maybe not," I said. "But you still said it. And if this is how you handle one question at one press conference, what happens when it actually gets hard?"

Silence settled heavy between us.

"I've been with men who couldn't stand in the light with me," I said. "Who needed me to be smaller. And I swore I wouldn't do that again."

His eyes searched mine. "I'm not asking you to be smaller."

"Maybe not intentionally," I said. "But that's what it felt like yesterday."

He stared at me for a long moment.

"So what are you saying?"

"I'm saying I need to step back."

Pain flashed across his face. "Step back?"

"I need space."

He swallowed. "I don't know what to do with this."

"I know," I said.

"For how long?"

"I don't know."

His voice dropped. "That's not fair."

"I know," I whispered. "But it's all I have right now."

He looked at me like I was breaking something he didn't know how to fix.

"Quinn, I—"

He stopped. Swallowed hard.

The words hung there between us, unfinished.

I knew what he almost said. I could see it written all over his face—the way he looked at me like I was everything, like saying it might change my mind.

And God, it hurt.

Because I loved him too.

But even that couldn't change what I needed.

When I stood, he didn't reach for me or try to stop me from leaving.

I walked to the door, my throat tight.

"Quinn."

I stopped but didn't turn around.

"I'll give you the space," he said, voice rough. "But I'm not giving up on this. On us."

I closed my eyes for a second, then kept walking.

When I stepped outside, the door closed softly behind me.

I let myself cry in the car.

Chapter Forty-Five

Benny

The treadmill droned beneath my feet, steady and relentless.

Metallica pounded through the basement, heavy drums and grinding guitar pushing me forward. The sound filled the space, vibrating through concrete and bone, something loud enough to drown out everything else. I turned the speed up another notch and fixed my eyes on the wall in front of me.

I'd set the space up recently—nothing fancy, nothing finished. Just a space to work things out of my system.

Except none of it was leaving.

I'd already logged eight miles and had no plan to stop anytime soon.

This was familiar. Physical pain I could measure. Control I could wrap my hands around. My lungs burned, sweat soaked through my shirt, and my calves protested with every strike of my feet against the belt. Good. Let it hurt. Let it demand my attention.

I pushed harder, jaw clenched, arms pumping, breath coming sharp and fast. My body could take it. It always could. I'd learned early on how far I could push before something actually gave out—and I was nowhere near that line yet.

No matter how hard I pushed, the same images looped back in.

Quinn stepping past me at the door.

The way she hadn't flinched or hesitated.

The calm in her voice when she said she needed space.

The treadmill display blurred for a second, and I swore under my breath, forcing my focus back to the numbers. I didn't slow down.

"Jesus Christ."

Cat's voice cut through the music, sharp and close.

I jerked my head up at the voice and stumbled.

She stood at the bottom of the stairs, arms crossed, eyebrows raised, taking in the scene like she was cataloging evidence. She wore leggings and an old hoodie, hair pulled into a messy knot that said she hadn't planned on leaving the house today.

I slowed my pace before stepping onto the sides and hitting the stop button. I bent forward, hands braced on my thighs, breath coming in harsh pulls.

"How long have you been running?" she asked.

I wiped my face with the hem of my shirt. "Not long."

"You're dripping. That's not 'not long.'" She walked over and squinted at the display. "Thirteen miles?" she said. "That's a half marathon, not a casual workout, Benny."

I grabbed the towel and wiped my face. "What are you doing here?"

"Checking on my brother." She crossed her arms. "You've been dodging my calls and texts all week."

I hesitated, then shrugged. "I figured it was better if I stayed out of the way."

"Of what?" she asked.

"The kids," I said. "They don't need...this."

Her expression shifted—not alarmed or angry. Just understanding.

"So something happened."

I didn't answer right away.

She sighed. "Of course something happened."

She said it more to herself than to me.

Her mouth pressed into a thin line. "You look like shit."

"Gee thanks."

"I mean it," she said, softer now. "You look like someone who hasn't slept or eaten in days."

I shrugged. "I've been busy."

"With what?" she asked flatly. "Punishing yourself?"

I dropped the towel onto the bench and leaned back against the wall. The cool concrete seeped through my shirt, grounding me. "I messed up."

"What happened?"

"Quinn asked for space."

Cat nodded once. "Okay."

I stared at the treadmill. "I answered a question. At a press conference. One sentence."

"And?"

"And somehow it was enough to blow everything up."

There was a pause. "What'd you say?"

"I said she writes the checks. That's it." I exhaled sharply. "I was shutting them down."

"And instead," she said calmly, "you shut her out."

"That's not what I meant."

"I know," Cat said. "But that's not what she felt."

Frustration tightened my chest. "I've always kept baseball and my personal life separate."

"But Quinn isn't something you can separate when it gets uncomfortable."

I looked away.

"She thinks this means I'll do it again," I said.

Cat studied me for a long moment. "Will you?"

The answer stuck in my throat.

"I don't want to," I said.

"Good," she replied. "Then remember this feeling."

I let my head fall back against the wall. "I miss her."

"That's also good," Cat said. "Because once you get her back—and you will—don't forget how this felt."

I nodded, eyes on the floor, chest tight.

I won't. I'll never forget this.

Silence stretched between us.

Cat glanced at the treadmill again, then back at me, her jaw tight.

"So," she said, pushing off the wall. "I'm guessing I should probably go before you decide to see how fast that thing really tops out."

I huffed out a breath. "I'm fine."

She arched her brow. "You're a few miles past fine."

I didn't have it in me to argue.

She walked back toward the stairs, then stopped, one hand on the railing. "Can I trust you not to run yourself into the ground if I leave?"

The question wasn't accusatory. It was careful. Sisterly. Like she knew the answer could go either way.

"I need to shower anyway," I said. "I've got an interview in a couple hours."

I grabbed the towel from the bench and followed her up the stairs, the ache in my legs dull and heavy as I took the steps one at a time. Each one felt deliberate, like I was choosing something instead of avoiding it.

Once we stepped into the kitchen, she turned, studying me, her expression shifting as if she were recalculating.

"An interview," she repeated.

"Yeah." I glanced down at my sweat-soaked shirt. "And this isn't exactly the look I'm going for."

Her mouth tipped into a small, knowing smile. "Probably wise."

She walked to the door and opened it.

"Whatever they ask you," she said, "just tell the truth—not what makes you most comfortable."

The door closed behind her.

Chapter Forty-Six

Quinn

I sat curled sideways in my office chair, one leg tucked under me, a notebook balanced on my bent knee.

I'd filled three pages already—short lines, half-thoughts, words that didn't need to make sense just yet. None of them were good, but all of them were honest.

My pen hovered over the page as I let my gaze drift to the other notebook on the shelf above my desk—the one Benny had given me for Christmas. Still unopened.

I should probably be dumping all of this in there, considering it was all about him.

Looking back down, I kept going, the words coming faster than I could write.

My wrist had just started to ache when a knock sounded at the door.

Standing on stiff legs, I set the notebook aside and went to see who was there.

When I opened the door, Cat took one look at me and winced.

"You look as bad as he does."

I opened my mouth, then closed it again.

I'd seen myself in the mirror. I wasn't going to win that argument.

Cat reached into her bag and pulled out a magazine, a yellow page flag sticking out near the middle.

"Read the article about Benny," she said. "All of it."

I hesitated, then took it.

My throat tightened. "Cat—"

"Just read it," she said

She turned and headed back down the walk before I could say anything else.

I stood in the doorway for a moment, the magazine heavy in my hands, then closed the door and went back to my chair.

The yellow flag marked a two-page spread. A photo of Benny took up the top of one page—leaning against the dugout, arms crossed, his steel-blue eyes looking directly into the camera.

Beneath it sat the title.

Benny Reed and the Long Build: Inside the Lagerheads' reset under their new manager.

I took a breath and started reading.

It was thoughtful. Grounded. About the work—renovations, staffing changes, the long view instead of quick fixes. Benny talked about culture more than wins, about patience, about earning trust in a town that had learned to be skeptical. He didn't oversell anything or promise miracles.

The questions shifted from renovations and staffing to leadership and accountability. About how much of himself he was willing to put into this team.

I kept reading.

My breath hitched when I saw my name.

It's well known by now that you and Quinn Logan are together. With the demands of the season—and the attention that comes with it—how do you make something like that work?

My fingers tightened on the page.

"Every relationship has challenges, and ours is no different—especially during the season. I love Quinn, and I'm focused on being there for her the way she deserves. That means doing the hard things—being honest when it matters, showing up publicly, and not pulling back when it gets uncomfortable."

I pressed my lips together, blinking away tears, then read it again. Then a third time.

The rest of the words on the page blurred, except those three.

I love Quinn.

He hadn't explained me away or protected himself at my expense.

I lowered the magazine into my lap and stared at the opposite wall, my heartbeat steady but insistent.

Closing the magazine, I stood. I didn't need to read anything else.

I slipped into my shoes and grabbed my keys on the way out the door

The lights were on in the living room of Benny's house when I pulled up. My hands rested on the wheel, heartbeat steady and sure. I cut the engine and got out of the car.

I walked up to the door, raised my hand, and knocked.

It took a few seconds, then the door opened.

Benny stopped short when he saw me.

For a heartbeat, neither of us moved.

Cat was right...he looked as bad as I did.

"Quinn," he said.

"I read the article."

"Yeah?"

I nodded.

Silence stretched between us. Not uncomfortable. Just full.

"I didn't expect you to—" he started, then stopped, exhaling. "I meant every word of it."

"I know," I said softly. "That's why I'm here."

His gaze searched my face, careful, like he was afraid to reach for something fragile too fast.

"You said you love me."

"I do," he replied immediately. "I love you."

Something in my chest loosened completely this time.

"I love you too," I said.

He let out a breath then stepped forward. His hands came up to my waist, grounding, familiar, like he was anchoring us both. My arms slid around his neck, my forehead resting briefly against his.

Then he kissed me.

Slow. Steady. Deliberate.

I kissed him back, fingers threading into his hair, and everything else faded—the doubt, the space, the what-ifs that had been looping for days.

When we finally pulled apart, his hands lingered at my waist, thumbs brushing soft circles like he was grounding himself as much as me.

"I'm not asking for easy," I said. "I just needed to know you wouldn't disappear when it got hard."

"I won't," he said. "Not again."

I believed him.

He kissed me again—softer this time, unhurried. When we finally pulled back, he rested his forehead against mine.

"Stay," he said. Not a demand. An invitation.

I smiled. "I was planning on it."

Epilogue

Benny

Opening Day

The air smelled like hot dogs and fresh-cut grass, and the stands buzzed with that particular kind of noise that only happened when a stadium was full and ready. Bergmann Stadium looked good—better than good. New scoreboards glowed, the grass was green, and every seat in the house was packed.

I stood in the dugout, arms crossed, watching my guys warm up. Stretching, laughing, loose in that way you wanted to see before the first pitch. Marin was out by the cage with our leadoff hitter, tweaking his stance. The bullpen was active. Everything felt ready.

My headset crackled. "Five minutes, Coach."

We were opening the season against the Carolina Waves, Sam Cherry getting the start. Nothing we hadn't prepared for.

I nodded to no one in particular and pulled in a long breath.

All the work—the hiring, the training, the press conferences, the goddamn renovations—came down to this.

The national anthem started, and I stepped out onto the field with my team. Caps off. Hands over hearts. Forty thousand people standing in unison.

I didn't let myself look toward the owner's box.

Not yet.

The anthem ended and the roar that followed was deafening. I walked back to the dugout, the adrenaline kicking in now, sharpening everything.

"Let's go!" I called out as our starter headed to the mound.

The first pitch was a fastball down the middle for strike one. Always a good way to start a game.

I stayed where I was, eyes on the field, letting the inning find its rhythm.

A flyout to center. A strikeout looking.

Then a grounder to short. A clean scoop and a throw to first.

Three outs.

That was when I finally let myself look up toward the boxes.

And there she was.

Quinn sat in the owner's box beside Tessa, leaning forward slightly, hands pressed together like she was holding her breath. She wore the Lagerheads jersey I'd given her for Christmas and her hair was pulled into a low ponytail that swayed when she turned to speak.

She looked...right.

Not like she was trying to fit in or play a part. Just herself. Comfortable. Present.

Something settled in my chest.

For years, I'd kept baseball and my personal life separate. It was easier that way—cleaner. Work stayed at work. Personal life stayed personal. No overlap. No complications.

But with Quinn, there was no separating anything.

She was part of the stadium, the team, the noise, the pressure, all of it.

And it didn't feel complicated.

It felt easy.

Like she was always supposed to be here.

I turned my attention back to the field as our lead-off hitter, Brett Collins, stepped into the box. He dug in, took the first pitch for a ball, then fouled off two fastballs.

The crowd was on their feet now, clapping in rhythm.

Collins settled again. Sam Cherry wound up.

Crack.

The ball shot through the gap between first and second, clean and sharp. Collins flew down the line, rounding first and sliding into second just ahead of the throw.

The dugout exploded. I clapped once, hard—and couldn't help looking up toward the boxes. Quinn was on her feet, clapping. She caught my eye and smiled—not a big, showy thing. Just...her.

I smiled back.

Then I turned my attention to the field, where it needed to be.

But I knew she'd still be there when I looked up again.

And for the first time in a long time, I wasn't worried about keeping things separate.

With Quinn, it all just fit.

Bonus Epilogue

Dane

The clubhouse didn't look anything like it had when I first toured it.

Two months ago, it had been all exposed concrete and plastic sheeting, wires hanging where walls were supposed to be. Now the lockers gleamed, the floors were finished, and everything looked shiny and new.

If I'd walked into this room a few years ago, I would've clocked it automatically—the training tables, the flow of traffic, where guys would naturally drop their bags and lean into conversation.

Now, I found myself trying to look at it differently. Not because it came naturally yet, but because it needed to. I caught myself wondering where conversations would happen, where someone might hang back without drawing attention, how easy it would be to observe without hovering.

It felt deliberate. Slightly awkward.

A reminder that I was stepping into something new whether I felt ready for it or not.

I wasn't a player anymore. But I wasn't fully a coach yet either—not until spring training started and the job stopped being theoretical. For most of my career, my arm had done the talking. Soon, it would be my eyes. My judgment. My ability to explain what I saw in a way someone else could actually use.

That part didn't scare me.

But it did make everything feel real in a way it hadn't before.

Benny was inside when I arrived, leaning against one of the locker banks, mid-conversation with Tessa Bergmann.

"On paper it worked," Tessa said, glancing toward the seating area, "but it was so hard to picture." She looked around again, taking it in with a sharp, assessing gaze. "I'm glad it works in real life."

Benny smiled. "Me too." Then he spotted me and smiled. "There he is," he said. "Perfect timing. We're just wrapping up here."

"Hey," I said.

Tessa turned.

She wasn't dressed in the business clothes I'd seen her in before. No blazer, no heels. Just dark jeans and a soft sweater, the kind that looked practical until you noticed how well it fit. Her pixie cut was looser than usual, softer than I'd seen it before.

Even like that, she still looked like she was mentally ticking through a never-ending to-do list, juggling a hundred things at once.

I could think of a dozen ways to slow her down.

None of them were appropriate.

Benny's phone buzzed. He glanced at the screen and shook his head.

"I've got to grab this," he said. "Be right back."

Tessa shifted her weight.

"It looks great," I said. "A long way from what it was the last time I was here."

"I'm happy with it," she said. "It's good to have it done."

"Yeah," I said. "That's a win."

She took it all in once more, then back at me. "So are you all settled in?"

"Pretty much," I said. "Most of the boxes are unpacked."

"That's good," she said. "Living out of boxes is never fun."

I huffed a quiet laugh. "No kidding." I hesitated, then added, "And thanks for the realtor recommendation. She was great and helped both Marin and me get sorted fast."

"I'm glad," she said. "I knew she'd take care of you."

A quiet pause followed, comfortable rather than awkward.

Benny's voice carried from across the room as he headed back toward us, phone still in hand.

"Sorry about that," he said. "You ready to go over the invite list?"

I reminded myself why I was here—to sit down with Benny and talk through which guys from the system we wanted to bring to spring training.

"Yeah," I said.

Tessa was already shifting gears. "I'll let you two get to it."

She stepped past me, her arm brushing mine, and froze.

For a second, neither of us moved. Her gaze lifted to mine, something unreadable flickering there before it disappeared.

"Sorry."

"No problem," I replied.

She nodded, pulling her phone back out as she stepped

away, her attention shifting seamlessly to whatever was next on her list.

I watched her go for half a second too long.

Then I looked back at the lockers and exhaled.

Attraction was manageable. Inconvenient, but manageable.

Acting on it wasn't.

So I wouldn't.

Lost in the Chorus
by Quinn Logan

Verse 1
I see you in the hallway, you're laughing with your friends,
I'm just a shadow on the wall, waiting for this day to end.
You don't even know my name, but oh, I know yours,
You're the star of my dreams, but I'm lost in the chorus.

Pre-Chorus
Every time you walk by, my heart skips a beat,
I wonder if you'll ever notice me.

Chorus
You're the song I keep on replay, in the back of my mind,
I'm the girl who's just a whisper, always left behind.
You're the reason for the smile, and these silent tears,
Hoping someday you'll see me, and I'll face my fears.

Verse 2
I write your name in my notebook, surrounded by hearts,
I picture us together, even though we're worlds apart.
I hear your voice in my dreams, it's like a melody,

But when I open my eyes, it's just a fantasy.

Pre-Chorus
Every glance that you don't see, feels like a rainy day,
I'm waiting for the moment you'll look my way.

Chorus
You're the song I keep on replay, in the back of my mind,
I'm the girl who's just a whisper, always left behind.
You're the reason for the smile, and these silent tears,
Hoping someday you'll see me, and I'll face my fears.

Bridge
Maybe someday, you'll catch my eye,
And I won't be invisible, just passing by.
I'll gather the courage to say hello,
And maybe, just maybe, you'll want to know.

Chorus
You're the song I keep on replay, in the back of my mind,
I'm the girl who's just a whisper, always left behind.
You're the reason for the smile, and these silent tears,
Hoping someday you'll see me, and I'll face my fears.

Outro
Till then I'll keep dreaming of a chance we'll meet,
And I'll keep singing this song on my lonely street.
You're the melody I crave, the star I can't reach,
But maybe someday, you'll walk with me on this beach.

About the Author

As a tween, Tina Gallagher and her best friend would create happily ever afters for their favorite soap opera couples. Eventually, the soap operas lost their appeal, but the writing never did.

Before living her dream as a full-time author, she worked a spectrum of jobs ranging from baking and cake decorating to marketing and project management.

In between creating memorable characters, traveling, and taking pole dance lessons, Tina enjoys spending time with her two grown children and Golden Irish named Thea.

www.ingramcontent.com/pod-product-compliance
Lightning Source LLC
Chambersburg PA
CBHW030132310726
48970CB00005B/1405